THE LAST CREATION

THE LAST SHE SERIES

THE LAST SHE

THE LAST CITY

THE LAST CREATION

THE

LAST

CREATION

H. J. NELSON

wattpad books **w**

wattpad books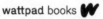

An imprint of Wattpad WEBTOON Book Group

Content warning: violence, murder, fighting, animal death

Published in Canada by Wattpad WEBTOON Book Group, a division of Wattpad WEBTOON Studios, Inc.

36 Wellington Street E., Suite 200, Toronto, ON M5E 1C7 Canada

www.wattpad.com

First Wattpad Books edition: December 2024

ISBN 978-1-99885-499-8 (Trade Paper original)
ISBN 978-1-99025-983-8 (eBook edition)

Library and Archives Canada Cataloguing in Publication information is available upon request.

Printed and bound in Canada

1 3 5 7 9 10 8 6 4 2

Cover design by Jill Caldwell
Images by christannafzger, Krailath, Enrique González Avilés/Wirestock
Typesetting by Delaney Anderson

For Travis,
who knows why the dog howls at the moon

SERIES RECAP

WHEN WE LAST SAW ARA . . .

She had left the ruins of Boise and journeyed to The Last City—the lone surviving metropolis surrounded by massive walls and sustained by their production of the red 'plague flower,' a plant that, when ingested, offers protection from the virus. The city is ruled by her grandfather, Walter, who insists that her father and sister never arrived. When she befriends Talia, who has lived in the city for years, she discovers that beneath the city, Walter hides many dark secrets: an army of emotionless human clones called the Creation, who are expected to finish what the plague began: the complete annihilation of the human race. Ara finds her father, who confirms her worst fear: that her family is responsible for the plague that ended the world, and that the cure has been hidden in her blood all along. Her father dies helping her escape, and she vows to bring the cure back to Boise. And put an end to it all.

WHEN WE LAST SAW KADEN . . .

He had journeyed with Ara to The Last City, only to find it more treacherous than he'd imagined. He is assigned as a tracker to an elite guard duty searching the ruins for a rogue fugitive. Except the guards have a different assignment: killing Kaden. At the last moment, he's saved by the very fugitive they were tracking, a man named Septimus, and together they hide in the ruins surrounding

The Last City. Kaden learns that Septimus is a Creation who was marked as a flaw but escaped before he could be destroyed. Together they break back into The Last City, intending to save Ara, only to discover the hidden Creation army led by Sevyn. Together Ara and Kaden escape, armed with the knowledge that Ara's blood holds the one true cure, and that an army of Creation is headed toward Boise. Kaden vows to fight for humanity along-side Ara—until the bitter end.

WHEN WE LAST SAW SAM . . .

He had survived the downfall and burning of the Castellano clan. He teams up with a mysterious girl named M, and together they make their way through the ruins of Boise to the flooded downtown. Despite M's nightmares, and the sense that she isn't telling him everything, Sam can't help but fall for her. He helps her make her way downtown, where they access an old computer still connected to The Last City. Sam helps M unleash the force of human clones known as Creation. Only after this does M tell him that the Creation are intent on finishing what the plague began and destroying humanity. They are led by Sevyn, a Creation who despises humanity for holding him prisoner. Worse, M is one of them, and is actually Ara's long-lost sister, Emma. Emma deserts him and, heartbroken and angry, Sam heads back to the new Castellano clan with one purpose: to turn the new tech back on and restart the world.

IT BEGAN IN BOISE, AND NOW IT ALL ENDS HERE . . .

PART **ONE**

CHAPTER ONE—SAM

Today, I changed the world forever.

The wind howled through the crumbling ruins of Boise. It wound over shells of long-forgotten airships, through shattered windows and gaping doorways, over carpets of leaves. Green shoots pushed through the mud, vines finding new handholds to climb abandoned structures. The scent of fresh rain, wet earth, and new growth mixed with the stench of rotting wood, crumbling stone, and decaying flesh.

In the weeds to the left of the street we walked lay the carcass of a deer. *That wasn't here last time.* Yet when I came closer, I saw its eyes were white, weeping blood. Infected.

"Should we burn it?" one of the men behind me said.

"No," I said quietly. "Leave it."

It was too dangerous to burn it here—not when we were this far from the clan and in enemy territory.

It had been five years since the plague had first begun. Five years since my life went from that of a boy living in the suburbs to one more survivor trying to make his way through a dangerous world. Boise had changed in that time. All around us nature reached out from the earth like fingers from a grave, reclaiming buildings, streets, and houses. Even the corpse of the deer would be devoured by predators or covered in green shoots soon.

The small group of eight men continued forward, making our way through a forest of trees growing between decaying buildings. A flock of birds burst up before us, and I pulled my bow tighter—the scars on my back aching in pain as I did—before I let it go slack again.

"Keep moving," Gabriel said. His eyes were wide, flicking from the buildings to the trees and back to us—as if he saw enemies everywhere. Since the burning of the Cabela's, where the Castellano clan was originally based, Gabriel had changed. He was more cautious. But also more paranoid.

Our group crossed out of the late afternoon shadows of a brick building. An enormous grinning skull, graffitied onto the wall, leered at our group as we passed. We'd left Castellano clan territory hours ago, our team of eight men moving quietly through the ruins into Skull clan territory. An hour ago, we'd passed real human skulls marking the edge of their territory. Even I couldn't find a good joke about the gruesome markers.

Gabriel startled; somewhere in the ruins a broken door thumped, likely blown open by the wind. His hands shook on the gun in his hand, his eyes darted from one thing to the next, and I had to bury the impulse to take the weapon from him. He'd lost weight over the winter, a haunted look to his eyes that hadn't been there before. Last year, when the clan burned, and Ara and Kaden had slipped from his fingers, well . . . something inside him had finally snapped. The new Castellano clan was based in the Old Penitentiary—the significance of its location was not lost on any of them.

My fingers itched to pull my bow a little tighter as I followed him. What would one little arrow really hurt? I could say it was an accident. Or that one of the Skull clan had done it. *It's not like he's even really leading, looking back every few minutes for me to point out the way. He didn't even say anything about the deer.* But no. Today I couldn't afford to indulge fantasies. Even if he was a pretentious bastard, I needed Gabriel.

He was going to help me change the world.

The wind caught my hair, whipping it across my face. I thought I smelled something rotten in the breeze, but when I turned to stare into the vast ruins, the scent disappeared. *Maybe just the scent of the deer?* Nothing but rising buildings, gaping doors, and broken windows stared back at me.

"Sam?" Gabriel had stopped at the edge of a three-story brick building—a jam of rusted vehicles blocked the road before us. "Which way?"

"Through the car jam." I pointed over the rusted heap of metal and tires to where another group of buildings loomed. "We won't have much cover."

There were some low murmurs from the other men, weary glances exchanged, but Gabriel ignored them. The fact that he insisted on leading a group when he didn't know the final destination pretty much summed up Gabriel.

"You came this way before? Alone?" Gabriel said.

"All winter. How else do you think I fed the clan?"

His eyes flashed, a hint of that cold anger, but it didn't rile me up like it once had. It wasn't nearly as fun messing with Gabriel now that he was losing it. *Kaden would still like it though.* My chest tightened when I thought of Kaden. It had been a year since I'd seen him—memories were all I had of him now. "You're welcome to keep leading," I said, looking over the ruins like I didn't have a care in the world.

My bluff worked. Gabriel's brow began to sweat, even though the day was cool.

"You take the lead for this section," he said.

I stepped past him, resisting the urge to give him attitude. It didn't matter if he was a paranoid, inept ruler. Today, everything would change.

The team followed me now. The last of the snow still clung to a few dark corners of the city, but spring had sent green tendrils snaking over buildings, cars, and roads, as if determined to erase us altogether. I'd once told myself that the apocalypse only sucks if you let it. That was when I believed my brother Kaden might still come back and save me.

Now the question I asked myself was this: What if the apocalypse didn't have to last forever?

Beyond the car jam, giant plastic sheets stretched over makeshift shelters between buildings. Bright orange signs still stood. This was one of the original failed containment areas in the city. Men didn't come here. Which is exactly why I had.

"Sam?" Gabriel called out.

I stopped, burying the urge to leave them all behind. The looming steel-gray building we'd been seeking stood just visible at the end of the road. "We're almost there," I called back, feeling like a parent dragging along a whiny child.

"You go first," he said, the fear apparent in his voice. "Make sure the building is clear, then come back and we'll join."

"Fine."

I turned and left the group behind gratefully. This was the way I preferred it. Just me, my bow, and the scent of earth and stone. My skills versus whatever the world could throw at me.

The eyes of the men were on me, but it no longer bothered me as it once had. Loyalties had shifted in the clan—men looked at Gabriel with hard eyes while they watched me with respect. I was the one who'd kept the clan fed all winter. The one who'd roamed far past the safe boundaries to find food and supplies in an increasingly desperate city. Gabriel was the one who hid behind clan walls and imposed harsher and harsher restrictions.

Everything had come to a head the day Gabriel had strung me up before the clan and demanded thirteen lashes for keeping a gun for myself. Even through the pain, as the whip fell again and again, I remembered that swelling, angry silence.

Gabriel was like a crumbling building fading into the earth and mud. It was only a matter of time before he fell. But before he did, I could use him.

Unless he uses you first. Her voice came to me now—as it often did in the ruins. I rolled my shoulders, feeling the sting of the healing cuts, as I imagined what she might say about Gabriel.

Bastards stay rulers, until you bring them down.

Sometimes out here, in the ruins, I felt her presence as if she were around the next corner: her high-pitched laughter, her mocking voice, her ruthless smile. Only out here did I dare to remember, just for a moment, the way her lips felt against mine. The way it had felt, for just a moment, when we had become something more than just two people trying to survive.

Em's words echoed in my brain all winter. But how could I trust her advice when she'd lied about everything else? She was not Em but Emma, Ara's little sister, and she wasn't fully human.

She was something that had been designed and produced by the humans in The Last City. Something called Creation.

Together Em and I had found a way to release the Creation from the underground lab they had been trapped inside in The Last City. I'd thought we'd built something together in those weeks we spent crossing Boise. But it turns out that she used me. As soon as she had what she wanted, as soon as the Creation were free, she disappeared.

Her final words to me, written in a note still tucked in my jacket, warned me to run, to leave the city forever—but I was done running. I wasn't like her. I wouldn't take the easy way out. If the Creation were coming, they wouldn't find us so helpless. Not after today.

Soon the mammoth building stood before me, the tallest in this section of the city. The front doors had been blown off, so that the entrance gaped, jaws of a sleeping giant, the interior dark and ominous. The smells of the outside faded beneath the musty, damp interior.

Leaves crunched beneath my feet as I stepped inside. The last time I'd been here, I'd scraped some of the leaves and dirt away from the marble floor, enough to make out the seal of an eagle. It had once been some sort of important government building. Now all that remained to mark its importance were the metal detectors and shriveled bodies hidden in the rubble.

In the back of the building lay an unmarked stairwell I'd found last visit. A musty odor drifted out when I opened the rusted door. A dripping noise echoed from somewhere deep within. I slung my bow back around my shoulder, dug my flashlight out, and then, with a deep breath, stepped into velvety darkness.

Following my previous path, I ignored Gabriel's order to

check for threats and return. I wanted a chance to see the room one more time without him. The stairwell bottomed out, and I pushed open the final door, then stepped into a long, thin hallway. There was only one door at the end of the hallway.

"Hey, Phillip," I called out into the darkness. "How's it hanging?"

The dripping noise grew louder as I drew closer to the body of the security guard I'd found last time I'd been here. As far as threats went, Phillip didn't qualify—he was dead, after all. The beam of my flashlight hit his chest, and his head was slumped forward over his neat military uniform. It looked almost as if he'd gone to sleep in uniform and had never woken. I wasn't sure if the cold down here had somehow preserved him. His name tag read: PHILLIP CONSTANTINO, CLEARANCE LEVEL 10. The door he was slumped next to read: DANGEROUS: AUTHORIZED PERSONNEL ONLY. Which was exactly why I'd broken in.

"You're looking pale, Phillip," I said. "You really should get out more. Mind if I borrow your card again?" I reached forward and pulled the card away from his body. Then I held it to the card reader, before I let the small string return it to his chest. Maybe it was strange, superstitious even, to leave the card on his body, but in the eerie darkness, it felt right. I'd read more than enough comic books and stories to ever want to disrespect the dead.

A green light flashed on the door, some deep internal locking mechanism grinding within. Some sort of backup generator powered it, not new tech, but a clear signal that what lay beyond was important. I turned the handle and pulled the massive door open—it was as thick as a bank vault door.

"Sam?"

I spun, flashlight dancing as I grabbed the knife at my waist.

Oh hell no.

Gabriel strode through the darkness toward me, his flashlight swinging all around. He drew closer, enough for me to make out his missing ear and his eerie gray eyes. Against his umber-colored skin, they seemed almost hollow.

"Is this it?" he said, motioning to the open door.

"I thought you were going to wait?" I wanted to step inside and slam the door in his face. *That wouldn't be fair to Phillip.*

"I figured you might need backup."

His eyes moved past me, to the open door and vast room beyond. I wondered if he felt it too. It was as if the room held some kind of gravity, a siren call of death and power. It was a beckoning force ushering us forward and neither of us could resist the pull.

I stepped into the silence and Gabriel followed. Our flashlights revealed a cavern-like room, round and deep, spiraling down in darkness. Standing in the center of the dark hole was a massive rocket-shaped device made of the same shiny silver metal all the airships bore. Even in the dim light the weapon gave off a faint glow. Something proud and hungry rose in me as I stared at it.

It had taken me months to find it. Months of cursing this city and everyone who'd left me here alone. But I had done it. Me. Alone. I'd found salvation for all of us.

And now, everything would change.

"It's some kind of new tech weapon. Like a nuke." Even my whisper felt too loud. "It's powerful enough to take out a state—maybe a whole country. My dad talked about it before the plague. There was supposed to be some kind of new international treaty to stop people from making them, but he figured that was because we'd already made one and didn't want other countries making them too."

"Why is it here? It looks ready to launch."

"Maybe because it was." My flashlight ran over the weapon that somehow still held a reflective, glowing sheen despite the years buried beneath the earth. "Perhaps they meant to destroy the city, and with it the plague. At least, that's what it looked like from the last few computer logs."

"You got the computers in here to work?" His voice was full of surprise—all Gabriel ever did was underestimate me.

"There's some sort of old tech emergency backup generator—bare bones, to keep the door locked and a few lights on," I explained, "but I was able to use it to get one computer on. I read through the last few logs. It hasn't been manned for the last few years. I found a book about the new tech, and compared it to this system. The biggest problem with new tech is turning the city grid back on if it ever goes off. It takes a single, massive surge of energy." I paused, and took a deep, steadying breath, praying that I was right. "This was likely the backup the city had."

The following silence felt like the moment I pulled the bow back, sighting my kill, waiting for the right moment to release. Knowing that what came next changed everything. Finally, he spoke. "You think . . . this?"

I took a deep breath and released the shot I'd been lining up for months. "We could set it off—channel the energy into turning the new tech system back on."

His flashlight turned to me, blinding me, his voice disbelieving. "You can't be serious, Sam. Even if this really could turn the new tech back on, you'd kill us all first."

I turned back to the grim, lethal beauty of the weapon. *Maybe the most beautiful things are also the most dangerous.* But I wasn't thinking of the weapon—I was thinking of her. Her smile. Her lips. Her absence. She wouldn't have feared the weapon. She wasn't afraid of anything . . . except maybe the Creation.

I pushed his flashlight down, and then turned my own flashlight to the walls of the bunker. "This bunker can open at the top, but if you leave it sealed, it's designed to absorb the blow, to funnel it into the new tech systems. That's what it was built for: the dual purpose of defense and restarting the city's new tech if it ever failed. But I can't do it on my own."

"What do you mean?"

The slow burn of shame grew in my chest. No matter how I looked at it, this was the one part of the problem I couldn't solve. The real reason I needed Gabriel's help. "We need a new tech engineer and someone who has the codes. And there are two sets of keys you have to insert. Both need to be turned at the same time."

I talked for hours with the only other living soul I trusted to know about this, and we'd both agreed this was the safest way to pitch it to Gabriel. He didn't need to know I'd already found one of the keys, and wore it on a chain around my neck, or that I knew there had once been a new tech engineer in the clan. He had to want to help.

It was perfect, the world handed to him on a silver platter . . . still, he said nothing. He stared at the weapon in silence, as paralyzed and cowardly as he'd been all winter. I ground my teeth together, forcing myself to wait. Didn't he understand that if we could turn Boise back on, we could have the world back again?

"And if you're wrong?" Gabriel finally said. "If this bunker isn't made to absorb the blow?"

"I'm not wrong."

"But if you were?"

Then Phillip will have a hell of a lot more company. "I'm not. And even if I were, it's worth the risk. Think about it: We could restart Boise. And then the world."

All I needed was a little help finding the engineer and final key. Gabriel might have been obsessed with power and blinded by pride, but there had been a new tech engineer in the old clan. Surely he remembered that?

Still, he said nothing, till I could no longer take it.

"How much longer do you think the city will stand like this?" I said, my hands fisted at my side to keep from grabbing him—or my knife. "The clans are ready to rip each other apart. There's not enough food or supplies left. The Castellano clan won't survive another winter—it might not even survive the summer. This is our solution—the only solution."

"Did you tell anyone else about this?"

"A friend. They won't tell anyone." It was the first time I'd lied today.

"Can he get in?"

"No." I shook my head. "The guard out there has the only ID card I've found. I haven't been able to find another way in—I doubt there is one. They didn't exactly want people in here."

Gabriel fell silent again. I felt like I'd handed him the key to some great, secret power, but for all his reaction I might have been handing him a manual on horse dung.

"I can do this, Gabriel."

"Or you'll destroy the entire city trying."

"It's worth the risk."

"You're not the one who gets to make that decision."

"And you are?" Anger flared in my chest. "Because you're a clan leader? Is that why you're afraid? Because with the power back on, we won't need the clans anymore? We won't need *you* anymore?"

He turned to me, and without meaning to my hand went to the dagger at my waist. But that wasn't Gabriel's way. No, his way was endless, pointless talking.

"Men will always need leaders," he said, in that slow, calm way that had once driven Kaden mad. "And for now, I represent the best interests of the men of the clan. My answer is no."

A thick, ugly tension grew between us. My hand fell on the cool handle of my knife, but I didn't draw it—because what would that accomplish? Only now did I realize how badly I'd misread this whole thing. I should have disappeared from the clan, done it all on my own. Found the engineer and the keys myself. That's what Emma would have done.

Bastards stay rulers, until you bring them down.

Gabriel must have read the anger on my face, because he stepped forward, smiling at me, trying the charm that had worked on many. It had absolutely no effect on me.

"Sam, I appreciate everything you've done for the clan. The food, the supplies, the intel—the men have come to look at you as a leader. They admire you . . . but power is a dangerous thing. I'm not saying it's a no forever, just till we better understand the tech. We can discuss it more back at the clan."

He patted my shoulder as if I were some kind of puppy and not a man who didn't stand two inches taller than him. The problem with his platitudes was that I didn't believe him and worse, I should have known better. I'd lost everything because of Gabriel, and now he was taking this too.

But he wouldn't take anything else.

Kaden was gone. Issac was dead. Em had abandoned me.

Everyone I'd ever known had left me. It was only me now. So I straightened my back, and met his eyes dead on. "I understand."

"Good. Now let's go back and get the other men. I'll keep the card, and we'll discuss our options further, back at the clan. Till then, can we keep this between us?"

"Of course."

I followed him from the room, shutting the door after one last glance at the weapon. Then the door sealed behind us, and Gabriel reached forward and stole the card from Phillip.

Phillip's head hung heavy, judging me for my failure.

You're wrong, Phillip. I didn't give up. I won't follow another leader. I'm biding my time to go my own way.

But I felt his judgment as we walked through the dark. Because the problem with biding your time was, at some point, you ended up like Phillip. A corpse propped against the wall, forever waiting.

Gabriel led us through the darkness and back to the light.

"You'll remember what I said?" Gabriel said, as he pushed open the final door, light flooding over us, the bitter wind crashing over me. I could smell the decay, the earth reclaiming the cement and metal, and deep beneath, a city waiting to be exhumed. To be all it once was and more.

Ara had once risked everything to follow her father's words and go back to the beginning. But that wasn't what I wanted. I wasn't looking to the past—I was looking to the future. I wanted a new world. A new beginning. No matter what it took.

"I remember everything," I said.

Before this was all over, Gabriel would too.

CHAPTER TWO—ARA

I stepped into the vastness of the mall. Cold, ominous hallways stretched around me. Wind whistled in through the broken sky-lights above, a few birds swooping in and out. Their calls chirped high and bright, as if no one had told them the plague had come. Their calls echoed strangely in the openness.

Making my way slowly forward, I walked carefully through the debris and dust. It seemed like much more than five years ago that I'd walked these halls. As much as I tried, I couldn't fully recall the noise and vibrancy of life as it had once been. Before the plague had taken all the women and most of the men from us.

All around me hints of the past littered the ground: faded paper, discarded clothing. The sun had begun to sink toward the horizon, leaving me a few hours till night. Still, I couldn't help feeling that even in a year, Boise had changed. The city I'd once known had given up the fight, knowing there was no hope of return. I stepped over broken glass, walking with the silent hunter's tread my father had taught me, a sense of despair rising inside me.

Where are you, Kaden?

The walls of the mall stretched out around me in silence. It had been almost two years since I'd last been in this mall, with Kaden, Sam, and Issac. Back then we had all gathered around a fire, surviving together in a ruined world. I had begun as a girl looking only for her father and sister, but then found a strange sort of belonging with Kaden, Sam, and Issac in the Castellano clan. Gabriel's clan that I'd burned down to save Kaden and myself.

But a year had passed since then. In the time we'd been away from Boise the mall had changed, vines climbing all the way up to the ceiling, like some sort of indoor jungle. The once marble white floors were nearly invisible beneath dirt and debris. I crouched beside a patch of mud where several footprints had been left. So many that it was clear there were other men in the area.

There are no friendly men. Not in this world, Ara.

That's what my father had taught me. Only now my heart hurt every time I thought of him. He was dead and gone, entombed forever beneath The Last City. It felt cruel that I'd found him only to lose him again. Yet even with the pain, now I knew that Emma was alive, and here, somewhere in Boise. Everything my father had taught me had kept me alive and would help me find her and Kaden. In that way, he lived on.

The farther I walked into the mall, past old stores and faded signs, the more I felt something was off. This wasn't the place I remembered—though at least I saw no sign of the infected wolves Kaden and I had met last time. Dozens of mannequins had been dragged out of their stores and left distributed throughout the long hallways. It gave the feeling of being watched—alone and not alone in the same moment. They were all dressed, some with bags and hats, some with raised hands, a frozen, unsettling mockery of the humanity that had once filled these halls.

I passed one mannequin whose chest was full of holes, as if someone had used it for target practice. That, at least, made sense to me. Target practice was useful. What purpose did these mannequins have? *Unless they exist to unnerve and distract newcomers like me.*

I stepped ever more carefully, holding my empty gun aloft as I continued. Kaden, Septimus, and I had agreed that if we were separated on our journey back from The Last City, we would meet here. But I had never expected what happened the night we were separated. Creation had swarmed the small town we were staying in. I tried not to think about the screams, the gunshots, the way Kaden had been ripped away from me, the final glance of his terrified eyes before the crowd tore us apart. I'd run into the darkness, then stopped only to look back to see the town on fire behind me. I had been lucky—I still had my bag and gun—but I hadn't dared return to the town. Instead, I continued my journey to Boise alone, hoping to run into Kaden and Septimus along the river. But they'd never showed, and it was too dangerous to stop moving or linger long. I had to have faith they would find me here. I had to look to the future, not the past.

Yet walking these halls alone felt like an odd echo of the past: the last time I'd returned to Boise, it had also been with an empty gun, seeking someone I loved. The wind whistled through the hallways, and every time the clothing on one of the statues fluttered my heart missed a beat.

Something moved in the corner of my vision—I jerked to the empty storefront beside me. But no, it was only another mannequin, with a flowy dress fluttering in the breeze.

Keep moving. You'll find him.

He's here.

He has to be.

The winter had been long, and, if not quite happy, productive at least. Kaden, Septimus, and I had left The Last City, armed with the knowledge that my blood held the one true cure, and could be spread via the plague flowers. We'd found them growing wild down the river, and I helped spread the cure all winter. That was part of why I needed to return to Boise: to bring the cure here.

Knowing that I could help cure people here almost helped cover the wound that my father's death had carved into my chest . . . and the guilt that he and my grandfather had created the plague that had begun all this. My family had ended the world: it was only right that I helped heal it.

I leaned over the counter of an old Wetzel's Pretzels, then poked around in the back. There was nothing there but a few shredded cardboard boxes. I hadn't really expected to find anything, but it had been a few days since I'd had a proper meal. I'd chosen speed over comfort, hoping Kaden would be here when I arrived.

Yellowed papers and leaves swirled through the abandoned hallways, the low moan of the wind masking any other noise. Vines crept through the storefronts, the whole city more ghostly and eerie than last time. Or maybe that was just the lack of Kaden, Sam, and Issac.

Every time a new store came in sight, or I lined up the gun with yet another mannequin, adrenaline surged through me— but nothing and no one emerged. I wasn't even sure why I bothered—my gun was as empty as the vast halls. Except the farther I walked, the more a strange sense of paranoia rose in me. As if I were being watched. Or followed.

I made my way to where the hallway turned and glanced around the edge. I meant to pull back immediately, but then I froze. One of the mannequins could have lifted a hand and waved and I wouldn't have noticed.

Spray-painted onto a far wall, in vivid green, were the words: SAM WAS HERE. Blood pounded through me. It was suddenly hard to draw breath. My knees felt weak—relief, disbelief, and shock coursed through my veins.

Sam was here.

Kaden and I had found a video broadcast from Boise with Sam in it, and with Emma, my little sister, which proved they were alive and in Boise. But that had been months ago—we'd still been in The Last City when we saw it. The journey back to Boise had taken all winter and then some. I took a slow breath, checked the hallways again, and then made my way over to the wall. Running a hand over the letters, I tried to find some clue as to how old they were. It was impossible to know for certain—it certainly wasn't fresh. But it hadn't been here last time I was, so it had to have been at some point in the last year.

Sam might have been here . . . at some point. What about Emma?

I made my way to the old fountain Kaden had shown me when I was first here. Back then it had a working pump that pulled up fresh water. I was pleased to find the fountain still working now. Water splattered into the base as I refilled my canteen, the sound too loud in the cavernous space.

Had Kaden been there I would have bathed. For now, I splashed water on my face and used the reflection from the pool to watch for movement on the second level of the mall. I saw no one, but the paranoia had shifted to certainty. Someone was here.

So why don't they make a move already? What are they waiting for?

If it wasn't for the fact that this was where Kaden and I had planned to meet if ever separated, and Sam's words on the wall, I would have run. Instead, I decided to bluff.

"I know you're there," I said, my voice swallowed by the rising columns and drifting out into the shattered skylights. "You may as well come out."

The wind and birds were the only answer. But I couldn't help but wonder if someone had placed the mannequins throughout the mall as a form of cover. All you would need to do was stand very still, and from afar it would be impossible to make out a human from a mannequin. With that unsettling thought, I pulled out my knife, placed it under the hand that held the gun, and started off again.

No such thing as friendly men. Not in this world.

But I wasn't that same girl who'd left the safety of the mountains and journeyed down into the city to find my father. I belonged to Kaden, and my blood belonged to the world. I wouldn't run. Not this time.

How I didn't see it, I couldn't say. The mall, the city, everything was different now. I expected the attack, if it came at all, to come from above.

One moment I was walking, eyes trailed on the mannequins placed at irregular intervals on the escalators to my left, when a snapping sound came from below, and the ground beneath me gave way. There was only panic, then the horrible sense of falling. I smashed into the ground. Pain and rising dust blinded me.

I lay there, dust swirling in thick clouds, the breath knocked out of me, trying to think through the disbelief. My right knee throbbed. Razor-sharp pain lanced down my side. Hot, sticky blood ran down my face.

You're all right. You're all right. You fell into a hole.

And then, immediately after, *So stupid! Why weren't you watching the ground?*

I tried to think, to figure out what to do now. But there was so much pain and confusion, all I could do was look at the shaft of light above me and struggle to draw breath. My chest felt hollow, refusing to draw air, and it was several long minutes before I finally felt able to breathe again.

By this point the dust had settled. I worked to throw off the debris and wooden boards that had fallen around me. Clearing it off brought me to the cold realization that this wasn't an accident—this was some sort of trap. The hole was too perfect, and the floor above had seemed so solid and unbroken from above.

My hands trembled as I finally checked over my body, wincing as I did. My leg was sore, and I had a gash on my forehead that throbbed. Blood ran into one of my eyes, but a tender touch told me the cut wasn't deep. I'd live—at least until I met whoever had set this trap.

A shadow fell across me.

I froze and looked up. I was right—I was being watched. I wondered if there were more of these traps throughout the mall, and if Kaden might have also been caught in one.

A man came into view above. Most of his face was covered in a bandana—I could make out only dark hair and pitiless eyes. My heart began to beat ragged. Then another man emerged. And another and another, until I'd lost count, until a group of men encircled the pit and stared down at me.

"It's a girl," one of them said.

"Should we kill her?" This from another man. "She might be infected."

More words were spoken, most in low, swift Spanish I couldn't discern.

Cold, clear fear pumped through me. Things had changed: once being a girl meant I'd been protected. Now they discussed killing me without remorse.

No such thing as friendly men. Not in this world. Not for you, Ara.

My fingers twitched—where was my gun? I'd dropped it when I fell—it had to be somewhere under the debris surrounding me at the bottom of the pit. But I'd hardly have any more bargaining power with an empty gun in my hands.

"I'm not infected," I called up to them. "I was cured."

This was a lie Kaden and I had come up with and used in a few of the small mountain towns we'd passed through. Safer to claim the plague flowers had cured me than admit the cure ran through my blood. But the reaction I'd had in the small mountain towns was nothing like the one I got here—sudden silence fell.

All the men turned to look at the first man who'd come out. He stared down at me, and I had the chilling feeling that whatever he said they would do.

"There is no cure," he said.

"There is," I said, wiping the blood from my eyes yet again. "A flower, from The Last City. It's in my bag. I can give it to you and prove it. Please, I used to be part of the Castellano clan. Someone there can vouch for me."

Dead, wallowing silence. This time I knew I'd said something wrong.

"She's with another clan," one of the men said, not bothering to whisper now, raising his gun, my heart thundering ever faster. "We should kill her."

The man, who could only be the leader, pushed the other man's gun down, then said down to me. "There is no more Castellano clan. Whatever peace treaties the clans had were broken when it burned. It's every clan for themselves now."

No more Castellano clan? That wasn't what Sam's message had said. Before I could ask more, he said, "You have this supposed cure with you?"

"Yes, it's in my bag, and the flowers grow down by the river. If you just let me—"

"Send it up," he said, cutting me off. A moment later a rope was sent down. *Shit.* I stared at the rope—what if I sent it up and then he left me down here to rot? But what else was I going to do? The plague flowers *worked*. Once they saw that, they'd let me out . . . right?

Failing to see an alternative, I tied my backpack to the end of the rope—but not before removing my full canteen. At the very worst, I could survive down here a few days as long as I had water. I tugged twice and the rope ascended, taking my pack, and the plague flowers inside, with it.

As soon as the pack disappeared over the lip of the hole, the men faded away too. I waited—surely they couldn't just leave me here? They were probably talking, making a plan . . . But the only sound was the low howl of the wind, the call of birds and the thud of my heart in my chest.

As if they'd never been here at all.

"Wait!" I called out, my voice echoing. The walls seemed to press in around me. "Please don't leave me here! I know where hidden supplies are in the mall! I know Kaden Marshall and Sam Preston—I was part of the Castellano clan! I can help you!"

The steep walls of the pit rose around me, offering no escape.

No answer came.

CHAPTER THREE—SEVYN

The dreams always begin the same way.

At first, there are only two sisters: one with red hair, the other's nearly black. The location differs—the mountains, the city, their house, somewhere beneath the blue sky—but always they are together. Sometimes they are singing, sometimes dancing, sometimes laughing, sometimes fighting, but it is clear there is a bond between them. A bond that should be impossible between a Creation and a human. It is peaceful, an idyllic childhood, an Eden before the fall.

Then the dream changes.

The father steps in from the background. He has the same auburn hair, the same hazel eyes as one daughter. He watches one daughter with love and devotion, but the other he watches with caution. As if he is waiting for her to become a monster.

Instead, he becomes the monster.

He leaves the dark-haired girl to die, and no matter how she screams, he never returns.

And then there is the other dream.

Green water surrounds me. It's peaceful, bubbling, and warm, covering every inch of me. The breathing tube in my mouth feels strange, the air stale and dry, but plentiful. The Creation surround me, in their glass tubes. There is a frustration beneath the peace, that my fellow Creation are so close yet I can never touch them.

Then the air stops.

I drag on the tube, trying to fight the panic. There is always air, the air cannot stop. But it has. I try to pull in air, again and again, but there is nothing.

Fear.

Panic.

Pain.

My body begins to jerk and my eyes snap open as I pound on the glass.

Finally, too late, I see them watching me. The humans.

I am suffocating.

I am dying.

I slam my hands against the glass. I choke—pleading, begging, dying, but they do nothing. I thrash against the respirator in my mouth and pull it free, trying to drag in air, but there is only water, choking me, drowning me, rushing down and filling my lungs.

I drown in pain and hatred, and when I wake, covered in sweat, screaming, all that's left is a reminder of who has done this.

Why they must pay.

Today I wield my hatred like a sword.

Smoke rose in dark plumes all around me. Someone screamed to my left, the noise quickly cut off by one of the Creation. I've told them to kill the humans quickly—even if it's far less than they deserve, far less than they gave to my many brothers and sisters who died in that underground lab where they made us.

Walking alone through the ruins of the small town, I realize that the sounds of screams, gunshots, and clashing weapons have all faded. It always surprised me how the humans fought to survive. Hadn't the plague shown them that their time was over?

Bodies littered the way. Black birds I had no name for were already swooping down and mounting the closest buildings and trees, watching me with beady eyes. Sometimes I wondered if even the animals here could sense we were something different. Something created, not born. The wind swept through the burning town, and even here, in the midst of death, there was an aching beauty to the land and the vastness of the sky.

It almost filled the hole in my chest.

The Last City had fallen so easily. Even I hadn't expected the ferocity of the Creation. For so many years we had been kept as prisoners beneath the city; for so many years our hatred had festered and grown so that when the first of us escaped, it was like the first drop of a rainstorm of blood. I gave the order, and they left behind nothing but a graveyard of charred bodies.

Yet when we'd left The Last City and journeyed south, I had expected some resistance. Not this . . . nothingness. How could I ever become a great and glorious conqueror when my opposition fell so easily? I stepped over yet another charred body, arms and legs twisted in a final gruesome dance.

Disappointment.

That was what I felt.

Not regret. Not some weak, human emotion like sadness or pity.

Disappointment was the weight settling on my chest. These

great humans—whom I'd spent years hating, who had destroyed the Earth and each other without thought, these vicious, violent predators—had fallen like saplings before the storm. Like a child silenced in the night.

Was this to be my fate? A grim reaper forever doomed to squash bugs?

A fire blazed in a barn to my right, and I stepped closer to crouch beside the body of one of the humans, almost wishing he were alive so I could ask him the questions that haunted me. For so long humans assumed the right to choose—assured in their right to lay waste to a beautiful world—but now they faced their final reckoning.

Was it so much to ask them to at least make it a challenge?

Even the redheaded girl—the one with the cure that pulsed through her veins, humanity's last hope, the last she—had left an easy path. She and the green-eyed man had followed the river, spilling her blood into the escaped plague flowers and distributing them to people along the way. I'd followed, killing those they'd given the cure to. A few humans escaped, but it hardly mattered. Not when I was the plague that humanity couldn't escape.

I left behind the field of bodies and continued to walk. The Creation watched as I walked among them, heads bowed, everyone moving out of my way as I went. I knew they would bury the bodies, as we did with all the dead, and then we would move on and repeat the process all over again. Outside the town, thick pines stood impervious to all. Out there, I met the only human left alive. At my order.

She stood directly in my path, glaring at me. Today her hands were unbound, and she clutched a knife in her hands. The emptiness I'd felt in the town slipped away as I approached. *Perhaps the world would not be so dull and boring if more humans were like Talia.*

"Talia," I said, enjoying the way she flinched when I said her name. Talia had been friends with Ara and Kaden in The Last City—until she betrayed them both to Walter, Ara's grandfather and the city ruler, to try to save her sister. A sister she would never get back because she was already dead. It made it more fun to string her along now, knowing that she would have a front-row seat to the demise of her former friends and their city. "Should I turn my back now, or were you planning to wait until nightfall to try to kill me?"

Her eyes were hard. She wasn't easily broken, this human. "Now would work."

"So innately human of you to stab me in the back."

"You shouldn't joke about me killing you. Someday I will."

I laughed at this. If nothing else, Talia was an entertaining distraction in an otherwise unchallenging world. She had been my prisoner since The Last City, and had tried to escape and kill me more times than I could count. It was one of the few human diversions I enjoyed.

She followed as I climbed the hill that grew increasingly steep. I could have outpaced her easily, but I moved slowly, flipping over small rocks covered in moss. I pocketed one with an unusual shape that glinted with flecks of silver and gold. *So much beauty in this world that the humans took for granted.* As expected, Talia didn't notice anything as she crushed small plants on her path to the top.

"You shouldn't climb with a knife in your hand," I said, taunting her when she finally drew closer.

"I know my way around a knife."

"If that were true, I wouldn't still be breathing."

She glared at me but tucked the weapon into her belt as we continued to climb. It seemed I would be spared an assassination attempt for the moment.

The farther we climbed, the quieter the thoughts of the other swarming Creation below became. It was a heavy burden, this mission that had been placed upon me. Even when the Creation followed me completely, I resented the constant barrage of their thoughts, especially where they concerned Talia. They didn't understand why I kept Talia alive. But to me it was obvious. If you wanted to destroy your enemy, first you had to understand them.

High overhead a bird soared, as if mocking our slow progress up the hill. I forced my feet to move at a human pace. The greatest accomplishments took time, patience, and the ability to see a problem from every angle. Humanity was more than a problem: they were the swarming, disgusting maggots feeding on the corpse of the world.

The top of hill was close now, Talia at last drawing near. I pushed ahead, and topped the crest . . .

. . . and was left breathless.

Wind blasted against me, like it was trying to tear me free. For a moment I thought of lifting my arms and seeing if it really would. The breeze wrapped around me, bursting with stories of the richness of the land: sagebrush, river trees, wet earth releasing new growth after a winter spent asleep. The flooded downtown lay far below us, the water like a glorious golden mirror reflecting the sun. A river snaked through the city that began at the base of the foothills and stretched far into the distance.

It was perfection.

It was everything I had been denied when forced to exist

underground. Everything *we* had been denied. Seeing it all brought a rising sense of purpose: this was what was at stake. Humans had destroyed this and each other, and would again if I didn't stop them.

Talia finished the climb, breathing hard as she came to stand beside me. For a moment I couldn't decide if I was happy I'd brought her or not. She was the enemy.

"Boise won't be like the other towns," Talia said. Even without turning, I could picture the way her eyes flashed, the way her hair caught the sun, the way her fingers wrapped white-knuckled around the knife in her belt. "They'll have weapons. Defenses. Ara told me they have organized clans. They'll fight you. It won't be like the other places you slaughtered."

Slaughter. Was that all I'd become? A butcher overwhelmed at the sheer harvest before him. But no, this city would be different—even Talia declared it.

"You think they'll fight?" I said softly, more to myself than her.

"Yes." Her voice was confident. "Your Creation aren't as perfect as you think. They let some of the men escape on horseback. They'll go down to Boise. Warn the others. They'll be ready."

Now I couldn't help it. I laughed. Talia watched me in shock. Then I stepped forward and stole the knife from her belt. Before her body had even registered what I'd done, I'd flipped it in a smooth arch, the sun glinting off the polished edge. Her eyes tracked the progression of the knife, not quite managing to hide the fear there. Her voice was softer, less certain when she said, "They'll band together. Even with the whole Creation army at your back, you can't defeat an entire city."

"Will they? Or will they fight among themselves as they always do?" I waited for her to answer my question, but the way her eyes went from the city and back to mine was answer enough. I tossed her back the knife, which she caught with deft fingers. Let her have her small weapon—it wouldn't do any good.

I turned back to the city. Soon I would fill the emptiness inside me. The humans would fear me, respect me, and finally reap what they'd sown.

In the beginning, God created humans from the dust.

In the end, humans created me, with one purpose: To return them to it forever.

CHAPTER FOUR—SAM

"C'mon, Liam. Think about it. We could turn the whole world back on. Why does Gabriel get to be the one who says no?"

We'd returned from our expedition three days ago, but still Gabriel hadn't even tried to talk with me about it. Which meant I'd gone to his second-in-charge, Liam. We sat tucked in the edge of the courtyard, where the weekly bonfire cast his face in flickering shadows. On the other side of the courtyard, the sharp crack of the whip and the corresponding scream rang out in the open space. The man at the whipping post had failed to report a small handgun he'd found in the ruins. His screams both sickened me and made me more determined than ever.

"This isn't the clan you and I joined," I pushed when Liam said nothing. "We used to be a family—not whatever the hell this is." I gestured to the whipping post and Liam sighed, his normally smiling eyes tight and unhappy. Ever since we'd moved into the Old Penitentiary, things had changed for the worse. Men patrolled the high walls not just to keep out invaders, but also to make sure no one inside tried to escape. There were no more clan games, no more laughter or singing. The roses that bloomed here in the summer had been crushed and cut away. Maybe it was how close Gabriel had come to losing everything. Whatever it was, the clan was run more like a prison than a community now.

The whip cracked again, and Liam flinched. He didn't like the whippings, but he also didn't speak against them. No one did—not unless you wanted your own collection of stripes on your back.

Liam shook his head, speaking low so his voice didn't carry. "If he said no, there's a reason for it. A weapon like that—imagine what it would be like in the wrong hands. Maybe we're better off without it. We've survived so far."

"*Survived*, Liam." I couldn't hide my frustration. "Do you really want to spend the rest of your life like this?" I gestured to the slinking shadows of the courtyard, the screams, the moans of the man at the far end, the guards pacing the perimeter wall. We were *definitely* living in a prison. "Think about what we could create." He had to be able to imagine—he'd helped build the clan after all. I knew there was still hope in him—it was just buried beneath fear. "We could build a better world, a new world."

"Sam . . . the world before, it wasn't much better than this. You're too young to remember—"

"I remember enough," I said, cutting him off, then forcing myself to lower my voice. It wasn't wise to draw attention, even here. "But I remember a clan where men used to smile and laugh. We deserve more than this." *Why couldn't he understand?* "I'm not asking to rebuild the old world. I'm asking you to help me build a better one."

Liam didn't answer me until after the final strike had fallen and the man was pulled down and carried away by his friends. "The clan isn't what it once was—but neither is Boise. Things have changed, and not for the better. Do you know what happened the last time I tried to deliver peace treaties?"

"No," I said, feeling mutinous.

"They killed the other two men I was with. I barely made it back. Gabriel hasn't sent anyone else out."

Cold ran down my back. "I didn't know that." *Why hadn't I known that?* The answer came to me immediately. Because Gabriel had ordered him not to tell.

"Exactly. Because Gabriel knows more than you do. We need to move carefully, Sam. If this weapon has the type of power you're talking about, it's dangerous."

"That's my point. We need to move fast—before someone else does."

"I'm sorry, Sam." He shook his head again, regret in his eyes. "My answer is no. Trust Gabriel. If he said no, it's because he has another plan."

"Liam—come on—wait—" But he had stood up and was striding away from me. Anger blazed in my chest as he left me stranded there. The only thing that stopped me from standing up and yelling were the two letters folded and tucked away, one in each breast pocket.

Bastards stay rulers, until you bring them down.

There is only the peace we find.

Emma's words versus Issac's. The girl I loved—and lost—versus the man who'd become my father after the plague. I carried the two letters wherever I went. Issac's unopened letter in my right pocket; Em's read and refolded a thousand times in my left. I liked to imagine they were the devil and angel on my shoulder.

Seeing as I'd only read Emma's it probably gave some hint as to whose voice was louder.

But how could I open Issac's letter? How could I read his final words to me? As long as I didn't open it, there was still some small part of him that lived on. I couldn't surrender it, so I carried the letter everywhere, keeping that small piece of him alive.

Sometimes when I was alone, in the city, it felt like the dead called out to me with soft, sinuous voices, trying to drag me down with them. That was why I couldn't think too much about the past—it was full of the dead. I could only look to the future, to what we could create and build.

I sat there brooding for some time. Finally, the cold grew too much, and I had no choice but to go inside.

The cafeteria was crowded, warm with the geothermal heat and thus where most of the men hung out at night.

"Sam, how are the ruins lately? Any monsters?!"

"Any fresh meat tonight, Sam?"

"Sit here, Sam! Drink with us!"

Men called out to me when I walked in. Usually, I sat and talked with them. Tonight I nodded and kept walking, not in the mood for conversation when I couldn't talk about the one thing that really mattered.

The last few months had brought me a newfound popularity here—surprising because I'd always assumed it was Kaden people liked, not me. But in my brother's absence, I'd become the man who brought back much-needed supplies and food, doubly necessary as many of the clan's supplies had been lost when the old building had burned. The hungrier men became, the more they loved me for bringing food. Even Gabriel was careful around me—which was why I'd gotten cocky. I hadn't really expected him to whip me for trying to keep a gun. Yet even that punishment had changed the way the men looked at me. I was one of them now more than ever.

It was a strange thing—power. For so long I thought I didn't want it. Now I saw that if you wanted to change things for the better, you needed power. And it always came with a cost.

I got in line for food—usually some kind of stew featuring mystery meat that I'd learned better to not ask about. As I waited, one of the other expedition teams approached me. They all wore black leather jackets like some kind of motorcycle gang, even though they traveled on foot like the rest of us. Their entire team brought back consistently less than I did alone. Kaden would have inspired them to do better somehow. I wished they would ignore me.

"Not a bad batch this time, Sam," one of them said, shoving a mug of whatever awful alcohol they'd brewed into my hands. "Here, try it."

"Thanks." I took a sip, then winced. It tasted awful.

"Find anything on your expedition, Sam?" one of the men in line said. Others turned to listen, all the men nearby waiting for me to speak.

Resentful anger flared in my chest, and the words were out before I could stop them.

"Nothing Gabriel will let me share."

The scars on my back twinged as if in warning. The men nodded and muttered, exchanging looks with each other, all of them shaking their heads.

"You hear that another team was attacked?" one of the men said.

I hadn't heard this—but it wasn't a surprise with the way Gabriel tried to lock down bad news. "What happened?"

"One of the Gonzalez brothers came back full of bullets. Doc couldn't do anything to help him." His voice dropped. "Gabriel didn't even send anyone out to find out who did it. This clan isn't what it once was." The other men shook their heads, agreeing, but carefully, glancing around as they did. The Castellano clan wasn't the home it had once been, but life outside these walls was even harder.

When I got to the front of the food line the cook gave me an extra scoop of soup—even though I knew he could get whipped for it. *But why not? I'm the one who brought the food in.* The thought was cold and bitter. Even though I wanted to sit alone, men joined me at the table I chose. I ate quickly and left.

Outside the wind was still sharp, but I could smell spring, see the green buds blooming on the trees. *Another spring without Kaden, Ara, and Issac.* Once thoughts of them had brought memories of warmth and happiness—now it churned a vast, dark, angry hole inside me. They had all left me. Abandoned me. Sometimes it scared me, the amount of bitterness that lived inside me—like it might consume me. As I crossed the courtyard, more men called out to me and I nodded, but said nothing. I'd already said too much.

A guard stood outside one of the smaller buildings in the corner of the Old Pen—it was one of the newest buildings, having been added later as a sort of tourist shop. It was also the only building, besides Gabriel's, that was guarded because of the person who lived within. Darkness had fallen completely as I made my way to the door.

"Good to see you, Sam." I didn't like the knowing smirk on the guard's face—but I also didn't really have a choice. He knew the deal here, same as me, and both of us would hang if either of us broke it.

"I'll put your payment on your cot tomorrow," I said grimly. Then I passed him by and opened the door to the only building in the Old Pen that didn't look like a jail inside. Full of lush carpets, colorful wall covers, and fresh flowers. Tonight candles lit the room in a flickering glow.

She had her back to me, hunched over something on the table. She didn't turn at my entrance, and I buried my annoyance. There was an instinct in me that flinched at every noise, saw every movement as a potential threat. I couldn't imagine being so protected that you didn't even turn when someone came through the door. *You were once innocent too. When Kaden and Issac protected you.* The thought didn't warm me.

I cleared my throat. "Hello, Addison."

At my voice, her head jerked up, her black curly hair bouncing with the movement. She grinned, and despite my earlier irritation, I smiled back.

"Sam! Finally! You got back days ago."

She crossed the room and threw her arms around my neck, pulling me into a hug. Even if she was only a year younger than me, she was so delicate and so . . . female. She wore a pale pink dress that showed off her slight but nevertheless feminine figure. I awkwardly patted her on the back, then quickly extracted myself from her embrace.

"I couldn't risk coming earlier." I walked over to the table. I was careful with Addison—not just because she was a lone woman in a world of men, but because she was Gabriel's little sister. If he caught me here, with Addison in my arms, the lashes on my back would look like child's play. And even if I'd never admit it, I was sometimes uneasy with Addison. She looked at me in a way Ara never had.

"How did it go?" she prompted. Like her brother, Addison was used to getting her way, and quickly. I settled heavily into a chair, and, seeing my face, she said, "That bad?"

"Worse. Not only did he say no, he took the access card that unlocks the bunker door." At least he didn't know I already had one of the keys hanging on a chain around my neck.

"I told you that you shouldn't have left the card on the corpse."

Phillip. His name was Phillip.

"It wouldn't have mattered." I shook my head, and suddenly felt exhausted. "He came down early, and I couldn't hide it from him. He said he'd talk when we got back to the clan but he's been avoiding me since we got back. We need to make another plan. Maybe I should go look for the engineer myself?"

"Maybe. Did you try talking to Liam?" Addison took a seat beside me, her dress just brushing my leg.

"Yeah. It went about the same as with Gabriel."

Her table was spread with papers and diagrams and projects that Addison was allowed to dream up—but only that. She left this room only for a single morning walk with her brother, or when he wasn't available, Liam. I'd seen Addison and Liam together a few times, talking and laughing, a touch of jealousy curling in me. The trust Gabriel extended to Liam would never extend to me.

"We have to start looking now, without him," she said. "Gabriel is stubborn—he thinks that what he's doing is best for humanity. If he said no, he won't change his mind. Maybe if we find the engineer, we can convince him to help us."

"Are you sure?" Even though I had wondered if it would some-day come to this, it still took me off guard. Blood was still blood.

She nodded, her face set and resolute. Watching her now, I saw the real reason we'd become friends. Addison had also changed since Ara and Kaden had disappeared. She'd gone from a child to a survivor. She'd been forced to see her older brother wasn't the perfect hero she once believed. We had a lot in common.

"I've read all the books you brought me on new tech front to back," she said. "If we can find the last key, and the engineer with the codes, then we can do it. Gabriel will come around."

We weren't moving against him . . . exactly. More working behind his back and then bringing him on board. *Though I doubt he'll see it that way.* Still, it could work.

It could also blow up in our faces. Literally.

"We need to find the engineer then," I sighed. We knew he was in the original clan, and that Kaden had known him, but beyond that I'd hoped Gabriel would know where he might be. "Any idea where he'd be now?"

She shrugged. "Sometimes people signed their original address when they joined the clan. The clan charter survived the fire. I'll make up some excuse to look there—I can probably get Liam to show it to me without him getting suspicious. And I'll have to get the key card back from Gabriel."

I tried not to consider all the ways this could go wrong. "What if you asked Gabriel to help? You could show him the book and our plan? Maybe that would go over better than with me asking."

She paused, seeming to fall back in on herself for a moment. "I don't see how I could without admitting we're friends . . . you think he'd be okay with that?"

"Absolutely. I bet afterward he'd name me the new leader of the clan and take me out for ice cream." The truth was, Gabriel's presence hung over our every interaction. For all her innocence, Addison understood what would happen if Gabriel found me here.

"I guess it's just me and you," she said. Her hand fell on top of mine, and I froze at the sudden physical contact. I was usually careful to keep a circle of space between us. But today I didn't pull back. How could I when she was the only person in the whole world who was on my side?

"So," I continued, "I'm reading a book about the American Revolution." Em would have mocked me, but Addison only watched me in silence. "And you know what the author keeps talking about? How young all the American leaders were. They weren't educated. They were outnumbered, outgunned, pretty much outmatched in every way. Most of the world thought they would fail. But *they* believed in their cause. They kept fighting for the kind of world they wanted to create. To them, that world was worth dying for."

"I'd like to read that book."

Was there a deeper message in her words? I gently pulled my hand away from hers, and said stiffly, "I'll lend it to you when I'm done."

A different sort of quiet settled between us; not uneasy, but charged. A silence I wasn't entirely sure what to do with.

"Do you look for her in the ruins?" she finally said.

Shock surged through me, and my gaze flashed up to her, a dull panic filling me. *How does she know about Em?*

She gave me a searching look. "Ara?"

I gave a shaky laugh at my own stupidity. Of course she was talking about Ara: she often did. They had been friends back when Gabriel had kept Ara captive in the old clan. I tried not to think about those days. It wasn't healthy to linger on plans that went poorly, or people you loved who disappeared without a trace. Which made it all the more pathetic that I still searched the ruins for Em. Still dreamed about her touch.

"I look for a lot of things in the ruins," I said.

"I've heard the men talking about how you've been almost single-handedly feeding the clan this winter." She laughed. "One of them said you've taken down three elk and a moose with your bow—is that true?"

Her words were a peace offering, but one I took gladly. "It was actually three elephants and a dragon with nothing but a sharpened pencil." I winked. "Nobody saw it, but trust me, it happened."

She grinned. "What did you bring me today?"

"Spoiled much? Always expecting something."

She held out a hand and I smiled as I slung off my small pack and searched through my survival supplies—tent, wires, knife, flint—for what I'd brought her. Unlike the other goods I'd brought back to the clan, Gabriel's goons never confiscated books. Books were the most precious resource left now—and even if others didn't understand, Addison did. Reading had created a bond between us I'd never expected.

When I'd decided to rejoin the Castellano clan, I'd found it very different from the clan I'd joined with Kaden. Addison and I were the two youngest members of the clan, both of us knew and loved Ara—but I'd thought that was all we had in common. She was, after all, the younger sister of Gabriel—something that I'd counted against her.

Then, only a few days after I'd rejoined, I saw Addison looking through a lone window in the back of this house—a window set with bars. Something about her reminded me of the summer I'd spent alone and friendless in Boise. Looking at her I knew she was in need of escape. Not literal physical escape—Gabriel guarded her like a dragon guards a princess—but the kind of escape that had saved me. Books.

That night I'd left her a book on the windowsill, and the next night it was back, with a small note tucked inside. For a while that had been it, me leaving her a new book I'd found in the ruins each night, returning the next night to find her letter tucked inside. I'd taken to writing back, until at some point, we became friends, and it was her, book in hand, waiting at the windowsill. We had become friends in our own right, and when I entered this room, I set aside the rivalry Kaden and Gabriel had begun. Today was the most we had ever discussed him—maybe that was why things felt different tonight.

"Is this a war manual or another alien adventure?" Addison took the small book I held out and examined it.

My cheeks heated at her question. I usually chose books I liked: about monsters or aliens or bloody wars. But lately I'd tried to pick books I knew Addison would enjoy too. "It's technically not a book—it's a play. *Romeo and Juliet.*" And, because I didn't want to sound like a total sap, I added, "It's still got epic sword fights, and betrayal . . ." Quieter, I mumbled, "And love."

"Thanks, Sam. I can't wait to read it."

I stood to go, but before I could, she slid off the chair and did something she'd never done before: she pressed a kiss to my cheek. My entire body froze, unable to move. The look she gave me—of adoration and longing—was one I couldn't return, as much as maybe I wanted to.

How could I tell her that when I dreamed at night, it wasn't of her? It was of a girl with flashing blue eyes, dark hair, and anger to her core.

"I should go. Lots to do. The clan won't feed itself." I cringed at my words—*could you sound more stupid?*—then slung my pack on, ready to make a hasty escape when her voice stopped me.

"Sam?" I paused with one hand on the doorknob, worried. But her next words weren't about me. "Gabriel is a good person, even if everything he's done lately with the new clan hasn't been. I know it's not fair that he blames you for Kaden's mistakes—"

"It wasn't Kaden's fault that he kept Ara captive. None of this is Kaden's fault. It's Gabriel's. He's the one who won't help us. He's the one who turned our clan into a prison."

My words were as sharp as a knife, and I saw the hurt on Addison's face. This was why we didn't talk about Gabriel.

"All I'm asking," she said softly from behind me, "is that if we do this, that you won't forget he's my brother. And I love him the way you loved Kaden."

Loved. Did she know that word twisted in my gut like a knife? The happy feeling I'd had when I handed her the book was gone, replaced by a dark, angry hole churning in my chest.

"When it comes to Gabriel," I said coldly, "I forget nothing." Issac's death. Kaden and Ara's disappearance. The whispered stories that Gabriel had murdered his own older brother, Emerson, for control of the clan. The history between Gabriel and myself was a wedge that had always existed between Addison and me—a chasm even books couldn't span.

I tried to smile, but it felt false, even to me. "You work on finding out more about the engineer and getting the access card back. I'll ask around the clan and see if anyone has any leads. Good night, Addison."

Then I pulled the door closed and made my way across the dark clan. I didn't want to fight with her, not when she was my only ally in getting the new tech back on. Still, I couldn't erase the way she'd looked at me as I left.

As if I'd disappointed her.

CHAPTER FIVE—ARA

I jerked awake as something heavy hit the ground beside me. For a moment, my head spun, and panic flooded my body. Where was I? How had I gotten here?

Darkness had fallen. My body ached. My forehead throbbed. I reached up and then winced when my fingers touched dried blood.

"Still alive down there?"

I looked up, just able to make out the dark outline of a man's form. A vast, cavernous darkness loomed beyond him, crowned in a strip of starlight. It all came back to me in a painful rush: I was in the mall. I'd fallen asleep in the pit. Whoever had left me down here was back.

The beam of a flashlight hit me in the face, and I winced away from the brightness.

"Hurry up and climb out," the man said. He sounded annoyed—as if helping me were a massive inconvenience to him.

"How?" The light moved, illuminating a rope ladder that must have been the sound that woke me. I checked that my empty gun was tucked in the back of my belt, my knife in my boot, my canteen across my body, then started to climb.

The flashlight clicked off again as I drew closer to the top. He didn't step forward to help me, and it took me a few moments of struggling to pull myself over the edge. When I stood free from the hole, his flashlight clicked back on, the light creating a space between us. It was the man the others had looked at earlier—the one I had guessed was the leader.

Beyond the bandana he wore around his neck, he had dark hair, scruffy facial hair, and deep, shadowed eyes. One of his hands rested on the pistol at his hip and he watched me with a sort of coldness, like I was a wild animal he expected to attack. Even in the dark I could tell his tan, weathered face placed him as an older survivor—maybe fifties, maybe older. His light was attached to the end of the gun, which meant if he raised the light, I'd be staring down the barrel of the gun."

"You still have the gun you had earlier?" he said.

"Yeah." I opened my jacket, revealing the gun without reaching for it. Something about his cold, careful gaze made me think that he could draw his weapon and have me dead before I blinked. In addition to the gun he carried, a rifle was slung over his back, and his jacket looked as if it held myriad weapons, ammo, and supplies.

"Any bullets?" he said.

I hesitated, wondering if I should lie. "No."

"What caliber?"

"Nine-millimeter."

He reached into his jacket, then tossed a small box at me. It rattled when it hit me in the chest. Ammo. He was arming me?

Before I could thank him, he said, "Don't waste them, that's my last box. Get your backpack. Hurry."

His light shone on my backpack, resting next to the edge of the hole. I hesitated only a moment before I stepped forward and swung it on, the weight reassuring. Then I knelt, shoving bullets into my gun.

"My name is Ara," I said carefully, cocking the gun but not returning it to its holster. I felt better with it in my hand.

"Didn't ask for your name." He turned and the moment he did, the light swung away from me, casting me into darkness. "Come on," he said over his shoulder.

I didn't move, the vastness of the mall rising all around me. The few stars cast little light, but I knew these halls well. I knew where to find the supplies Kaden had left hidden here. Now I had a loaded gun, and, if the man had left everything in my backpack, I had everything I needed to survive. I could leave right now . . .

But what exactly would I gain by doing so? Kaden could be anywhere, and this was where we'd planned to meet. This man was clearly a leader among his people, and he hadn't threatened or forced me. He'd armed me. Judging by his retreating figure, if I walked away right now, he wouldn't stop me.

Plus, he'd taken the plague flowers from me. Did that mean he'd used them?

Curiosity got the better of me.

I followed.

His light pierced the thick darkness of the mall, lighting the uneven floor littered with the scraps of humanity. He moved carefully, weaving a path through the debris that told me he knew this path well. Twice an animal cried out in the night, and he stopped, holding his hand over the light for several long heartbeats before he dropped his hand and moved forward again.

After a few minutes we passed through one of the old department stores, then through a side door and out into the cool night. He glanced at me for only a moment, then said, almost critically, "Are you hurt?"

My forehead throbbed again, but I resisted the urge to touch the wound. The cool breeze blowing across the parking lot felt good against it. "I hit it when I fell. It's not too bad."

"Is it still bleeding?" he said, again not seeming able to look at me.

"No. It's scabbed."

"Good. There are still some predators out."

He started across the parking lot that now held a small forest of trees and weeds growing between abandoned cars and airships. After a winter in the mountains, the spring night felt mild, full of the scents of wet earth and blooming plants. Coyotes yipped in the distance, but the sounds didn't concern him. I wanted to ask him what had happened to the infected dogs that had lived in the mall, but decided they must have died—no one could live here full time if they were still here.

Despite wanting to keep a distance from him, I needed his light, so I found myself walking only a few steps behind him.

"You know, it would be nice to know your name," I said. "Or where we're going."

It took him a long time to answer. "Matteo. No more talking."

Right. Sorry. He gave no indication where we were going, but it wasn't toward the burned remains of the old Castellano clan. We crossed out of the parking lot, down a slight hill, and through several businesses that had been burned down. The yips of the coyotes grew closer.

I was about to press him for more information when he stopped before a single-story nondescript building. It was one I had never been inside—in fact, I wasn't sure I'd ever been in this part of Boise. Unease grew in my stomach. Why were we here?

Matteo spent a few moments before the front door, his gun pointed at the ground as the sound of metal tinkling came. Then he put his shoulder against the door and shoved it open, revealing a gaping darkness inside. Matteo turned back to me and said in a gruff voice, "Get in."

Part of me wanted to refuse, but then an animal howled behind us—an animal that sounded much bigger than a coyote. I stepped inside and he followed.

The door closed and his light illuminated a small waiting room with a few chairs and in the corner a counter covered by glass. The only window had been boarded over. There was something familiar about the space, despite the fact I was sure I'd never been here. Matteo made his way to the door beside the counter, finding yet another key in his key ring, when I suddenly realized where we were.

"Is this the county jail?"

He gave a gruff noise that I took as acknowledgment, but when he swung the door open and motioned inside, I froze. Gabriel had once kept me captive—I wasn't doing that again.

"Listen, thanks for the gun and all," I said, glancing down at the dark corridor beyond him, "but I'm not going in there with you."

I thought he would try to persuade me—that's what Gabriel would have done. Instead, he removed the flashlight from the top of the gun and slid the gun across the floor to me. I stopped it with my foot, and then stared up at him, shocked. But then my gaze hardened.

"As if I believe that's your only gun."

"Not very trusting, are you?"

"No."

He sighed, and then tossed me the keys too. I was so shocked I dodged them, and they clattered to the dirty floor beside me. Still, I didn't move.

It looked like it pained him to speak, but he finally said, "I'm not going to hurt you, girl. I need to show you something."

"Ara. My name is Ara."

"Fine. Ara. I need to show you something."

I pocketed the keys, then picked up his gun, holding both before I nodded. "All right. But one wrong move and I shoot. And leave that door open."

He nodded and I followed him into a dark room lined with cells. The rank smell of too many bodies in too small a place filled the air. But even though I'd just walked into a jail, with a man I barely knew, that wasn't why I was suddenly terrified.

The cells weren't empty.

They were full of infected.

Men or women, I couldn't tell—because they were like zombies. Some sat, slowly shaking back and forth. Others lay on cots, motionless, so that it was impossible to know if they were alive or dead.

I lowered both guns, my blood cold, the hair on the back of my neck standing on end. Each cell, on the left and right, held a single person, with white, bleeding eyes. It was so quiet I could hear the rush and pulse of my blood through my veins. Feel the impact of each footfall on the cement floor.

"Here," Matteo said, and I jumped at the sound of his voice. He was standing before the final cell, the beam of his light pointing inside.

I wanted to run, but I forced myself to keep walking, to see what he wanted to show me. At the last cell I knew instinctively something was different. The man inside, though skeletal as the others, turned his head to face me. Twin tracks of blood ran down his face.

But his eyes were clear.

"Matteo?" the skeletal man said, his voice hoarse. "You did it. You found the cure. You've saved us."

"It wasn't me," Matteo said. "It was her."

CHAPTER SIX—KADEN

"This has got to be the dumbest thing I've ever done." I held the zip line and glanced down at the roaring river below. If the line snapped, or I slipped, there was a good chance it'd be the last thing I ever saw. But if it worked it would also save us days of hiking and I could see Ara all that much sooner . . .

"Dumber than riding an old roller coaster that hadn't been serviced in years?" Septimus called out from behind me.

I laughed. Trust Septimus to remember my stupidest moments. "You're right. This is practically safe in comparison." I took a deep breath, tightened my grip on the metal bar, and felt the excitement and fear grow in my chest. "Well, we're burning daylight."

Then I jumped.

The line twisted as I went plunging straight for the roaring river, so fast I braced myself to crash. I went careening over the white-faced rapids, flying for the other side far faster than I'd anticipated. The water was so close beneath me I could feel its icy spray.

Then I was free of the river. Before I could crash into the tree the line was anchored to, I let go, falling hard and rolling several times on the bank before coming to a stop, flat on my back, staring up at the blue sky. I lay there, stunned for a moment. I hadn't expected the zip line to work. Septimus called to me from the opposite bank, and he was already pulling the zip line back to him with the wire he'd wisely suggested we tie to it beforehand.

"Kaden? Are you all right?" His voice barely carried over the roar of the river.

"I. AM. INVINCIBLE!" I shouted, jumping up and throwing my hands into the air.

"You should have seen yourself!" he yelled, his voice choked with laughter. "You looked like a squirrel in a rainstorm!"

As always, Septimus's analogies were completely unique. No matter how many times I tried to teach him human sayings, he preferred his own.

I cupped my hands and shouted, "QUIT STALLING AND GET YOUR ASS OVER HERE!"

We had found the zip line yesterday at dusk. I had been searching for a good place to ford the river but hadn't had any luck. Septimus was terrified of the water—sometimes he woke screaming from dreams about drowning in green water. The river was high and dangerous with spring snow melting off the mountains. The zip line was a gift. Or, as I'd like to see it, a dare.

"AUGHHHHHH!!!!" Septimus screamed, as he came soaring across the water.

"OPEN YOUR EYES!" I shouted, but he either didn't hear me or was too terrified to let go. Before I could move to stop him, he crashed into the tree the line was anchored to.

"Septimus!" I rushed over rocks and brush to get to him. "Are you okay?"

He lay on the ground, staring up at the sky. "Can I do it again?" he said with a glazed, wondrous look in his eyes.

I couldn't help it, I started to laugh. After a few moments he joined me, then I pulled him to his feet and dusted him off.

"You all right? Anything broke?"

He shook his head. Creation were different from humans—stronger, faster, but I guessed also less breakable.

"Fine. But I don't want to cross the water again."

"You won't have to." I grinned. "We're on the right side of the river now. Boise isn't far. As long as nothing else gets in our way, we'll see Ara soon."

I should have known better than to tempt fate.

~

We spent the day making progress as quickly as we could. After we'd been separated from Ara, we'd been hit by so much bad luck that when I'd first noticed the zip line I was tempted to think it was just another trick. I tried to believe it was the sign that our luck was finally changing. We would make it to Boise soon and find Ara. From the progress we were making, I'd hoped we were in front of the Creation now.

"Tell me more about Boise," Septimus said as we walked.

He did this often, almost like he was a child, which, I supposed, in some ways he was. He'd been grown in a lab under The Last City but had managed to escape. He had been hiding in the ruins that surrounded The Last City when he found me about to be executed and saved my life. During our time together he'd told me that there was some kind of computer program that ran on a constant loop, which taught the Creation the basics of human language and behavior from within their tanks. He had only been in the real, outside world for less than a year. Because of that I did my best to answer every question he asked me. Partly because he was my friend, and we'd saved each other's lives multiple times, but also because things would be different when we reached Boise. No one could know what Septimus really was. No one could know he was Creation.

"Before the plague, it was a really beautiful city," I began. "People used to float the river in the summer, and there were lots of hiking trails in the foothills. Lots of different people came to live there. It's where Sam grew up—and I spent a lot of time there, too, before I went to live with my dad."

"And now?" he said.

I sighed. That was the question, wasn't it? Ara, Septimus, and I had spent the last few months spreading the cure to as many small towns and settlements as we could. And then Septimus had woken, screaming, telling us that The Last City had fallen. Every night after that went the same way, him telling us they were moving, coming, killing.

Then, we'd actually run into a small group of them.

It was like nothing I'd ever seen before. Screaming. Fire. A wall of Creation, pressing in on the town, killing everyone they encountered.

I'd taken a bullet wound to the leg. It wasn't deep, but enough that I'd been distracted for the split moment it took for Ara to be separated from us. The last I'd seen of her she'd been running into a dark forest, and I hadn't dared call her back. Septimus and I had barely escaped ourselves, then we were forced to hole up for three horrible weeks while my leg healed. Septimus had searched into the night, trying to figure out where Ara had gone, but I knew he wouldn't find her. Ara knew how to survive, how to disappear. She would have followed our plan should we ever be separated: make it back to Boise. Get to the mall. Start spreading the plague flowers and telling others about the cure.

Now there was a new goal: Let everyone know the Creation was coming and burning everything in their wake. Find a way to stop them.

Septimus was watching me now, waiting for an answer like an expectant child. I chose my next words carefully. "Boise is different now," I said. "We'll have to be careful."

"But the clans are bringing peace?" Septimus said. He liked to hear about the clans far more than I liked to talk about them. I think he liked the idea that humans could organize and work together—it went against everything the Creation believed. That humans were evil, brutal, and not worth saving.

Unfortunately, sometimes I believed that too. "The clans are doing their best," I said uneasily.

Septimus smiled. He was getting better at reading my moods—the things I said without saying. "You don't like the Castellano clan leader, Gabriel, because, he is, in your words, a spineless prick?"

I laughed at this. "Yeah."

"You do know pricks do not have spines?"

As much as I missed Ara, life with Septimus was never dull. I had to imagine this was what having a kid would be like—a curious boy who always questioned everything. It made me want more than ever to find a safe place we could all live in peace.

My legs ached as we walked, the stiffness and pang from the

wound flaring up. I was lucky, the bullet hadn't hit bone. Still, hiking for hours every day across rugged mountain terrain wasn't exactly helping it heal. I refused to let Septimus give me another piggyback ride—even though he was delighted the first time I told him what we called carrying someone on your back. He'd demanded a thorough explanation for why it was called that— and I just invented one to stop his questions.

I hadn't noticed Septimus had stopped walking until he said, "Kaden."

I froze, my hand going to the gun at my side. But he shook his head and pointed up ahead. I followed his gaze and saw, in the light of day, what we'd missed in the night.

Smoke, rising from the forest before us.

~

"Did you see this in your dreams?" I said, all the laughter and humor from earlier today gone. Septimus stood beside the neat row of freshly turned earth. Graves. Row after row of them, spaced with eerie neatness, like someone had used a ruler to measure the space between them. The small town was a charred mess behind us. A few fires still smoldered, putting up some smoke, but it looked as if the worst of it had burned in the night.

We were too late.

"No," Septimus said, walking between the rows. He knelt beside one of the smaller graves, as if it contained a child. He had picked a wildflower earlier, and he laid it on the grave now.

Why did they bury them? I'd asked Septimus the question at a previous settlement just like this, only to wish I hadn't.

To return humanity to the earth forever.

A cold wind blew, mixing the smell of pine with the scent of burning wood. Today the forest held a strange, empty silence—like it too grieved the people who'd been here.

The progression of the Creation was the opposite of when the plague came. Back then you could trust no one. It was a world of gunshots, explosions, chaos. This was quiet, clinical, brutally clean. They never killed any animals—they set them free and then burned anything that humans could build to the ground. The violence was always buried beneath the earth.

"You said they were going to go north?" I whispered, turning away from the graves.

Septimus swallowed hard. "I . . . I may have been wrong."

"We need to get back to Boise. As quickly as possible."

I lifted a handful of dirt and trickled it over the grave. "Ashes to ashes, dust to dust," I whispered. Then I said a prayer over the lost town like Issac would have. There was nothing we could do for these people now.

The Creation couldn't be stopped. Boise would be our final stand. I looked down at my leg, already feeling the pain. We couldn't beat them in a race to the city.

But I hadn't been the best expedition leader in the city for nothing.

I looked to the trees and then limped over to where I'd seen some prints in the mud. The Creation always released livestock. Septimus said they didn't understand the animals or their uses. Their loss.

The mud at the edge of town held the deep hoofprints of several horses, and I could see that the gates had simply been opened. The horses had likely smelled the fire and run, but I doubted they had gone far. Not when they knew food and shelter were here.

"Change of plans," I said, following the tracks now. "We need a faster way to get to Boise." The city needed to be warned that the Creation was coming. As much as I hated to admit it, I hoped Gabriel was still in control. He had connections to all the other clans. He could get messages out to everyone, warn the clans, unite them in defense of the city.

"They burned all the cars," Septimus said. "Unless you think you can get an airship working?"

"You remember those stories I told you?" I said. "About cowboys?"

"What of them?"

"Get that rope. We're going old school. I might not be able to beat the Creation to Boise walking. But I can damn well beat them riding."

CHAPTER SEVEN—SAM

The crickets and cicadas' song rose, wavering and lonesome, as I paced down the small walkway that encircled the Old Pen. The stars and moon were so bright tonight it was as if they had crept closer. I hated it. The peacefulness. The sprawling, cruel beauty of the land. The way nature didn't care whether we lived or died.

I tried to remember all the sounds of the before world— sounds others had insisted we'd never get back. Airplanes, and sirens, and car engines, and cell phones. Horns and speakers and dogs that wagged their tails and didn't try to kill you. The way you could flick on a light switch and burn away the dark, or the white streaks the airplanes had made through the sky.

I wouldn't forget.

I would remember, even if I were the last one, until I brought it all back.

I stared up at the sky, suddenly transfixed by the trailing light of a satellite. Even with the city falling beneath nature, everything we'd once been was still there, waiting for someone brave enough to bring it all back.

The satellite disappeared from view, behind one of the few clouds in the sky, and I sighed and continued along the walkway.

The Old Pen had four guard watchtowers, one positioned on each corner of the walls, and a walkway connecting each of them. Tonight, there were three of us on duty. The sun had set hours ago, and even with the blazing stars above, I could still make out only twenty feet in front of me. We'd been given flashlights but had strict instructions to use them only in case of emergency. *Because of course Gabriel would assign people to walk around a perimeter when they couldn't see shit.*

Then something moved in the brush beyond the wall. I flicked on my flashlight, eager for something, anything, to happen.

My light hit two shining eyes—a coyote. I sighed and flicked the light off and kept walking. Night patrol was about the best torture Gabriel could have assigned me. Out here, walking the perimeter all night, bored out of my mind, I couldn't talk to the other men about how we could build a new, better world together. More importantly, I couldn't ask if they'd known the new tech engineer who'd once been a part of the clan.

Night after night, I walked in endless circles, knowing that the key to our survival was out there, unguarded. Waiting. I couldn't even leave on the pretext of a supply run—not when I was assigned to guard duty every night. If I did leave, it would be seen as desertion, and I wouldn't be welcomed back. I would be leaving the clan, and Addison, forever.

The deep hoot of a barn owl called out, his bold, unbothered call mocking me. I met the end of the walkway and turned, making my way back, feeling like one of the tigers I'd once seen pacing his cage at the zoo. But what else could I do? Even if I did manage to find the engineer and he had both the final set of keys and the launch codes, I still needed the access card Gabriel had taken to open the door. As much as I hated Gabriel, he was still my best hope for finding out more about the engineer.

The longer I walked, the deeper the night stretched, the more my thoughts warred, and the more the anger churned in my chest.

Em wouldn't have let this happen. She would have taken what she needed. She would have crushed everyone in her path. *Like she crushed me.* I thought more about the letter Em had left me, folded against my chest. *Leave the city, Sam. Run as far and as fast as you can. I've seen what they're planning. The people in the green water are coming—and they're going to kill everyone.* She'd thought I was a boy who would run from a fight, who would leave his city, his home.

I'd prove her wrong.

I'd prove them all wrong.

On the other side of the wall, a flashlight flicked on and off, three times. All thoughts of the Creation and Em abruptly disappeared. I stopped, watching as the deliberate flashes of lights came again.

Was that Morse code? If it was, I had no idea what it meant. I turned my own flashlight on then took off running in the same direction of the lights, toward the front gate. *Please don't be another infected coyote.* The only exciting thing to happen while on guard duty was when animals killed each other outside the wall—or when we saw who could piss the farthest.

I reached the front gate a moment before Malik, another guardsman who'd lost a hand in a farming accident. Ricardo, our third night guardsman, was already there and looked panicky—an emotion I'd never seen on his usually calm, unworried face.

"What's going on?" I said.

Ricardo motioned to the darkness beyond the front gate. "Down there," he said.

I joined the two of them leaning over the wall. For a moment I thought it was the coyote again, until my light hit on shining red.

Then it felt like the breath had been knocked out of my chest.

"Is that—" Malik began.

"It's a man," Ricardo said. "He looks like he's been . . . attacked."

More than just attacked. The man looked like he'd been dragged through the trenches of hell before being deposited on our doorstep. Just before I could ask if he were dead, he moaned and lifted a shaking hand. He seemed to be muttering something, but from this high up on the wall, I couldn't make it out.

I sent the beam of my flashlight up the road and farther down. There was no one else there. Or at least no one I could see. "Is he alone?" I asked.

"Looks like it," Ricardo said. "What do we do?"

To my surprise, the question was addressed to me. Ricardo and Malik had both been night guards much longer than I had. They were both older than me by at least ten years. But they both stared at me now.

What would Kaden have done? Issac would have let the man in, of course. The Good Samaritan was one of his favorite Bible stories. I knew Gabriel's rule—never open the gate after dark. Breaking almost any rule these days resulted in a whipping.

We couldn't live like this anymore. I'd seen the angry looks men had given Gabriel last time—the clan was a pot about to boil over; maybe it was time to let it. When Gabriel heard what I'd done, he'd be forced to stop ignoring me and call me to his office. Then I would lay down the law: either he gave me the name of the new tech engineer and relieved me of guard duty, or I would tell the whole clan the truth about the new tech. He'd have to give me the access card and let me go. Even if he didn't give me the name of the engineer or a way to find him, there were others in the city who might.

"Let him in," I said. "I'll go down and carry him through."

There were two main gates, with an enclosed chute between the two gates, so that you had to pass through both to gain entry.

Ricardo exchanged a look with Malik. "You'll be whipped again, Sam."

I rolled my shoulders, ignoring the flash of lingering pain from the not-quite-healed scars. "So? My others are starting to heal."

I made my way over to the wheel that controlled how the gate rose and fell. I threw my weight against the wheel, and a dull creak sounded from below as I turned it.

Usually two or three men helped turn the wheel, but the other two watched me, likely not wanting to be part of this. I didn't ask them to join me—I liked the feeling of doing it alone anyway. When I knew the first gate was high enough for me to slip under I stopped and looked back to the other night guardsmen.

Ricardo sighed. "You go out and get him. Once you're clear, we'll let you through. But if anyone else shows up, if it is some kind of trap, we're sounding the alarm, and you'll be stranded in the Chute."

The Chute was the enclosed space between the two gates. "Understood." *No good deed goes unpunished, right?*

I climbed down the ladder that led to the front gate and slipped beneath the gap I'd opened. It creaked closed behind me, sealing me into the Chute. I made my way quickly to the second gate, trying to ignore that creeping, panicked feeling I sometimes got in enclosed spaces.

The sounds of the night, peaceful and melodic from the top of the gate, sounded ominous down here. The tension built higher and higher as I waited by the second gate. I wished I would have brought my bow with me. *Too late now.* The second gate opened and I slipped through.

Up close, the man was in even worse shape. I'd helped bandage a few wounds with Kaden and Issac over the years, but this was different. I could smell blood, fresh and hot, and beneath it something rancid, like rotting fish. For a moment I hung back, afraid the man had died in the time it had taken me to get here. But then he groaned, and I forced myself forward.

I knelt beside him, reaching out a hand and placing it on a small patch of unbroken skin on his arm.

"Hi, I'm Sam," I said, not sure what else to do. "It's going to be okay. You're at the Castellano clan. We've got you now. I'm . . . I'm going to help you inside."

He made another groan I took as assent. He was a big man, too large for me to lift alone, so I put his arm around my shoulders and then worked to get him upright. I managed to pull him to his feet, half dragging and half carrying him to the gate. Blood coated my jacket, and I wondered if that was why the coyote had been nearby. *He's lucky more predators didn't find him first.*

"We're in," I called up to the wall when we cleared the first gate. A few moments later I heard the gate shut behind us. When we reached the second gate that opened into the clan, I saw that, despite it being the middle of the night, a few others had heard the commotion and had come out to see what was going on.

Shit. I'd hoped that we could get him to the doctor before news spread, but there were no secrets in the clan. I guessed I had only a few minutes before one of Gabriel's loyal followers ratted on me. *Well, then, I'll just have to put the plan into action quicker.* But I suddenly worried that maybe I should have put a bit more thought into this plan.

None of the crowd stepped forward to help as I dragged the man the final few feet, but at least Malik and Richardo opened the gate. Around twenty men had gathered, forming a wide circle around us.

"Someone get the doctor," I ordered. Two men immediately left the circle. Unable to hold the man upright on my own, I tried to lower him to the ground, but he collapsed into a heap with another moan. Not knowing what else to do, I unzipped my jacket and draped it over his shivering form. He stared up at me, eyes wide and fearful, but blessedly clear of the white, bleeding eyes of those infected.

The other men were watching us, waiting. I felt like I needed to do something. "Are you from one of the nearby clans?" I asked.

His lips were chapped and bleeding, his voice a croak when he said, "He sent me to warn you. To warn all the clans."

Cold ran down my back. The letter in my pocket suddenly seemed to weigh heavier. "Who?"

"He said to tell all the clans that the Creation are coming. That no one will survive."

My heart stopped in my chest. Suddenly I'd gone back in time, to the moment I'd seen a Creation body suspended in green water. Em and I had freed her, watching the water drain lower and lower . . . and then watched as she punched the glass, again and again, till blood ran down, till it shattered.

They're coming, Sam. Run as fast and far as you can. The same words Em had written in her letter to me. Warning me that the Creation were coming. All winter I had wondered if her words were a lie. Now I had my answer in the bloodied face of the man before me.

It was too late to run now.

They were nearly here.

And that changed everything. We didn't need the new tech to build a new world. We needed it to survive.

"Where are they?" I said to him, shaking him just a little when his eyes closed for a moment. "How far away? What happened?"

"I was in a small town outside of Boise. An army came through—they look like people but they aren't. They're"—he shivered and closed his eyes before he whispered—"monsters. The leader, Sevyn, he spared me. Sent me to deliver his message. But everyone else . . ." He trailed off.

A sort of dull ringing sounded in my ears. What kind of monster sent a message ahead to his enemies? Why warn us at all? *And yet, Em warned me too.* None of that answered my question. "Do you know how long we have?"

I didn't get an answer, because just then the doctor paced through the circle of men, all of them parting before him. He was a short man with a neat beard, and he had been some kind of foot doctor before he'd come here. Still, he knew how to stitch up wounds and was braver than most. He joined me and crouched next to the man.

"What happened?" he asked in a clear, assertive voice.

"I-I don't know," I said when the man on the ground failed to answer. "He's covered in blood. He says he was sent to deliver—"

"That's enough!" Gabriel's voice rang through the night like a peal of thunder.

The group surrounding us had grown to maybe forty men, and a ripple went through the crowd. At least half of them simply melted away into the darkness. The rest of them drew back, leaving the doctor and me stranded alone with the bleeding man.

Foreboding filled me with every stride Gabriel took closer. His eyes blazed in cold fury—I couldn't even find it in me to make fun of the fact that he was wearing a button-down shirt. He gazed from the bleeding man on the ground, to the doctor who had pulled back from him, and to me—like I was the source of all his problems.

"What is this, Dr. Sullivan?" he said.

"Apologies, Gabriel," the doctor said in the dry, unaffected way he had. "I was told there was an injured man out front—"

Gabriel held up a hand and the doctor fell silent. The few men who'd remained seemed to draw even farther away. I should have been afraid. But I wasn't. I was angry. "He was injured," I said defiantly. "So I opened the gate—"

"You know that's against the rules."

"Screw your rules. I told you this would happen months ago."

"And I told you I would handle it. You forget your place here."

I felt my fury like a blade, honed sharp and cold, like a wire stretched so tight it would take only a whisper to make it snap. Gabriel had taken everything from me. He wasn't the right leader of the clan. He was a coward keeping us from a better life.

It was time everyone knew the truth.

"He's lying to you all," I said, raising my voice so it carried into the courtyard. "I found a way to turn on the new tech—a way to save us all. But he's too cowardly to use it."

Silence filled the courtyard.

I waited—for them to rise and throw off their oppressor. For them to finally see the truth and grasp their power. For us to bind together, to save our city as one . . .

Nothing happened.

Nothing happened, and some naïve, childish hope inside me broke forever. I heard only her voice, whispered and mocking.

We're all alone in the end.

Gabriel took a step closer to me, and each one of his words drove the knife of betrayal deeper.

"Just because your brother was almost a clan leader you think that you can do whatever you want. My rules are for the good of the clan. That man could have been infected. Or he could have been a decoy for an ambush. You're as short-sighted and arrogant as Kaden."

"Kaden was ten times the man you are."

"Then why isn't he here?" He shook his head. "Kaden got men killed. He was good at finding things and nothing more. We're better off without him."

Kaden believed in this clan. That's what I wanted to say.

But how could I when Gabriel was right? Kaden was gone and I was alone.

I turned to the few men who remained in the circle, desperate now. "This man came with a warning. The same one I gave to Gabriel months ago, that he's chosen to ignore. There's an army coming. But I found a way to turn the new tech back on. We can have our world back. We can fight them. Gabriel is the coward here. He will keep you in this prison forever under his thumb. But it doesn't have to be that way. We can build a better world together—without him."

My voice echoed over the courtyard as the last sliver of hope inside me died.

All the men who had whispered support to me in the shadows now stood in silence. None of them would even meet my eye.

As if he sensed my desperation and sought to deliver the final blow, Gabriel motioned to Ricardo. "Open the gate."

Without looking at me Ricardo nodded, leaving me there, stranded before all the men. Watching all my plans fall to pieces. *It wasn't supposed to go like this. I was supposed to leave with the card and know how to find the engineer. I was supposed to convince the men of the clan that this was the right path forward.* Yet the gate inched up, each tick mocking my stupidity and naïvety. When it stopped Gabriel pulled his gun from his waist and leveled it at my head.

"Sam Preston," he said, his voice ringing over the clan, "on my authority as clan leader, I hereby banish you from the Castellano clan forever. Put your flashlight on the ground and leave. Return, and I will kill you."

He cocked the gun and my hatred blazed—for him, for the cowardice of these men, for a world that only rewarded villains. His lips twitched into the grim mockery of a smile, probably thinking that this would break me. I tossed the flashlight at his feet, knowing what it meant. I had no plan. No friends. No light, or weapon, or supplies to survive the ruins. My jacket was now draped over the bleeding, broken man on the ground.

I had nothing and he had everything.

"You will regret not killing me," I said, then dropped to my belly and crawled beneath the gate.

It didn't matter if I had no weapons.

Hatred was more than enough.

~

I forced myself not to turn, to see the receding form of the Castellano clan behind me. *It doesn't matter. That place wasn't your home.*

Even so I couldn't deny the bitter taste in my mouth, the betrayal at the men's silence, the way it all felt poisoned now: every plan, every path forward. I wanted to turn on the new tech to save the men of the clan—now I wasn't sure if I ever wanted to see them anymore. I remembered when I first came to the Castellano clan. It felt like the pinnacle of adventure. Like all my boyhood dreams come true. A gathering of men, working together, living in what looked like a massive hunting lodge. Hunting, fishing, scavenging through the ruins; Kaden made it all feel like one big game. One grand adventure.

When he disappeared, only then did I realize that this game had rules I'd never known.

I'd been a fool. I'd tried to rely on others, tried to play by Gabriel's rules. Now I realized that this wasn't a game for Gabriel.

If you didn't kill your bastard, he'd kill you first.

I froze beneath the branches of an oak as a chilling sound rose through the night.

Baying dogs. Bloodhounds, several of them. I knew them because Colborn and his men had brought them to the clan. But it had been a long time since they'd been used. I knew what Colborn had used them for.

To hunt men through the ruins.

No. He wouldn't. Not even Gabriel . . .

But then Em's imagined voice cut through my thoughts. *Grow up, Sasquatch! I don't know how you survived in this world without me.*

Gabriel didn't leave loose ends. Everyone who'd ever threatened his leadership had disappeared. His brothers, Kaden, and now me.

He was hunting me.

The men tonight had chosen him, not me. Which meant if the men tracking me caught me, they would kill me.

The baying of dogs grew louder.

I took off into the night.

I kept running, and without a light sometimes I fell hard. I let the hatred, pain, and fear fuel me even as my lungs seared and my legs ached. Speed and my knowledge of the city were all I had now. Every painful step reminded me what Gabriel had taken from me. Everything I owned: my bow, arrows, knife. All the books I'd left in my room. Every friend I'd made in the clan.

Addison.

My heart tightened as I thought of her. She would think I'd abandoned her and our entire plan. I wondered if she'd think I was mad at her for what she'd said about Kaden. Why had I left things that way? Now Gabriel would feed her some bullshit story, if she even dared to admit we'd been friends. He would win again.

Gabriel had the card, Addison, the clan: he'd taken everything from me. Worse, I'd trusted him, even asked him to help me.

My thoughts grew as dark as the sky above. The dogs continued baying in the distance, but I didn't slow or stop. Hatred drove me forward through the dark, unforgiving city.

~

Hours passed like that until finally dawn approached, weak light filtering through the trees. I ran flat out now. My whole body screamed in protest, but I didn't listen. I'd started to see flashes of the dogs in the distance. They were catching up.

Only one of Issac's old tricks had kept me from being caught.

Kaden was all about the horses, but Issac knew dogs. *You'll never outrun the dog, but you can outrun a man.* In the growing dawn, I'd gained a bit of space, but not nearly enough. Which was where Issac's second tip had come in handy. Every time I saw a fence that was locked, I jumped over it, crisscrossing my way through neighborhoods. To follow my trail they'd either have to circle around, cut the lock open, or toss the dogs over the fence.

All night we'd played this game, but I hadn't been able to shake them. Now it was time for my final move.

There was only one place I would be safe from Gabriel now.

I cut across an overgrown lawn with dew heavy on the blades. The house had a red X across the front and seemed to sag in on itself, but the fence still looked solid enough and a rusted lock held it closed. My fingers burned as I jumped over it. The back-yard was even wilder than the front, yet there, right in front of me, was a rusted bike leaned against a shed. As if someone had taken it out, intending to ride it, and never came back.

I paused, looking at the bike. A few years ago, early on in our days with the clan, Issac had found a bike and fixed it up. We would ride it through the mall sometimes, just him and me. I swallowed hard as I stared at the bike—part of me wanted to see if it still worked. The dogs would have a hell of a time tracking me then. I touched Issac's letter still in my breast pocket. For a moment a pang of grief rose beneath the anger, but I buried it quickly, forcing myself to turn away and continue on.

Issac was dead. It was easier to be angry than sad.

The baying cries of the dogs had grown ever closer, when I saw the human skull sitting on the crooked remains of a fence, grinning at me. Behind the skull, dark clouds hung in the sky, promising rain.

As I passed, I reached out with my left hand. One of the times I'd fallen, a rock had left a deep gash in my palm. Now I smeared my blood across the skull. The dogs would find the blood—and their handlers would understand the message. Crossing this boundary would mean blood.

I set off into Skull clan territory. The dogs continued baying behind me, louder than ever before, growing into a frenzy, and then suddenly dying off. They wouldn't follow me—not after what had happened to the last men who'd walked into Skull clan territory. Crossing over this line with a pack of baying dogs was all but declaring war. Gabriel wouldn't risk it, he couldn't afford to.

I kept moving, pushing deeper into enemy territory. Decrepit houses, rusted cars, overgrown airships: it wasn't much different from the other clan territories, except for the Skull paintings that had been added on the sides of buildings or vehicles. Some were cartoonish, some creepy, some gruesome—but in a strange way, I liked them. In a world of fading colors, of vines and earth reclaiming all, they were a bold, vivid declaration of humanity . . . and death.

The sun climbed higher, muted behind the heavy clouds. I should keep running, but my legs ached, and my feet felt like they were made of cement. I forced myself to continue at a steady walk, just in case one of the more motivated men followed me without the dogs. Fortunately, Kaden had taught me well. I stepped carefully, leaving no sign of my presence.

The sun climbed higher, lighting the ruined neighborhoods in a golden light. *Just a few more hours*, I told myself, *till the day warms up. Then you can find a nice house to crash in for the day. Find some blankets. Get a new jacket, a lighter, some kind of weapon. Just a few more hours . . . just a few more hours . . .*

One foot in front of the other, again and again, heavier and heavier each time. The city awakened around me, birds calling, leaves rustling.

One moment I was walking through an alleyway, thinking about sleep, and where I might bed down for the day, then, a quick snap at my feet. The ground twisted and moved beneath me, and I was hoisted into the air. Between one breath and the next I was suspended ten feet in the air, swinging back and forth, trapped in a thick net.

Adrenaline cleared the fatigue, my heart racing as the net continued to sway back and forth. *No. This is not happening.*

The birds continued to call. The sun continued to shine through the thick clouds. No one and nothing in the world cared that I was an absolute and total idiot.

When the net stopped swinging, I laughed, hysterical from pain and exhaustion. I didn't have a way to escape—no knife or way to cut free. Yelling for help was out of the question, what if one of Gabriel's men was looking for me? What if the Skull clan came? I'd walked straight from one death sentence into another.

Ahh, yes, thank you, God. I was starting to think it couldn't get worse.

I needed to find a way out, yet I doubted even Kaden or Issac would have a helpful tip here. No weapon. No jacket. No supplies. No friends. I was exhausted. The way the net held me, I couldn't even reach my jacket pocket to read Issac's letter—I'd die without ever having read his final words to me. After a few minutes of pointless thrashing, I decided to close my eyes and rest. The best thing I could do was regroup. Just till my head stopped pounding, then I'd figure a way out. *Yes . . . that's what Kaden would do, right? . . . Conserve energy . . . a few minutes . . . then a new plan . . .*

Hours later, I woke to the sun high above, the dark clouds gone, knowing I'd slept longer than I'd intended. But on the plus side, I no longer needed to figure out a way to escape.

The Skull clan had found me.

A group of men with faces painted into grinning skulls stared up at me.

"Should we cut him down, boss? Or let him rot for a few days first?"

Their question was directed to a small man on horseback. When he turned to look at me, I started: his face was covered in a cheap cartoon Halloween skull mask. Alone it might have been comical, but in conjunction with the group of men surrounding me, all leering up at me; well, I suddenly wondered if maybe I should have tried to outrun the dogs in any other clan territory.

"Please," I rasped, "I didn't mean to come into your territory, I'm just passing thro—"

The net plunged to the ground, and I slammed into hard earth, unable to break my fall. My thoughts were disjointed, warped by pain and fear. The sun glared down on our small group, and from my position flat on my back, the men painted with skulls seemed monstrous.

Footfalls sounded on the pavement, but I was stuck, trying to remove the net, trying to make my lungs fill, trying to see beyond the sun blinding me.

Then the sun disappeared. I blinked as the man from the horse blocked the direct light. Lit from behind, the dark holes of the skull mask seemed bottomless.

He lifted his hands. I sucked in a breath, bracing myself for whatever horror would come next. Would they kill me and put my head on a stick like the others? Would I meet Issac before the day was up? My heart pounded as the mask lifted free.

Then, once again, I couldn't breathe.

Not from fear; from shock.

Dark hair. Angular, feminine features. Ice-blue eyes I would have known in any heaven—or hell.

Her lips lifted in a mocking smile. "Looks like we caught ourselves a Sasquatch."

CHAPTER EIGHT—SEVYN

The horse bucked and kicked beneath me as I struggled to bring it into submission. Why couldn't it see this was a great honor? The Creation all followed my orders exactly, like an extension of my hand. When I'd told them all to break into groups and scout the city for weaknesses, they had obeyed without hesitation or deliberation.

Unlike this unruly beast.

Talia's arms wrapped tight around my waist, the closest she had ever been to me. And the closest I had ever been to a human I wasn't trying to kill. The feel of her hands, the warmth of her body: I couldn't decide how I felt about it. Shock? Disgust? Or something else I had no name for?

"You stupid beast," I hissed, digging my feet in and trying to get it to move straight. It went in a circle. "Doesn't it know this is a great privilege?" I kicked it again. It ignored me, seeming determined to fling us both from its back. I yanked back on the reins and the horse danced sideways, its hoofbeats making a staccato rhythm on the cement.

"It's a horse—I don't think it knows anything but that it doesn't like you," said Talia, as dry and unhelpful as ever. I'd seen images of humans sitting atop the beasts, looking like glorious conquerors. But this one must have had a death wish.

"Why won't it obey?!" I yanked the reins back, trying to stop the beast, but it only danced sideways. *You stupid, worthless creature. After I master and destroy the humans, you four-legged beasts are next.*

Then Talia's hand reached around and landed on mine. "Stop fighting it . . . relax."

I stiffened at her touch. "Relax?"

"Yes, Sevyn, relax." She sighed. "It's a thing humans do."

"I don't want to be anything like humans."

She pulled her hand back like she'd been stung. "Fine. Let a *horse* beat you. Good luck destroying humanity after that."

Even though I didn't want the creature, or Talia, to think they had won, I did as she suggested, and after a moment, to my immense shock, the horse did settle.

"Now what?" I said, immediately wishing I hadn't. Creation didn't ask humans for help.

But Talia didn't gloat. She said nothing, simply reaching around and taking the reins in her hands. Then she made an odd sort of clucking noise, squeezed her legs, and the horse started off. Faster, and faster. Soon in a bounding run that was at once smooth and terrifying.

We tore through the ruins. The ground flowed beneath us in an exhilarating rhythm. Unable to resist, I let out a laugh.

"You're welcome," Talia said from behind me.

"I would have figured it out," I said, refusing to thank a human. For all I knew she and the horse were working together. After all, they were both contrary, difficult, strangely beautiful creatures. But I let them be, because the ruins of Boise stretched all around us, glorious even in decay.

Soon it would all be mine. The Creation would find a weakness here, or I would, and the plague that was humanity would be ended.

Skeleton trees reached out bony fingers, green just beginning to creep back into their limbs. The horse raced down the wide road, clear except for the occasional rusted car. Mountains rose to the north, still topped with snow even though here, in the valley, it had long since ceded to fresh sprouts and new growth.

It was beautiful, this world the humans had destroyed.

After years beneath the surface, years held captive in swirling water, able to only see the others but never touch them, there was unspeakable pleasure in feeling the wind on my face, the power of the horse beneath me, even the touch of Talia's arms—though I tried not to dwell on the latter.

Finally, the horse slowed, more because it seemed tired than from any signal from me. I was neither sure how to instruct it nor willing to ask Talia for instructions. As the creature slowed, Talia drew back from me, the separation once again making us human and Creation. For some strange reason, I wished the horse would run again.

"You haven't tried to escape in some time," I said. The horse's slow, swaying motion made me feel restless once again. "Given up?"

She was silent for a frustrating amount of time. Finally, just when I was about to demand an answer, she said, "No."

"No, you haven't given up? Or no, you're tired of escaping?" Were all humans so frustrating? Perhaps I should stop killing them long enough to find out.

"No, I decided to try a different approach."

A different approach? I wondered if that meant I needed to be wary of some new weapon, or some new subterfuge. Humans were creative in their killing. That I knew well. Dark memories rose in me, of all the Creation who had not escaped from beneath The Last City. Of all those of us they'd destroyed.

Let her try. I'll be ready.

The horse's hooves made a steady clomping noise as we made our way down a cracked pavement road. As it was going the direction I wanted, I let it continue. Though the colors had faded from most of the city, many of the strange metal signs the humans had erected still remained. I read all of them with interest.

Some bore words like YIELD or STOP; others held arrows or symbols I couldn't assign meaning to. All of it seemed funny in a pathetic way. Had they really expected such simple, crude things to keep order in a chaotic world? It was a miracle they'd survived this long at all with the way they killed each other.

We passed beneath one of the junctions where roads met. Huge poles stood at each of the four corners where the roads met, with vines spanning between all four sides, so that it looked as if the plants had grown in oddly symmetrical shapes.

"Did you ever visit here, before the plague?" I said, glancing back at her. She watched the ruins with a very different gaze than mine—as if danger hid in every corner.

"No. I grew up in The Last City." There was a sort of tension in her voice. "My parents died when I was very little. I was raised by Walter. He became like a father to me, and my sister."

Ah. Her sister. In The Last City, when I'd first decided to spare Talia, I had promised her I would reunite her with her sister. And I had, but not in the way she wanted. Her sister had been one of the Creation, and I'd shown her another clone of the sister she'd lost. "I've noticed you haven't spent any time with your sister's clone."

Her voice, when she responded, was hollow. "You know that wasn't what I wanted." Then, as if it cost her something, she whispered, "What happened to her?"

The horse kept walking, the lone wind howling, when I told the truth I knew she didn't really want. "She was deemed too human. Many of the earlier versions of Creation were. The humans killed her."

For a moment, the memories threatened to overwhelm me. The rushing, green water. The air, as it grew thinner and thinner, until it disappeared. Slamming against the glass. Drowning, again and again. Creation shared some sort of connection—whether they'd intended it or not, every time they killed one of us, we all died a little with them. I'd both watched and felt the humans who kept us prisoner kill us, over and over, powerless to stop it. Powerless to do anything but watch, and plan, and know that someday, when I was set free, I would settle the score. I would avenge every Creation death with a thousand, a million of their own.

High above us, a bird wheeled through the blue sky. I wondered if it had fed on the many corpses that scattered the ruins. I wondered if it had even noticed when they died by the millions—and if they would notice when I finished the job. The horse continued his slow and steady walk, and though the sounds of the city were numerous—the creak of metal, the call of small birds, the wind making a door slam—all I could hear was the silence of the woman behind me.

"Do you know why they call me Sevyn?" I finally said.

"They ran out of names?"

I gave a cold, mirthless laugh. "They created six other versions of me. All of them were deemed unworthy to lead. All of them were too human."

"What happened to the other six?"

"They killed them," I said. "Except for the seventh. They took him out of his tank for testing and he woke early. He killed his human creators and escaped." *Septimus*. The traitor who would be punished. The traitor whom I'd been falsely named to replace—as if when I took his number, he would cease to exist. I could feel him somewhere in the ruins, but it wasn't the way it was with the other Creation. Somehow, it was as if he'd become more human, and therefore more difficult to access his thoughts. It hardly mattered—I would kill him along with all the other humans.

"Why are you telling me this?" Talia said.

I pulled the horse to a halt, and this time, to my shock, it obeyed. Maybe it could be taught after all. "Because you blame me for something that isn't my fault. Humans killed your sister. Not me. I offered you the next best alternative."

Her eyes blazed, even though I saw they were filled with moisture. "You offered me a lie."

A lie humans created, not me. But I didn't say that. I shrugged, and turned back to the ruins, uncomfortable with her show of weakness. Creation did not cry. We were not weak like humans.

I swung off the horse, wanting to feel the earth between my feet—or maybe just needing to escape Talia's touch. The horse didn't even turn its head to glance at me. I hoped it would wander away while I was gone. When I'd found it this morning, I'd thought it would be a faster, more efficient way to explore the city and plot the best way to weed out the humans with the fewest

Creation casualties. Now I wondered if humans weren't even stupider than I'd originally thought. Why would they use such a temperamental beast?

"What are you looking for?" Talia said from the back of the horse. *Speaking of temperamental beasts.*

"None of your concern."

An old railroad track ran across the earth to my left, and the blackened shell of what might have been a house or business lay to my right. The humans had used some sort of program to raise the Creation: flashes of images, like memories, training and showing us the world beyond our underground prison.

But those images weren't the ones that shaped me, the ones I clung to.

No. It was the memories from the other Creation. The first Creation, who had escaped and was raised by a human. The dark-haired daughter. If it weren't for her, for the images of the beyond world, we would have all died beneath the earth. But she gave us life—more than the tubes with air. We called to her, and when she dreamed, she heard our voices. She had finally answered us, set us free . . .

But where was she now? I could feel her in the ruins, just as I could feel the betrayer. We were like planets, circling each other, gravity drawing us closer and closer with each rotation. Today I'd allowed myself one moment of curiosity, of selfishness, seeking out a place I'd once seen in her memory. While I'd sent the Creation to find and access the weaknesses of the city, my goal today went deeper.

I wanted to know what it was like to be human.

I walked farther down the road, seeking out the building I'd seen only in memory. It was difficult to follow the memory, trying to compare the way things once were to the overgrown trees, the rusted train tracks, the sad buildings. But then I found it.

"What are we doing here?" Talia said. She'd rode the horse, which, to my annoyance, obeyed her completely.

"You'll see." I left the road, making my way toward the building.

"What about the horse?" she called out from behind me.

"I have enough creatures in my possession that don't obey me."

She laughed at this, and I couldn't help the way my lips tugged upward at the corner, even as I made sure not to let her see. I'd purposefully turned my back and left her with the horse. She could leave, she *should* leave . . . yet I was relieved when I heard her follow after me.

Weeds blocked the front door, but I pushed them aside. When the door didn't open, I kicked it in with a single blow. Then I gave Talia a stately bow, gesturing her inside. "Humans first."

She rolled her eyes but stepped inside without argument. Most of the windows had been boarded over, but pale sunlight still managed to leak through in slits, illuminating swirling spirals of dust. Scents of wood and leather and rot permeated the place. The hallway held a few turned-over chairs, some yellowed paper, and not much more.

"What are we doing here?" Talia repeated.

I walked confidently down the hallway. *Being human.* "Come see."

The hallway opened into a deep room. The roof had collapsed in the far corner, sunlight streaking across what would have once been smooth, wooden pathways, but were now coated in dust and debris. There were chairs and tables at the end of each of them—and a strange sense of waiting.

A collection of heavy-looking balls, roughly the size of a

human head, stood at the end of each row. I picked up one of the balls and turned it over—there were three holes in it. Part of me wanted to ask Talia what to do but pride stopped me. If a human could figure it out, so could I.

I approached the lane, lifted the ball, and threw it in an arch in the air. It hit the ground with a crash like thunder. I laughed. *Humans really are insane.* I started collecting and throwing more of the balls.

"That's not how it works," Talia said. "You're supposed to *roll* the ball."

"This is better. Besides, isn't the point of everything humans do destruction?" I launched another ball, and it crashed into the wall so hard it left a hole behind. I smiled.

"Not everything," Talia said.

I sent another ball flying just so I didn't have to see the look I knew she was giving me: one of blame and hurt. As if it were my fault her sister was dead. Humans were like that, always blaming others for their problems, instead of understanding that they were the root of all evil and destruction on this planet.

I inspected one of the balls I'd picked, wiping the thick coat of dust free. Beneath it looked like the night sky—one more thing the humans had kept from me. Suddenly I didn't want to throw them anymore.

I spun back to her. "Tell me one thing the humans did that didn't end in destruction or death?"

"Art? Literature? Love?"

"Humans locked up art, charging prices to see it. Their literature was weak, pointless, and most often about killing one another. And love—well, I see no evidence of it here."

"And if you did, would it stop you?" Talia said.

"Nothing will stop me."

She shook her head, glaring at me in frustration. "You're wrong."

Wrong? I almost laughed. The dust muffled my footsteps as I drew closer to her, my words reverberating in the enclosed space. "I've already been proven right a million times over. Humans destroyed all this." I waved a hand at the sad remains of this place.

But her eyebrows only drew together, making a wrinkle in the middle of her forehead. "That doesn't mean you can just kill them all."

"Why not? Is that right only reserved for God?" Somehow my feet had carried me within inches of her, this perplexing, infuriating human. We glared at the other, neither of us backing down.

I needed her to understand. Humans were the villains here, not me. I was no more evil than death—I was simply the final breath in humanity's existence. I waited for her to argue with me, but she seemed determined to do the most frustrating thing possible. She stayed silent.

Such a disappointment. Like all of them.

I turned away from her. "It's time to go," I snapped.

Outside, back in the sunshine, the horse was still waiting for me. *You stupid creature, you should have run while you had the chance.* But I wouldn't allow it to defeat me, not while she was watching.

I swung up onto the horse's back, and then turned back to Talia. Her eyes were as hard and angry as ever. Something strange shifted in my stomach as a new possibility presented itself to me. I could leave her here. Ride away and never see her again.

She would be safer without me. Safer away from the storm that was coming.

But I didn't want to leave her.

"Are you coming?" I held a hand out to her. It wasn't a demand—it was a question. Our eyes locked and for the first time, I understood why God had given humans autonomy. Why He hadn't simply bent humanity to His will. It was exhausting, killing over and over again. But letting something, or someone, come to you because they chose it—that was a feeling I didn't yet have a name for. A feeling that grew in my chest the same way the sun climbed into the sky, with a surety and blazing heat that was undeniable.

She took my hand, and I pulled her up onto the horse behind me. I pushed him forward, ready now to find the other Creation and see what they had learned of the city and the humans. To make our plan to root out and destroy the humans from this place.

This time the horse didn't fight, didn't protest. Maybe the creature felt what I did.

That even if I was Death, and she was everything I sought to end, something here was right.

CHAPTER NINE—SAM

"Em?" I said in disbelief. I lay flat on my back, staring up at her. Her ice-blue eyes seemed to laugh as she looked down at me. It felt as if the last few months were nothing, and no time had passed. It was her and me again—the two of us against the world.

Then I remembered we were surrounded by men with faces painted as skulls.

"I assumed you'd be halfway to Mexico by now, Sasquatch." She shook her head, and I noticed she'd cut her hair to just past her chin. "I see you didn't take my advice."

Her advice? She stepped away from me and beckoned to some of the men. They came forward at once, working to untangle me from the net. Only as the men worked to free me did my hand go to her letter, and I realized what she'd meant. In her letter she'd told me the Creation were coming. She'd warned me to flee Boise.

The net fell free and I scrambled to my feet, trying to regain a bit of dignity—difficult to do when none of the men seemed to view me as a threat. Most of them fell back, leaving Em alone beside me. Now that I was standing eye to eye with her, I realized more than just her hair had changed. For one, she looked older. There were bruise-like shadows under her eyes that hadn't been there before. *Still beautiful, though.*

The same dialogue I'd been replaying in my head for months rose up now. She'd used me, then left me, but the way she looked at me now . . . "It's good to see you again, Em," I finally said, feeling like that was at least safe.

She looked me up and down. "You got taller." She sounded almost annoyed. "You really should have left the city, Sasquatch."

"What can I say? I'm a rebel."

She laughed at this, and despite myself, I couldn't help but smile back.

"Ah, Sasquatch, I've missed you." She turned abruptly, making her way back to her horse and missing the dopey smile her words had brought to my face. *She left you, remember that!*

I sized up the men around her—fifteen in total, a mix of young and old, some with plastic skull masks and others with skull-like features painted on their face. They were well armed, with guns, axes, bows, and arrows—and all of them parted before her without question. In contrast, I stayed exactly where I was.

Em and I had run into a group like them last year. That time the men had all worn skull painted faces and had been pulling a prisoner with white eyes weeping blood—someone infected. Em had revealed to me one of the few details of her life. She had been infected, taken captive by men who thought her blood bore the cure, then eventually took her revenge and escaped.

But that didn't explain why these men looked at her as if *she* were their leader.

Em mounted the black horse I'd seen her ride earlier. Even if horses had always been Kaden's thing, I couldn't deny that this one was especially beautiful—a perfect match for Em. She rode straight up to me, so that I was forced to retreat a few steps. "What was that stupid thing you used to say about the sun—"

"We're burning daylight?"

She held out a hand. "Come on, Sasquatch. We're burning daylight."

I swung onto the horse's back. There was no saddle, but it didn't matter. I'd rode bareback plenty of times with Kaden.

"Head back to the Skull clan!" she said to the men. "We'll meet you there later."

Then she pushed the horse forward and he sprang to life, eager to run.

It had been a long, horrible night. But as we rode, I did something far more dangerous than leaving the clan or venturing into Skull clan territory—I put my arms around her waist.

She didn't pull away.

~

We rode deeper into Skull clan territory before she stopped the horse. A single glance back was the only communication I needed. I slipped off and she followed, leading the horse behind her as we continued on foot. The brush grew thicker, the branches lower, until I heard the river.

A small game path led us out onto a sandbank, the river beyond fast and high with spring snowmelt. Massive cottonwood trees overhung the area with shade, and a collection of sun-bleached, river-smooth logs crisscrossed the bank. Em led the horse down to the flow, where she tied him loosely, giving him access to the water and grass. Then she sat on one of the logs overlooking the river, and after a moment of hesitation, I joined her.

"I like to come here," she said after we'd sat in silence for a few minutes. "Watch the river. It's easy to pretend the world is the way it once was here."

I gave her a strange look. Of everyone I'd known, Em seemed to thrive in life after the apocalypse. Yet I saw what she meant: the river was as beautiful as ever, the water cold and clear, the stones beneath smooth and polished by its flow. It was a source of life in the city—and therefore a source of contention. Almost every clan fought for access to this river. These waters had flowed red more than once.

"I didn't know you wanted the world back the way it was?" I asked.

"Not the same. Better. That was the whole point of the Creation. That was why I released them."

Emotions slid over me fast as the river flowed. "We. *We* released them."

She turned to meet my gaze. "All winter, every time I dreamed, I felt them. Felt what their leader is doing. He's in the city, Sam. I can feel him looking for me." She swallowed hard, looking even more exhausted than I felt. "I thought if I trained the Skull clan, if I made them into weapons, we could fight the Creation."

She wants to fight the Creation. Even though I knew I needed to move carefully, I couldn't help the hope in my voice. "We set them free together. We'll stop them together."

"They can't be stopped."

"I don't know, all that skull paint was pretty scary."

She tilted her head back and laughed, but it was an exhausted sound. There was a desperation, a hollowness to her eyes. Like she'd already given up. The temptation to reach out and take her hand was so strong I crossed my arms firmly in front of me.

"Well, lucky for you," I said, "I have a plan to fight them. And it's foolproof." *Even if that idiot Gabriel couldn't see that.*

"You and your plans, Sasquatch."

It was my turn to laugh. "I didn't hear you complaining when I came up with a plan to get us downtown."

"All right. I'll hear your plan when we get back to the Skull clan."

"We aren't going back now?"

"No."

"What are we doing?"

She stretched her arms over her head and gave an enormous yawn. "Playing hooky." She winked at me. "Being a clan leader is a lot more work than I thought it would be."

She's leading the Skull clan. I wasn't sure why that shocked me—it shouldn't have. What Em wanted, she took.

"Yeah, I'm done with clan life for a bit too," I said.

She smirked at this, seeing straight through me. "Gabriel still a dick? I thought I gave you a solution for that."

"I'm not the best listener."

"How did you survive the apocalypse without me, Sasquatch?"

The words were teasing, but they still made my insides clench. Because I had survived—when she'd left me. So why was I here, sitting next to her, wanting more?

She pulled off her jacket and placed it on a patch of sand the sun had warmed. I would have copied her, but I didn't have a jacket, having left mine on the bleeding man at the clan. But that ache of pain and betrayal felt distant now, like it had been weeks, not hours. *Maybe because there's a new betrayal right in front of you, waiting for you to slip up again.*

Without looking at me she lay on the ground, using the jacket as a pillow. "You can share my pillow if you want."

I had a sudden flash of déjà vu—of all the nights we'd spent together where she'd woken screaming. All the nights I'd held her trembling body against mine. All the mornings where she pretended it had never happened.

But she left. She left . . . so what does this mean now?

I decided I didn't care. The long, exhausting night had finally caught up to me. Even Kaden admitted women were a mystery that men had never solved. I'd make better decisions once I rested. So I laid my head down on the jacket, my back pressed against hers.

I thought maybe she'd already fallen asleep, but then, after a minute she whispered, "I haven't slept well since I last saw you."

It wasn't an apology. But it was as close as I'd get with her. I turned over and wrapped my arms around her, bringing her body flush against mine and breathing in her scent.

"Neither have I," I whispered in her ear.

She shifted, pressing even closer. I held her like that—the river sliding by, the sun watching over us—and wondered what it would have been like if we'd met in a different life, a different world.

~

It was nearing dusk by the time we approached the Skull clan. We'd slept for several hours, and woken when the horse, having eaten all the grass he could reach, began to nuzzle Em's pocket searching for treats. She still hadn't told me where exactly the Skull clan was located, but as we drew nearer, I realized I knew where we were.

Two men stood outside the front gate, the skull paint making their eyes too big and smiles too deep. *Not quite as family friendly as last time I was here.* They showed the same respect as the other men Em had led yesterday, bowing their heads as Em passed.

"Come on, I'll give you a tour," Em said.

Crowning the gate we passed under, and lit by the last light of day, stood the words ZOO BOISE. Vines grew all along the outer perimeter fence, but it all still looked to be standing. I suppose it made sense: a fence ran along the entire zoo, and a small outlet of the river flowed through it. Why not have a clan here?

Em led me past the entrance and into an area that looked very different from the last time I'd been to the zoo. For one, the entrance was a minefield of metal spikes that we wove through to gain entry. A few were tipped in what looked like blood. Farther in, I began to realize that the Skull clan had taken over and repurposed the entire zoo. Farm animals had replaced exotics. There were chickens in the exhibit that once held ocelots, horses where there had once been lions, and sheep in the giraffe enclosure. As giraffes were my favorite animal, I decided not to ask what had happened to them.

But for every exhibit that held animals, there were ten more than had been repurposed for men to live inside, or, as in a few of the more covered ones, to store food. There was a tent pitched beneath the old giraffe slide I remembered going down as a kid, lean-tos made against informational signs, a smokehouse in the penguin exhibit, and the old monkey house had been turned into a bunkhouse that somehow smelled even worse now than when it had held monkeys.

Unlike Gabriel's organized clan, chaos reigned here, and everywhere I looked I saw some new form of madness. Em wasn't much of a tour guide, and I had the sense she walked me around only to check that everyone was doing their jobs. The only consistent thing here was the treatment of Em: men fell silent as she approached, bowing their heads respectfully, as if she were some kind of royalty. I wondered if it was because she was female—I saw no other women here—or because she'd done something unspeakable to their last leader.

I decided not to ask.

"Why the zoo?" I said as we passed a pig roasting on a spit beside a sign that read, GET YOUR COTTON CANDY HERE!

She shrugged. "Water access. Big fence. Infrastructure. There was already a clan in here so it was ripe for the taking." She glanced over at me and grinned, seeming to know what I was thinking. "Don't worry—all your furry friends were long gone by the time we got here. The cages were all open. Someone had risked their life to set them free."

Sometimes freedom is worth dying for. But I didn't say that. Because I knew what Em would say: that I needed to grow up. And maybe she was right. The good guy didn't win in this world.

"If you had this great, unbeatable plan to beat the Creation," Em said as we walked, "how come I found you in my net?"

"I asked Gabriel for help."

She laughed, the sound high and clear, ringing out over the pathway before us. "Oh, Sasquatch. Did you listen to anything I taught you?"

"I'll admit my plan could use a bit of fine-tuning. But it *is* the only chance we have against the Creation."

We passed a rusted carousel that now held the drying carcasses of several deer, strung up by their back legs. I couldn't help but feel impressed. Even if the Skull clan didn't look nearly as organized as the Castellano clan, they clearly had more than enough food. It had taken the end of the world for me to realize that hunger, or the lack of it, was a powerful motivator. Maybe that was why these men were so in awe of Em—no one here was starving. *Or maybe it's that she's a beautiful young woman in a world of desperate men.*

"You hungry, Sasquatch?" Em said, noticing me staring at the deer carcasses.

"Always."

"I'll have them bring something for us."

Past the carousel was a large square building that looked like the downstairs had once been a kitchen—there were two deep freezers in the back, and several red buckets sat on the long counters with names like MEERKATS and ALDABRA TORTOISE still written on the side.

Above the kitchen Em took me to a room I assumed must have once been an office. A window looked over a large, empty enclosure below—I think it had once held camels. There was a desk with a chair on one side and a cot on the other. She gestured for me to take the chair, and almost immediately a man entered with two steaming bowls of soup. For a few minutes there were only the sounds of us eating.

"Almost worth being part of a clan, just for the food," Em said, tipping the bowl back.

"Not necessarily. I spent all winter feeding the Castellano clan and ate like shit. I had to bring everything back and share it before I got anything." Not that I always followed that rule, but it still stung to have given so much only to be left with so little.

Em sighed. "We may as well get this over with. What brilliant thinking got you kicked out of Gabriel's clan?"

"It's not his clan. The clan belongs to everyone."

"Really? So the whole clan kicked you out?"

"Fine. He threw me out," I said quietly. "You were right all along."

She set her bowl down and came to sit beside me. Her proximity surprised me. She was, after all, the one who'd left me. I'd laid it all on the line, I'd kissed her, and in the end I'd woken alone.

But her next words weren't about us. "I've been dreaming of the Creation again," she whispered. "They're looking for me."

The hair on my neck stood on end. "What do you mean?"

"Before I only heard them as whispers, calling to me for freedom." She wrapped her arms around her and shuddered, as if she were suddenly cold. "I thought they would take their revenge on The Last City, and that would be it."

"But?"

"But it wasn't enough. I can feel him in the city. He's making a plan. He's looking for weaknesses."

The hair on my neck stood on end. Weaknesses? He didn't have to look. All he had to do was point—the city was in shambles, the clans warring. I'd hoped to turn the new tech on, to unite the clan behind a common enemy. Instead, I was further than I'd ever been from turning on the new tech.

I reached out with my hand, threading my fingers through hers. "We'll find a way to stop them. There's always a way."

Her eyes flashed. "No there isn't. We made a mistake, Sam. We never should have released them. I've seen what they've been doing to the other settlements. The city doesn't stand a chance."

"But you're one of them, maybe you could talk—"

"I'm a traitor to them. They'll kill me if they catch me." She stood and made her way to the desk, uncorking a bottle of whiskey and pouring it into two cups. But instead of drinking hers, she left it on the desk, staring out the window. "I could train and prepare the humans in the city for a hundred years and we still wouldn't be ready."

"Why train them at all?"

An almost feral smile grew on her face as she turned to face me. "A final battle between human and Creation, good and evil, the last humans fighting for their lives, led by a Creation? It's like one of your stories. Who wouldn't want to be a part of that?" Then she shrugged, and said, in a softer voice, as if she didn't want to admit it, "I don't want to be a monster."

"You aren't a monster." She arched a brow at this, but I pressed on. "And if it comes to a big battle, then we can win. All we need to do is turn the new tech back on. We'd have access to everything again, including the new tech weapons."

"Last time I saw you, you said you only knew how to do it in theory."

"That was before I found the bunker with the weapon. I've already found one piece of the puzzle." I pulled out the chain I wore around my neck, revealing the first key hung on the end.

"And how many other pieces are there to this puzzle?"

"A few. And the first piece is in the clan. With Gabriel." Now, rested and with food in my belly, I saw the way forward. I wouldn't sulk in the ruins, aimless, searching for the new tech engineer when Gabriel had the knowledge, and the access card.

"Let me guess," Em said dryly. "Your plan involves going back to the clan and asking for him to give them to you, pretty please?"

"I'm done asking." I made my way to the desk and lifted the two shots of whiskey she'd poured. "Someone once told me if you want something, take it. And that bastards stay rulers . . ."

Her eyes met mine: vicious, beautiful, burning. She took her whiskey and clinked it against my own, and we both drank to her words.

"Until you bring them down."

CHAPTER TEN—ARA

A single light bulb lit the underground room. Row after row of metal shelves held boxes, misshapen lumps, rusted toys, forgotten holiday decorations, and dusty canned items. It was impressive, and a little unsettling. The ceiling was low, the ground uneven—it looked like it had been dug out, with only a black tarp between us and bare earth.

"Don't touch anything," Matteo said gruffly, his flashlight lighting the way as I followed him through the cellar-like room. He stopped only occasionally, taking the last of the canned food items and tucking them into his backpack.

"What is this place?" I whispered. It had been a week since I'd made it to the mall, a week since Matteo had pulled me from the hole and shown me the infected men in the jail, and every day Matteo surprised me. Which was a feat, considering he barely spoke.

"A group of Mormons stored all their supplies down here."

"How do you know that?"

"I lived around here in the before days. Enough questions."

Which of course made me want to ask a hundred other questions. Was he Mormon? Where was his house? How had he found this place—and kept it a secret? If the last week had taught me anything, it was that Matteo didn't like to talk about the past. Or really about anything.

"You know," I said as he passed me a giant can of green beans to put in my pack, "a horse or mule could carry ten times what we could."

"Don't like horses."

"What about mules?"

"Horse with bigger ears. Not bad eating though."

I laughed, not sure if he was joking. Probably not. Matteo didn't joke about food. Since the night he'd taken me to the jail, together we had cured seven men, all of whom Matteo had somehow kept alive. We'd also left bags of plague flowers with instructions on the borders of other clans—it was too dangerous to hand-deliver them with the state of the city. Not to mention we barely had time to keep our own clan alive. Turns out feeding a clan, half of whom had just woken from the plague, was extremely difficult. My own stomach tightened at the thought of food, but we never ate until we got back to the mall, and the others ate first. Every time we came back, I couldn't help that rush of yearning, hoping Kaden would be there waiting for me.

Every day he wasn't I grew more worried.

My back ached from the weight of the pack by the time we left. "Kinda sad, isn't it?" I said as we closed the door of the cellar.

"Sad?"

"They planned so thoroughly and then didn't get to use any of it." I was glad we hadn't gone in the house—I didn't want to see the pictures on the wall.

Matteo shrugged and set out across the yard. Weeds grew thick and it looked like some sort of animal was nesting in the back corner of the lawn. Had the sun not been an hour from setting, with a long hike back to the mall, I would have considered trying to flush it out for some fresh meat. I'd already shot several animals for the clan—even Matteo had grudgingly told me I was a good shot.

Together we paused at the edge of the yard and surveyed the quiet street ahead. Besides my pistol, Matteo had also given me a beautiful wood-stocked rifle. Maybe it was the full food on our back, or the awful silence of the neighborhood that reminded me of my own, but I couldn't stop the question. "Which house was yours?"

He kept walking, and I thought maybe I'd gone too far. Just because we'd cured a few people, shot some animals, and fed a clan together didn't mean we knew each other. Yet I thought this was how bonds were formed in the apocalypse—one bullet, one bite at a time. *Maybe he just sees me as someone to feed the clan.*

As we walked, I tried to imagine this neighborhood as it had once been. I imagined the grass, now waist high and filled with weeds, as short, neatly cropped, with kids laughing and chasing brightly colored balls. One of the houses had a porch. I imagined an older man and woman sitting there, smiling, or maybe scowling, at the noise. I tried to fit Matteo into that equation: Was he an accountant? Teacher? Engineer? I couldn't picture him in that neat, orderly world.

Matteo stopped so suddenly before a slate-gray house that I nearly ran into him. A giant red X had been spray-painted on the door. I lifted my gun at his abrupt change, surveying the empty street for danger.

But the street was empty. Matteo looked only at the house.

He stared and stared until I finally understood.

This was his house.

It was sagging, the yard gone wild. A large tree stood on one side of the yard, a frayed rope still hanging from it. Had a swing hung there? One of the front windows was broken, and the mailbox lay on its side. Buried in the high grass and weeds were the rusty remains of a red wagon.

The red X slashed across the door still seemed bright and new.

I'd gotten so used to seeing that X that it was easy to forget what it meant. But seeing it now, I felt those two slashes like they were pages of a story I didn't need to hear, because I already knew the ending.

"We'll need fresh meat soon," he said abruptly, "even with all these cans." He turned and kept walking down the street. I walked with him, because if nothing else, I understood that to survive in this world, you had to leave the past behind.

"We should stop and see Rahul on the way back," Matteo said as we drew closer to the mall.

I suppressed a groan. "Do we have to?"

Matteo didn't reply—which meant yes. Unlike Matteo, who I liked more with each passing day, I liked Rahul less every time I'd seen him. And I'd only seen him three times in the week I'd been here. Rahul lived in the mall but refused to join the clan. He was a leech, taking clan resources when needed, but not helping find food or protect the others. Yet Matteo tolerated him for one reason: he'd somehow found a way to access the solar panel grid on top of the mall and had connected it to a radio where he listened in for news from neighboring settlements. He had promised Matteo he could bring back power to a small portion of the mall, but so far all he'd managed to do was turn on the speaker system in the mall and play a few sad songs.

"You got it?" Matteo asked, and I pulled the tin from my backpack.

"Yeah."

At the top of the stairs, Matteo rapped on the door and said in a low voice. "Rahul? You there? We brought your food." A sound came from inside, and Matteo nodded to me. Together we stepped into a small room full of electronics with a single window that overlooked the mall below. I stepped forward, carrying the can of tuna we'd found for just this moment.

"Hiya Rahul," I said in a false, cheery tone. "We brought this for you."

"Set it there." He didn't turn, fiddling with the dials of the massive radio set up before him.

"Anything today?" I asked. He shot me a cold look, and I forced myself to wait in silence. Finally, he set the headset down.

Then he turned to Matteo and said, "Another town gone. Just like all the others." Matteo didn't say anything, his frown only deepening. Rahul wasn't done. "This is the first time there were survivors. One got on the radio. He said, 'They're coming for Boise next.'"

Matteo and I exchanged a look. I knew this would happen, yet somehow, I'd thought we'd have more time, be more prepared . . . And always I envisioned it would be Kaden standing beside me.

"How much time do we have?" Matteo said.

Rahul pulled out a map, and then showed us the red Xs that had spread across Idaho and the surrounding states; there were more than I could have ever imagined. "If they're moving at the same rate"—his fingers trailed over the red Xs and down to Boise—"they're already here."

The accompanying silence felt bitter cold.

"What are they waiting for?" Matteo said.

"I don't know—but it can't be good. And I doubt it's going to last." Rahul shook his head, staring out at the long stretch of mall when he said, "Which is why I'm leaving."

"You can't leave," I said at once. "We need your help! You can call others on the radio, organize the clans—"

Rahul cut me off. "There's nothing I or anyone else can do." He couldn't meet Matteo's eyes as he picked up the can we'd brought him. In the corner I saw a large, bulging backpack—showing me the truth of his cowardice. He'd already made his decision. "I'd suggest you move your clan as well, Matteo."

Matteo nodded, saying nothing, but I wasn't going to stand for this. "You're just going to leave? Matteo has fed and protected you! The clan needs you now more than ever! You're a coward for running."

"Cowards survive," Rahul said quietly. Then he pulled on his backpack, tucking the can I'd given him carefully away in one of the pockets. "I'll spread news of the plague flower if I can. I've been announcing it on the radio."

As if that will help us when we're all dead! I flashed a look at Matteo, expecting him to do something, to stop him, but he only extended his hand and shook Rahul's. "Thank you for the help you've given my clan, Rahul. I won't forget it."

Just like that, Rahul left. The second he was gone I turned on Matteo. "You could have tried harder to convince him to stay," I snapped. "You made it too easy for him."

Matteo stared down at the mall below, not reacting to my anger. "Rahul isn't a fighter. He was never going to stay." I was about to say that it didn't matter, that he still had a responsibility to help, when Matteo said, "Did you hear that?"

I thought he was trying to distract me, but then I heard it too: a noise from the hallways below. Someone below was being *loud*—I could hear the screeching of chairs and tables.

No one in the clan would be that loud.

Matteo pulled his gun free, and apprehension churned in my stomach as I came to stand beside him. Together we looked down through the glass, at the mall stretching out below, listening as the sounds grew louder, closer, more ominous.

Then the massive form of a grizzly bear lumbered into sight.

Its white eyes wept blood.

CHAPTER ELEVEN—SAM

"This isn't exactly what I had in mind when you said we should storm the Castellano clan," Em muttered. Her leg pressed against mine as we lay side by side in the tall grass. It was only the icy fear of discovery that kept me from savoring the touch. When I didn't answer, she said, "I imagined something a little more heroic. And bloody."

"No blood," I whispered. "We're the good guys. Remember that."

We'd spent the past few days perfecting our plan. Then last night I led her all the way up to the edge of the clan using only moonlight and memory. I knew from guard duty they couldn't see us.

Now my fingers were numb from cold, small rocks digging painfully into my side as we waited fifty feet from the entryway. The rest of the Skull clan was hiding farther away, ready to intercede—but that was only if the plan went very, very wrong.

Once I would have sent up a prayer to Issac's God that he

believed in so deeply. But if I were being honest, it had been a long time since I'd prayed. God had left me the same way Issac had.

"They're gonna open it soon—be ready." From where we lay, it was a short sprint to the gates. Gabriel's rule was that the two gates were never open at the same time—except for two times a day, at dawn and dusk, to move the herd of sheep they kept protected inside at night. If this was going to work, I couldn't let Gabriel have time to plan and control the situation.

"I still think we should just kill him," Em muttered. "He tried to kill you—you owe him."

"No blood," I said again. The clan—hell the whole city—was close to splintering and the Creation hadn't even begun their attack. Gabriel's death would cause chaos. The clan needed a leader.

"You know, I've never been used as live bait before," Em said. Today she wore tight jeans and a fitted T-shirt instead of her usual black, baggy hoodie. There would be no mistaking what she was.

"Happy to help," I muttered. A soft morning breeze waved through the grass, her hair brushing against my arm. I resisted the urge to reach out and tuck the lock of hair behind her ear. *Focus, Sam.*

A familiar rattling and metallic screech sounded. "It's opening," I whispered.

"Get ready."

Both gates creaked open. I shoved up from the cold earth, my stiff muscles protesting the sudden movement. Em and I sprinted across the open ground between our hiding place and the gate. I kept my eyes on the walkway above, but the men posted there were looking inward, shouting and cursing at the sheep. Farther down the road, hidden away behind a few buildings, was the Skull clan. All fully armed and ready to attack.

It won't come to that. All I needed was the access card and any information Addison had found about the engineer. Gabriel would never be able to resist the temptation of another woman in his clan—not when Ara had slipped through his fingers.

A sense of foreboding washed over me as we passed through the first gate.

"Remember, no blood," I said. Em nodded as we made our way into the Chute. My chest tightened, but I kept going, pushing through the sheep and then drawing near to the second gate.

Shit.

Gavin, the shepherd who watched the sheep during the day, stared at me in shock.

"Hey, Gavin." I gave him a friendly wave as if I were meant to be there. The sheep kept me from an all-out run, but I tried to keep smiling. This was the kind of nonchalant bluff that Kaden would have sold effortlessly. But I wasn't Kaden.

Gavin stared at me, only managing to speak as I drew level. "Gabriel said you weren't allowed back in. I-I can't let you pass."

"He'll change his mind when he sees who I brought with me."

Em stepped out from behind me and flashed him a razor-sharp smile. "Morning, Gavin." She stood on her tiptoes and pressed a kiss to his cheek. He looked at her with wide, shocked eyes, his mouth hanging open.

"Thought you'd change your mind," I muttered as Em and I slipped through the final gate and into the clan. Homesickness tightened my throat as I looked at the dawn lighting the stone buildings and walls. There was no such thing as home in the apocalypse—but hadn't this been something like it?

My gaze fell on the whipping post and my heart hardened. Gabriel had taken the clan from me—but he wouldn't take my chance to restart the new tech and save our city.

I paced forward, into the center of the courtyard. We'd made it only twenty feet when the first man noticed Emma. He did a double take, stopping dead in his tracks. Someone cursed behind him. He lifted his hand and pointed at Emma. The group of men fell abruptly silent.

This pattern continued, until men began calling out, "A woman! There's a woman in the clan!"

Confusion reigned but Emma and I stood unmoving, the calm center of a growing storm.

"Admit it, you're enjoying this," I whispered to her.

"Who wouldn't?" She reached forward and took my hand in hers. I felt her touch through my whole body, as if some sort of current ran between us.

Soon a crowd had gathered, the men in the back calling out what was happening, and the ones in the front answering, "Sam's back! And he brought a woman!"

The call echoed as more men gathered, leaving a careful circle around us. *So far so good*.

Gabriel pushed his way through the crowd. His stride faltered as he caught sight of Em. Her dark hair held hints of red in the light and her blue eyes blazed in the dawn, as beautiful as a freshly sharpened knife. *And twice as dangerous*. The men fell silent as Gabriel stepped into the careful circle of space left around us. His eyes went to Em, and then to our joined hands. I could almost hear the gears turning in his head.

"Sam," Gabriel said carefully, "We didn't expect to see you again."

"Turns out I forgot something," I said.

"Then I suppose we should go somewhere private to talk?" Gabriel gestured behind him.

"No, we can talk here. This is Emma." She smiled at him with the look of a predator sizing up its next meal. "We've come to negotiate a trade. The card you took from me, and any information about the new tech engineer who was once part of the old clan—and she'll stay with the Castellano clan."

I didn't say the alternative: that the entire strength of the Skull clan was ready to take it all by force.

I needn't have worried; Gabriel's voice adopted his smooth politician tone as he fell straight into our trap. "Of course, Sam. I will get that information to you immediately." He turned to Emma, a smile that I knew she would see right through. "I'm honored to meet you, Emma, I'm Gabriel Castellano—"

"The card and the info," she cut in before he could finish. "For me joining the clan."

Gabriel's calm gaze flickered. I wondered if he was thinking that the last time a woman had joined the clan she'd burned it to the ground. What he didn't know was that Em was Ara's little sister, if not by blood, by every other bond in this world.

And by far the more dangerous of the two was the sister standing next to me.

"Of course," Gabriel finally said. "It's in my office. Come."

The group of men parted before us. We followed Gabriel through a red dawn breaking over the clan. I'd gotten what I wanted, but the tension that sat on my chest only grew heavier. We were playing with fire and everything stood to burn.

~

"The access card." Gabriel held out the card to me in his office, the old warden's space. I reached out, but he pulled it back before I could take it.

"But first, Emma, I'd like you to sign the clan charter. It's one of the few things saved from the fire. It also has the only information I have about the engineer who was here before the old clan burned. If you'll have a seat."

"Of course," she said, demure and doe-eyed as she sat at his desk. Annoyance churned in my chest, even if I knew it was all an act.

Gabriel pulled out a massive leather-bound book and passed it to her. I wondered how many prisoners had once come through here and signed away their lives. She picked up the pen and then froze. It took a moment for me to understand, to see what she saw.

There, near the bottom of the list, was the name of the last girl to join the clan. *Arabella Edana*. Her sister.

"Ahh yes, you've seen Ara's name," Gabriel said, noticing Emma's hesitation. "We once had another woman here. She's since left, but my younger sister, Addison, is here. She'll be so happy to have another female here. She was, of course, devastated when Ara left."

Em stared down at the name, unmoving. I swallowed, suddenly nervous at all the ways this could still go wrong. Whatever emotion Em hid behind her ice-blue eyes, I couldn't tell. But then the spell broke and she leaned forward and signed her name with a flourish. I didn't have a chance to see what last name she'd signed. She couldn't exactly put *Emma Edana* without giving away Ara as her sister.

"And the engineer?" I said as she pushed the book back, wanting to move this along. "What do you know of him?"

"Quite a bit actually," Gabriel said. "I keep extensive records—but not in this room. The information is in one of my journals. I've got it up in the South Tower. Would you like to come with me and see if we can find it together?"

Something about his tone, and posture, set off warning bells inside me. The South Tower was different from the other three because the wall had crumbled on one side. I was used to seeing Gabriel up there, reading or writing, so I wasn't sure why that made me nervous.

"Yes, I would," I said carefully.

"Then come." He gestured for us both to follow him. "We can go get it now."

Again, I hesitated. He wasn't supposed to be in control here—I was. He paused and looked at me. "Or I could bring it to you later. It might take me some time to find my old reference to him."

I couldn't let him go alone—he would try to slip out of his end of the bargain any way that he could. Of course, we were planning to break our end of the bargain as soon as we had what we needed. Em had already assured me that she would make her escape that evening, and together we could regroup and make our final plans to turn on the new tech.

It was time to finish this.

"Let's get it now," I said. "But I want the access card first."

Gabriel smiled and passed me the card, then led us out of his office and across the clan, headed for the South Tower. I trailed behind them, trying to ignore my growing unease. Something about the way he smiled wasn't right.

"It really is fascinating, the clan you've built," Em said. There was a hardness to her eyes that Gabriel didn't seem to notice.

"Thank you. I really have the clan to thank for it."

I rolled my eyes at Gabriel's false modesty—he never resisted the chance to brag about the changes he'd made here. The guard tower could only be accessed from either the walkway or a rope ladder descending from the hole left in one side of the tower. Since we'd come from the ground, we would have to climb the ladder. Gabriel went first. Em gave me a reassuring wink and then climbed after him.

I cast a nervous look over the clan before I followed. Why did he keep his journals here? I wished I would have pressed him harder. When I gained the top of the tower, I found Em looking out of one of the windows and Gabriel in the far corner bent over boxes that held several massive journals. The tension winding in my chest eased a little. *It's fine. It's gonna be fine.*

"How do you get fresh water?" Em said, gazing out the window. Though it looked like she was enjoying the scenery; I was willing to bet she was assessing the clan for weakness. Or looking to where the Skull clan waited.

"We have a well."

Usually Gabriel took any excuse to talk about the clan. His brevity felt like a warning. I glanced back at the opening from where we'd just climbed, to the ground below. It was a far drop to the cement. The wind grabbed at my clothes and I stepped away from the sheer drop to approach Gabriel.

Only then, looking at the books, did I see they weren't journals. They were encyclopedias.

"Where's the journal?" I said, trying to bury the sense of panic, the sense of things spinning out of control. It wasn't too late. I could still make this right.

Gabriel pulled out his gun and pointed it at my chest.

Everything stopped.

You're a fool, Sam.

The steel glinted in the sun. My heart thudded, my mouth dry, as I stared at this man I hated more than anything. *Fool, fool, fool,* my heart seemed to beat.

I waited for him to berate and threaten me, but Em spoke first.

"Finally." She angled her head sideways, smiling as if this were all a fun new development. "I was beginning to think you were as boring as Sam said."

"I told you I would kill you if you ever came back here," Gabriel said. The barrel seemed to stare at me, like all the force in the world was focused on that small opening.

"Easy, now." I didn't want to move; afraid he would shoot. "All I need is the information about the engineer. We had a deal, remember? You don't have to do this, Gabriel."

"I DIDN'T WANT TO!" he shouted, the simmering calm he wore like a mask cracked at the edges. "What I want is to save the world, and the clan, from people like you." His eyes flashed to Em—but I didn't dare follow his gaze. "If you want her to live, you're going to destroy that access card, stop your pointless quest for the new tech and leave the clan forever. Em will stay here, and what happened with Ara will never happen again."

"We'll pass on that plan," Emma said dryly.

Gabriel didn't move the direction of the gun, but he turned to stare at her, incredulous. Had I not been worried I was seconds from death, I would have been in awe. She wasn't even looking at him, picking the dirt out from under her nails with a small knife.

"This doesn't concern you," he said. "You'll be safe here."

She looked up—her eyes flicking to mine for the briefest moment. Was there a warning there?

"That's where you're wrong," she said coldly. "The Creation are coming, and, as much as I enjoy this game, we don't have time to play it."

"This isn't a game!" Gabriel hissed, unhinged now. "I don't know what he's told you—"

"It doesn't matter what he's told me," Em interrupted, the knife pausing in her hand. "What matters is what I told him." The knife shifted. "I told him that bastards stay rulers—"

It happened in the space between one word and the next; so fast I barely saw the flash of her blade.

She threw her knife.

It hit the gun just as Gabriel fired—barely missing me.

I surged forward and smashed into Gabriel.

I fought against him, slamming him into the wall before he forced me back. *The gun, just get the gun!* But I couldn't. He was strong, and all pretension had fallen away between us.

The edge of the wall loomed closer as we struggled. I fought with all my rage, all my anger, and the knowledge that if he got another shot, he would kill me. Once he was stronger than me, but now I was the stronger one, pushing him, fighting back—

Then he was gone.

Time stopped.

My head felt as if it were disconnected from my body, unable to process what had happened. Just a moment ago he had been there.

I'd blinked and he had . . . he had . . .

I couldn't finish the thought. All I could do was look at the empty space in front of me, where Gabriel had been a moment ago. Where he should have been now. And beyond that space, the open wall. The sheer drop.

No. This isn't what I wanted.

I took a step forward, to the edge of the tower and Em came to stand beside me. Together we looked down.

There on the ground, far, far below, lay Gabriel.

Spread-eagled. Still.

No, Issac, I swear this isn't what I wanted. This isn't who I am. Help me.

But no one answered. God had long ago abandoned me. The cold wind swirled over me, a pool of blood around Gabriel's head growing, as I stared down at what I'd done.

"Until you bring them down," Em said, as if it were the final line in a play.

CHAPTER TWELVE—KADEN

The severed human head glared down from the fence post; the stench so powerful there was no debating its authenticity. Beneath it lay a spray-painted message: *Skull clan Territory. Turn back now.*

"Is that a real skull?" Septimus said curiously.

"Yes. Don't touch it."

Watched by the skull, I fished out my remaining bullets and loaded my gun. Dusk was falling, and I felt uneasy in a way I rarely was in Boise. We'd lost the horses yesterday. Even now, I couldn't shake the way the horse had screamed. Septimus had been riding a beautiful roan mare when it had fallen into a pit that fell away in the center of the road. A trap. Only the fact that Septimus was Creation, with faster reflexes than a human, had saved him.

Now all I could think was what had happened to Boise in the time we'd been away, that there were traps in the road, and human skulls mounted to fences.

It terrified me that Ara had returned here alone.

"I see another skull farther down," Septimus said, craning to look over the fence. "Do you think this is some kind of boundary? Are you sure it's wise to cross it?"

"No one ever said I was wise," I said, trying for lighthearted but failing. I wasn't about to let a severed human head stop me from finding Ara. Nothing would, no matter how dangerous. And dangerous no longer seemed a big enough word for Boise.

The city felt like a war zone—whatever fragile peace Gabriel had once managed here was gone. Septimus and I had passed several corpses since entering city limits—fresh, not the shriveled ones I was used to seeing. It was hard to say what had killed them, but it wasn't Creation.

Which meant we were killing each other before the real enemy even arrived.

Septimus followed me as we crossed the border—I had to bury the impulse to look back and see if the head watched us as we went. Septimus held only a knife, which was part of the reason I moved so quietly through the ruins. He refused to handle a gun, no matter how many times I told him it was necessary to defend himself.

A chill wind blew, bringing scents of cold earth and something rotten.

"Did you hear that?" Septimus said, his head whipping sideways. I'd gotten used to this—as Creation, his hearing was better than mine.

Unfortunately, his instincts were usually worse. "Just the wind," I said. "Let's keep moving."

Except when we turned the corner, there, lying in the center of the road, lay a human body. It was so fresh that his clothes weren't yet covered in dirt or debris—but the stillness of death was undeniable.

"Should we bury him?" Septimus said.

"No. We leave it."

"But shouldn't we—"

"I said no, Septimus."

My voice was hard, clipped, but we didn't have the time to bury every human body we came across. It was dangerous—who knew what diseases the body might have, or if whoever killed them was nearby.

I stepped around the body, keeping my eyes on the buildings all around, watching for signs of a trap. But when I turned back Septimus stood only a few feet from the body, staring down at the corpse.

"Should we not honor his body in some way?"

I wanted to drag him away, but when I looked at the body again, my breath caught in my chest. It was a man I recognized from my time as an expedition leader. I hadn't known him well, but I'd traded with him. He was known for making soap.

"I guess we can say a prayer," I said, and then, because Septimus was looking at me expectantly, I crouched and took a handful of dust. "Lord, we commend this soul to you and ask that he rests in your peace." I sprinkled the dust and we moved on.

Coyotes sang their lonesome song as the sun sank toward the horizon.

"What is that?" Septimus said, looking unnerved.

"Coyotes. They're scavengers, they won't attack." *Not when there is plenty of other rotting meat out there.* "It's the infected animals you have to worry about."

The sun was nearly gone by the time the mall loomed before

us. It wasn't the ideal time to approach—too many predators stirring—but if Ara was here, I had to know.

"Someone's living in there," Septimus said, surprising me as we drew closer.

"How do you know?"

He pointed to the rooftop. "Look at the roofing. There are solar rigs up there."

In the fading light I could make out nothing more than a basic roof—plus I couldn't imagine someone taking the risk to get up there now. "I'll take your word for it."

When we reached the mall, the door creaked open, and the smell of rot, stone, and smoke washed over me. *Please be here.* I'd already made it halfway down the hallway before I realized Septimus hadn't followed. I turned back, and for one half moment, seeing him framed there with the last light of day behind him, a warning flashed through me. One I quickly buried.

"What's wrong?" I said.

"I'm not sure . . . something smells wrong."

I stared down the beckoning hallway, aching to throw caution to the wind. "Wrong how?"

"I don't know . . . I've never smelled anything like it."

She could be here. What if she's in trouble?

And yet, Septimus was the one who'd warned us when others were ahead on the road. He was the reason we'd made it here in one piece.

"Then we go carefully," I said after a moment. Together we stepped into the mall, the walls closing in around us. Already the dying light of day barely reached inside. I wondered if maybe Septimus was right—maybe I should have waited for dawn. *Too late now.* Shadows lined the cavernous space, the escalator just before us, the food court behind it, and the last light of day coming in through the skylights above.

A strange rumbling sound came from deep in the shadows. Septimus froze and I saw his eyes fix on something and then widen in fear.

"What is—"

But I didn't finish the sentence.

A massive grizzly bear stepped into view, its white eyes weeping blood.

It was infected.

I unloaded every bullet I had into it before I could think. It did nothing except make it angry.

The bear roared and charged. I didn't hesitate, grabbing Septimus and shoving him forward.

"RUN!"

We ran, weaving between mannequins, fake potted plants, and fallen debris. The mannequins seemed to confuse the bear, who was flattening them one after the other, but still coming after us.

Then she was there.

Ara.

I almost thought I was dreaming.

Her eyes met mine. The world stopped.

Or it would have—if an infected bear hadn't been chasing us.

"This way!" she shouted; I followed her without hesitation. She ran so swiftly between mannequins and other obstacles I wondered if she had done this before. Then she suddenly threw out her hand, stopping Septimus and me even though the bear still lumbered after us.

"Go around the red lines," she said, pointing to the floor in front of us. I wouldn't have noticed till she said it—but I saw now that the ground before wasn't part of the original flooring. Septimus and I carefully ran around the red lines, but instead of continuing, Ara turned around and stopped.

The bear charged around the corner, and I took a step back. "Umm, should we . . . ?"

"Hold," Ara said, far more confident than I was.

"I don't have any bullets—"

"Don't shoot," she said. The bear charged.

"Plan? Ara?!"

"Hold!"

I could see its bleeding, white eyes now, its muzzle, the thick rolling muscles that were fully capable of tearing us apart. I grabbed Ara, about to drag her away, when the floor suddenly collapsed beneath the bear.

There was a final terrifying roar of pain.

Then everything was silent.

Ara turned to me and smiled. "It's about time you two showed up."

I stepped forward and pulled her to me, holding her as if I was afraid she would disappear. My heart thundered so hard I felt almost dizzy from adrenaline. She was here. She was safe.

"You'll be the death of me, Princess."

~

We gathered around a small electric heater in one of the back rooms. It was a very different group than the one that I'd once brought here with Ara.

For one, Matteo, the man Ara had introduced as the Mall clan leader, regarded Septimus and me with suspicion. His hand was never far from the gun at his hip. Had it only been me I wouldn't have minded—hell, I probably would have egged him on. But there was something a little too discerning about the way he watched Septimus. I worried he knew he was Creation, even as I reasoned there was no way he could know. Ara wouldn't have shared something like that with someone she barely knew. Either way, it wasn't like I could ask her now, while he stared me down.

Ara had given us a tour of the clan, the back rooms they used and the traps they had set around the mall for protection. Despite Matteo's coldness, the rest of the clan welcomed Septimus and me with open arms. They were clearly appreciative, if not downright worshipful, of Ara. They saw her as the reason several of the members had been cured, and beyond that, as the reason they now had a steady supply of fresh meat. When Ara introduced me and Septimus as the friends she'd been waiting for, they all seemed genuinely happy for us. I could deal with Matteo not liking me—it's not like I had some great record when it came to clan leaders.

Finally, Matteo yawned, and then stood, speaking to Ara and not me. "I'm gonna turn in for the night. Want me to find these two another place to sleep?" He said it like we were two stray dogs she'd picked up.

"I've got some extra bedrolls in my corner. They can stay with me," Ara said easily. The long room was lined with cots, bedrolls, and hammocks full of sleeping men—it wasn't like it was some huge imposition. Still, Matteo gave us both a final cold look before he made his way to his cot. Septimus, despite his occasional lack of social etiquette, seemed to understand I wanted Ara all to myself.

"I think I'll go to bed too," he said, and made his way over to the corner of the room where Ara had shown us she slept.

"Should I help him get set up?" Ara said.

"He can figure it out." I took Ara's hand and pulled her in the opposite direction.

The other men watched us, Matteo's gaze tracking our own, but I ignored them all. Before this mall housed their clan, it had belonged to me, Issac, and Sam. They might think they ruled it now, but I knew things about this place they never would. I loved it in a way they never would. I pushed open the final set of doors to the mall, and the vast cavernous space stretched out around us as if to welcome me back. Stars crowned the ceiling, and the night was warm.

"Where are we going?" she said, laughing as we went.

"Somewhere I can kiss you without everyone watching." As soon as the doors closed, I took her face in my hands. Every touch was a memory, and I stroked her cheek, soaking her in before I pressed my lips to hers. She arched into my touch. The vastness of the mall, the darkness—it all felt different. Not doomed, but full of possibilities.

She didn't pull back for some time—till my breath ran ragged. Then she grinned up at me. "You know what I need?"

"Me?" I said with a wink.

"A bath."

"I second that."

We made our way slowly through the mall, hand in hand, unhurried, the way I imagined couples once walked through these halls. Ara even pointed out a few things, changes and improvements Matteo had made. I was surprised at the admiration and respect in her voice.

"I have something to show you," she said as we walked.

"I'm yours to lead."

She only laughed. "Come this way first, then we'll go to the pool." Mystified, I let her lead me forward, till she stopped, pulled out her flashlight, and shone it on the words spray-painted onto the wall. SAM WAS HERE.

My heart thundered for a new reason, memories flashing by me like leaves swirling in a storm. Sam and I, running through the mall. Sam and I, practicing our aim, shooting mannequins. Sam and I, making plans about what we'd do when the power came back some day.

"Do you think it was him?" she said, startling me back to the present.

A final memory came, even more vivid than the others. Issac catching Sam and me spray-painting the walls, shaking his head, telling us it was disrespectful to the world—and then surprising us both by joining in. After that it became a private joke between the three of us, each one of us leaving messages for the others to find.

My voice was rough with emotion when I said, "Yeah. That's him." I glanced up and down the dark hallways. "Any other sign of him or Emma?"

"No. But Matteo said there are rumors that the Castellano clan moved into the Old Pen, like Sam said in the video. I figure we could go there. In a few days."

"A few days?" I said, surprised. Now that I was here, now that I'd found her, I wanted to go now.

She shrugged, a look of guilt crossing her face. "Matteo helped me. We cured people, and some of them are still weak. We can't abandon another clan. Not like we did last time."

Maybe I'd been naïve in thinking the mistakes I'd made in the past would stay there. Ara must have read the look on my face, because she turned back to the writing on the wall and said, "Apparently when the Castellano clan fell, so did several others. The city isn't what it once was. It's on the brink of war—and the Creation are coming."

I sighed. "Septimus says they're here. In the city."

"What are they waiting for?"

I paused. This wasn't exactly what I wanted to talk about right now, not when I finally had her next to me, but I saw the determination in her eyes. She wouldn't let this go. "He thinks their leader is waiting for some weakness—some way to kill us all at once. Like another plague."

I didn't like the silence that greeted my words—or the tension that now sat on Ara's shoulders. This had to be why she didn't want to leave Matteo's clan—because she felt some sense of blame for what had happened in the city. Her grandfather had been the one to design the plague in the first place.

"The city is falling apart," she finally whispered. "I tried to distribute plague flowers, but it all feels useless. I don't know where to even start." She wrapped her arms around me and set her head against my chest.

I laid my head on top of hers. "Only one place to start. With a bath."

She laughed at this, and then led me away from the message, and away from our worries.

At the pool Ara tugged my shirt off, running a finger down my chest and lighting my skin on fire. Then she backed up, her smile wicked as she stood next to the pump.

"Do you remember what you said last time we were here?" she asked.

"If I brought you to work or stare?"

She grinned. "I think I can do both."

We didn't return to camp for a long time.

CHAPTER THIRTEEN—ARA

The beam of my flashlight trailed over model airplanes suspended from the ceiling. It was almost homey, this small storage room in the back of the Barnes & Noble bookstore. Someone had definitely lived here, but if it was Sam, or Emma, I couldn't say. A small cot sat tucked in the corner, posters decorated the walls, and stacks of comic books lined the floor. A small table held a guitar coated in dust. Emma didn't play guitar . . . but I suppose it had been nearly five years since I'd last seen her in person. She had likely changed as much as I had.

"Do you think he was here?" I asked Kaden.

The only response was a click, followed by light flooding the small space. I turned in surprise. Kaden stood across from me, his right arm raised, holding a string connected to a small light bulb that now lit the entire room.

Kaden's smile matched my own. "Sam was definitely here."

I clicked my flashlight off, standing in appreciation at the warm, golden light. In the days since Kaden and I had been reunited, we'd spent our time exploring nearby, searching for signs of Emma and Sam, while bringing back food and supplies for Matteo's clan. Our next step would be going to the Castellano clan, but we wanted to make sure Sam and Emma weren't here first. After all, we'd heard from others that Gabriel still led the Castellano clan. We couldn't exactly expect a warm welcome after burning it down. And his note on the wall had said *Sam Was Here.*

So where are you now, Sam? The longer I was here, in the city again, knowing the Creation were coming, and yet not knowing where Sam and Emma were, it wound something tighter within me, like a coil that would soon snap.

Opposite the cot was a wall of plastic bins and Kaden rifled through these now. Again, there was nothing helpful to tell us where Sam might have gone.

"There's not much left," Kaden said, clearly disappointed as he went back to examining the room. Today he reminded me of the wind outside, tearing through the city, unable to rest, filling up the space with unbridled energy. I understood the feeling—the same ache grew inside me to find Emma. He ran a finger over the layer of dust on the cot. "No one has slept here for weeks. . . but it looks like he intended to come back."

"Maybe Emma was here too?"

He must have heard the despair in my voice because he stopped what he was doing and wrapped his arms around me. "We'll find them both. This is our city, and we know them better than anyone. We just keep looking."

I tried not to think about how much the city had changed since the last time we'd been here—and how much Emma would have changed too. Yet one thing felt the same: I saw her in my dreams, in shadows, always just out of reach, always dancing away from me.

"Wish he would have left a few more clues in that video," Kaden said, letting out a heavy sigh.

"Aren't you the best expedition leader in Boise?" I said teasingly. "You'll find them."

Kaden pressed a kiss atop my head and then gently pulled away, sucked back into whatever secrets the room held. Or maybe he just sought comfort, to be in the same place where Sam had once been, to stand where he'd stood.

Kaden knelt beside the bed, rifling through the comic books before he stood and returned to the plastic bins in the corner. He threw the lid off one, not gentle as he shifted through the contents. Clearly finding nothing helpful, he threw it sideways in disgust, and said, "Maybe it's time to finally face Gabriel."

I nodded, even though my stomach clenched in fear. The last time we'd escaped the Castellano clan, it had cost our friend Issac his life, and nearly Kaden's as well. And now we were just going to walk back in?

"I could go alone?" Kaden said in response to my silence.

"No," I said at once. "We go together or not at all."

"Have you talked with Matteo about it?"

"No." How could I? I'd helped heal all those people, and now I would abandon them—just like I had my sister. "He needs me here."

"He'll understand we need to go," Kaden said, though I wasn't sure that was true. "If the Creation strikes, there won't be any clans left to protect. For all his faults, Gabriel wanted to unite the clans. Maybe he'll have a plan to do that. It's worth a shot."

Worth a shot. Was that really the only plan we had?

After another hour we'd found nothing to help us, so we left the Barnes & Noble, and then made our way back.

Soon the mall loomed ahead of us. We walked beside an abandoned tank that I remembered seeing last time I was at the mall. The days were growing longer, but even so, we'd only just barely made it back in time. The sun dipped behind the horizon, painting the ruins in streaks of red.

I'd been quiet the whole trip back, thinking about Gabriel and what it would mean to see him again. Then there was Matteo. He had been kind to me, fatherly almost. What would he say when I told him we were leaving? He wouldn't try to keep me prisoner—he wasn't like Gabriel in that way. Still, I imagined the way his lips would press together in silent disappointment.

"Wait, Ara."

I spun at Kaden's words, worried something was wrong, but then saw, to my shock, he was down on one knee. I'd seen the wound on his leg, where the bullet had ripped through him, and for a moment I thought maybe he'd stumbled. But when I tried to pull him up, he said, "No, I want to do this from my knees."

My heart beat faster, even as I arched a brow at him. "You already proposed. I haven't changed my mind."

"I know," he said, something serious in his eyes. "But I love you, Ara. I want to spend the rest of my life with you. I want to build a family with you. I'm tired of waiting. Marry me."

"Right now?"

He grinned. "Right now."

I pretended to consider this. "Well, you'd better get off your knees then."

I pulled him upright, and he said, "Do you have the ring Issac left for you?"

I had kept the ring on a necklace around my neck, not wanting to lose it. I pulled it free now and he took it, taking my hand in his own as he held the ring over my finger.

"Ara Edana Marshall," he said, and I grinned at him adding his own name at the end of mine. "I have loved you through all our wild adventures together. With this ring I promise to love and cherish you, to protect you, and if needed, to lay down my life for you."

He slid the ring onto my finger, and now, looking in his eyes, it was all I could do not to cry.

"Kaden Marshall Edana," I said, and he laughed at this. "I promise to love and cherish you. I promise to laugh at your jokes, and always help you find the humor and goodness still left in the world. I promise to stand beside you no matter what comes." I paused, and then said, "By the power vested in me by everyone we've loved and lost, everyone who still remains, and the God Issac taught us to believe in, I pronounce us husband and wife. Kaden, you may kiss your bride."

And he did.

CHAPTER FOURTEEN—KADEN

Telling Matteo we were leaving went both better and worse than I'd imagined. Better because Matteo nodded and embraced Ara, telling her he understood, and then told her to go investigate the spare supplies to pack what we needed. Worse because, the second he sent her away he sat me down and glared at me, demanding to hear my full plan.

"We'll be going to the Castellano clan in the morning," I said, sitting straight-backed before him. I was glad Ara hadn't mentioned we'd just gotten married.

"We had a few men pass through this winter—deserters from the Castellano clan." Matteo kept his voice low so as to not wake the others. "They said things were bad. The leader was whipping men for trying to hide weapons or taking more than their share of food. And that most of the food and supplies came from a single man."

A single man? I wondered who had replaced me as expedition leader—and why he worked alone. Issac, Sam, Jeb, and I always brought back the most supplies, but we relied on each other. And each year scavenging the ruins became more difficult as supplies ran scarce and Boise became more dangerous.

"You sure that's where you want to go?" Matteo pressed.

"Yes, if my brother's there."

"You'll risk Ara's life to check?"

I understood him being defensive—Ara wasn't safe in this city. But she wasn't safe anywhere and we had to keep looking. "Ara's also looking for her sister. We've already discussed it—we're going together." I softened my words a little. "I would give my life to protect her."

"And if that's not enough?"

"It's all I have."

He shook his head, staring into the shadows of the room where Ara was packing and speaking to some of the other men. Ara had told me he had family. Maybe even daughters. I wondered if he saw in Ara the shadow of someone he'd failed to protect. *And maybe she sees in him the father who'd died to protect her.*

"I'm sorry," I said, meaning it. I knew what it was like to have those you loved most be ripped away from you.

He shrugged, even though I could see he still didn't like it. "I guess a man has to do what he thinks is best." His gaze was piercing as he looked me up and down. "But just so you know, I've already told her if she has second thoughts, she can ditch you and come back here with us."

I laughed, and decided that, despite his gruffness, I liked Matteo. "Good to know."

We sat like that, surrounded by the low murmurs of the other men, and the flickers of the coals, till Matteo spoke again. "She reminds me a bit of my oldest daughter. She wanted to join the

Peace Corps, change the world." He shook his head, staring into the fire as if he saw a different world flickering in the embers. "Maybe it's a good thing none of them lived to watch the world go to shit."

Something about his unexpected honesty touched me. "Sam—my brother—was like that too. He always believed in the best of the world and people."

We both sat there in silence, each of us bearing the weight of everyone we'd failed.

Then, to my surprise, Matteo said, "I have an updated map of the new clan territories. I'll give it to you before you leave. It'll help you get the Castellano clan without too much trouble."

"Thanks. I appreciate that." I stood, leaving Matteo by the fire, and then checked on Ara. She hadn't seen Septimus, so I made my way out into the dark recesses of the mall to find him, tell him the new plan, and have a moment alone. Something about the grief in Matteo's eyes struck a little too close to home.

The mall seemed too quiet tonight, the only noise a cool breeze whistling down from the broken skylights above. As I walked, I thought about my family. I'd buried my sister and brothers beneath the vast Montana sky—those goodbyes had ripped my heart out. But I'd always had Sam. And then Ara. I couldn't imagine losing your whole family. Like Issac had. Like Matteo had.

What kind of faith did you need—to lose everything and continue on? Did I have that kind of faith? I wanted to. I'd tried to. But there was a part of me that worried I wasn't strong enough. That if I lost Ara, like I'd once thought I'd lost Sam, I wouldn't be able to follow a god who'd taken everything from me. Except that wasn't how Issac saw it. He saw everything here as opportunities God had given us. He saw all this as a chance to do better. He believed death wasn't the end—that we would one day all be reunited.

I wanted to believe that too.

My flashlight lit a game trail that wove through dirt, debris, and the hundreds of mannequins that now filled the hallways. Whoever had moved those out here was either lonely or had a sick sense of humor. I wandered through the still caricatures of humanity, feeling aimless.

Ara had told me that Septimus had gone to look for some new clothes, but now, as I checked one store after the other, all empty, an explained sense of paranoia began to rise. The shadows, once benign, felt increasingly sinister. Where was he? Had he already gone back?

I turned the corner and stiffened.

There, standing on the lip of the fountain, lit by the moonlight, was Septimus. He stood oddly still, facing me. My heart thundered, but I pushed aside the uneasiness.

"I've been looking for you," I said, a strange, uncomfortable feeling rising in me as he stood there unmoving. The beam of my flashlight pooled at his feet, but still he didn't move.

"And I you," he said, his voice soft in the darkness.

His clothes were different—black from head to foot.

"I see you found new clothes," I said, more to break the silence, which seemed to billow and rise like smoke—suffocating me in a way I couldn't understand.

"Among other things."

I took a few more steps forward, staring at him, standing there above me. He reminded me of one of those stone statues in graveyards: a dark, avenging angel. I tried to tamp down that strange, horrible feeling in my chest. Even if he was Creation, Septimus had proven himself again and again.

"Why are you out here?" My hand dropped casually to my side

to where my knife was sheathed—I suddenly regretted leaving my pistol back at camp with Ara.

"I've always wanted to see this place." He tilted his head back, staring up at the shattered glass skylights. "Strange, isn't it? All these things the humans built, only for the few survivors to watch them crumble. Does it make you sad, seeing how quickly you are forgotten?"

The hair on the back of my neck rose. I felt like I was staring over the edge of a cliff, like I was caught in the gaze of a predator, watching it stalk forward but unable to move.

"It does make me sad," I said slowly, carefully. "But it also gives me hope."

"Hope," he spat, and his eyes met mine, cold and cruel in a way I'd never seen. "An annoying human trait. Wouldn't it be easier to give up? To surrender to your fate?"

He smiled at me, and only then, far too late, did I realize what I should have the first moment I saw him.

"You aren't Septimus," I said. His smile only widened, and fear crept up my back. There was a cruelty, a viciousness to his features I'd never seen in Septimus.

This was the leader of the Creation.

"The designation they gave me was Sevyn," he said dismissively. "So like humans to give a number instead of a name." In one fluid motion he jumped down from the fountain and closed the space between us. I drew my knife, holding it out between us, but even as I did, all I could see was Septimus's face, eyes, arms, body. Could I really hurt this man—this thing—that was my friend in every physical way?

"There's no need for that," he said, smiling at my knife like it were some kind of toy. "I've come to talk with you. And offer a trade."

"For what?" I said, taking a step back, already thinking of the fastest way to reach Ara. But his next words stopped me cold.

"In *four minutes*, the Creation will begin their attack on the mall. Unless you give me the traitor, Septimus. Should you fail to bring him, you all die."

"Or I could kill you now," I said, glaring at him over the knife.

His smile faded, and he snapped his fingers. From the shadows all around us, like silent specters, hundreds of people materialized. The hair on my neck stood on end as I watched figures I had thought were mannequins, figures I had dismissed as shadows in the darkness, move closer.

An entire army.

My heart pounded, and suddenly all I could think about was Ara, in the room where I'd left her on the other side of the mall. Four minutes. Could I get Ara and everyone out in that time? I knew the answer—no. There were too many weak men. Maybe Ara, Septimus, and I could run, but we would condemn everyone else here.

I decided to bluff. "We lost Septimus in the mountains. I haven't seen him in ages."

Sevyn shook his head. "How very human of you to lie. I know he's nearby. I can feel him, sense him in my dreams. You can't lie about this. Not to me. Not to us."

Us. I glanced back at the hallway—only to feel like the breath had been punched out of me. The Creation had disappeared as quickly as they'd come—but now I felt their presence like a hand pressed against my mouth. "I can't. I won't."

He sighed. "Then I'll kill everyone. It's your choice."

You'll find a way out of it. Make the deal and then get back to the others. "You'll let everyone else free?" I asked. "If Septimus comes to you?"

"I give you my word. Unlike with humans, that's actually worth something."

"What will you do to him?"

"What he deserves." Then, before I could ask what he meant he said, "Clock's ticking. I suggest you run."

I needed no other prompting. I spun, fleeing from the fountain, and flinched at every mannequin I passed. My flashlight bounced, barely able to light the way as I flew over the ground.

I burst through the doors to the backroom. Matteo instantly stood, turning to me as I shouted to the room, "Everyone get up! The Creation are in the mall! We need to leave! *Now!* Grab what you can carry and run!"

Chaos ensued at my announcement, but to my relief Matteo didn't fight or question me. He simply jumped up, ordering the others to pack.

"How many?" he said, as he shoved bullets and other supplies into his backpack. "Can we fight them?"

"An army," I said grimly. "We only have minutes."

"Are they going to follow us?"

It was my turn to be tight-lipped. "Just get them ready. I'll take care of it." It felt as if something had been wrapped around my chest, squeezing tighter and tighter. Could I really do this? Give up Septimus, my friend, to save everyone here?

I had hoped he wouldn't be here, that he had somehow sensed the Creation and run. But that wasn't who Septimus was. I guessed he had returned in the time I'd been gone. Now I watched as Septimus comforted an older man. I couldn't hear Septimus's words, but he helped the older man pack, and then lifted the bag onto the man's shoulders.

I can't give him up.

I won't.

As if he could feel my gaze, Septimus suddenly turned, his eyes meeting my own.

You have to.

I hated that, in that single glance, he saw the words I couldn't say. He gave one last reassuring smile to the older man, touched Ara's shoulder, and then turned to me. Each step that he took across the room felt like a nail driven straight into my chest.

I wanted him to stop—everything to just stop—so I could think. So I could find another way, any other way, out of this. Septimus and I had so many adventures together. We'd faced death together a hundred times. And always we'd found a way out.

But I couldn't stop time. All too soon he stood before me. "What's happened? Kaden, what's wrong?"

I felt sick—like the words were caught in my chest. "He's here. Their leader." *And I thought he was you.*

Septimus's face paled, but then his gaze swept over the room. "What does he want?" I heard it in his voice. He knew what I was about to ask him.

Don't say it.

You can still save him.

You can still save all of them.

But that was the problem, wasn't it? Life in the apocalypse had taught me, over and over again, that I couldn't save them all.

"He wants you, Septimus," I said, hating myself, hating all of it.

I saw the shift in his eyes—and the realization. He took a deep breath, staring at the door that led to the rest of the mall. This time it was me, waiting for him to pull out some wild plan that would save us. Instead, he said simply. "Then I know what I need to do."

"You can come with us. You don't have to—"

He set a hand on my shoulder, and this time it was him comforting me. "You once told me that no one survives the apocalypse. I am thankful for all the time I've had in this world and with you."

There was so much I wanted to say, yet words were stuck in my throat, and tears stung my eyes. This couldn't be it. This couldn't be the last time I saw my friend.

Time was spinning out of control, and now Septimus spoke again. "You said your friend believed in heaven and a forgiving God. Do you think God would welcome someone created and not born?"

"I know He would."

He smiled, just the way we both did before every stupid decision, every dumb plan we'd made together. For a moment it felt just like old times. Maybe he saw that I was a moment away from begging him to stay, telling him to forget the whole thing, because he said, "Well, we're burning the moonlight."

Then he turned and walked away from me.

I stared at his retreating figure, wanting to call him back, wishing for anything but this.

"Goodbye, Septimus," I said when the door closed. Then I turned back to the others. They didn't see the grief in my eyes, the agony in my steps as I yelled that we all needed to go now. I shoved it all down for a later time as I led the group out of the room, the opposite way Septimus had gone. I didn't know how long the truce would last, or if the Creation leader would keep his word, but I had to try.

I owed Septimus that much.

Our group went through the back exit, moving as quickly as

we could with a collection of weakened men. I held my gun level as I searched the dark shadows. I could feel them watching us. I thought only I could sense it until Matteo swung his gun sideways, to something in the darkness, and muttered, "What the hell are they waiting for?"

I didn't answer him. I couldn't tell him that I'd traded the life of a good man to save us.

Finally, we spilled out of the mall, our group crossing the wide parking lot. The moon shone down on our small group, and out here, the land rising around us, it hit me what I'd done. *I left him. I gave him up.*

Ara seemed to have the same thought. "Where's Septimus?" she asked, looking at the group and only now realizing he wasn't with us.

"Keep moving," I said, not able to meet her eye. We were nearly across the parking lot now.

"Look!" Matteo said, pointing back to the mall.

The group of us turned, and it felt like the world had inverted.

An army stood in the darkness, the moonlight casting them in an eerie glow.

Two of the figures separated from the group.

Two forms that matched each other in every way.

I felt like I was caught in a nightmare I couldn't escape.

"Septimus," Ara whispered in horror. One of the two identical men lifted a gun, pointing it at the other's head.

The gunshot split the night in two.

Ara screamed, and Matteo jumped, grabbing her as she tried to run forward.

"No!" she screamed. "Septimus!"

Matteo struggled to hold her back. I felt like I wasn't here, like

I was trapped in some kind of nightmare where all I could do was stare.

It felt like I was underwater, like all the sounds and scents of the night were dulled. Then Ara ripped free from Matteo and slammed into me, bringing me sharply awake.

"Kaden?" she sobbed. "What's happening? Was that . . . ?"

I forced myself to swallow hard and turn my back on the scene. It didn't matter that I wanted to charge forward screaming, to fight and kill every Creation standing before me. It didn't matter that I didn't want the burden of the lives of everyone here resting on my shoulders.

Septimus was dead—and he'd given his life to protect us.

I met Matteo's eyes, cold understanding passing between us. It felt like a different man, one colder and harder, who said to the others, "We need to move."

Ara was quietly sobbing, the whole group watching me now.

"Where to now, Kaden?" Matteo said. I heard the judgment in his voice, the weight of his words. If I failed, more than Septimus would die.

I turned to look out into the darkness, to where the river lay, and beyond it the clan I'd once burned. It was time to find out if Gabriel was in a forgiving mood.

"The Castellano clan."

CHAPTER FIFTEEN—SAM

"So much for no blood," Em said. A buzzing noise sounded in my ears, so that I heard her words as if from a great distance.

I killed Gabriel.

No matter what Emma said, no matter how many times she'd insinuated what I had to do, I hadn't really thought . . . it didn't seem possible . . .

I didn't mean to . . . right?

I didn't know. I kept replaying the moment, trying to wind it back. Trying to undo it. I hadn't meant to kill him. I wasn't that person. But he had attacked me. It was either me or him . . . right?

"We were supposed to be the good guys," I said dully. I thought I was prepared to pay any cost, but this wasn't what I wanted.

Em's voice sliced through my inner turmoil. "*You* wanted to be the good guy. I never claimed to be."

"I killed him," I said again. My mind felt like a broken record, repeating itself, unable to accept it.

I would have stood there, unmoving, for hours. But Emma

yanked me away from the ledge, and then her arms took hold of my shoulders, and shook me. Hard. "Repeat after me: I did what I had to do. No going back now."

My insides twisted. Bile rose in the back of my throat. But Em didn't give me a chance to empty my stomach—she took my face in her hands, her fingers digging cruelly into my skin. "Say it back, Sasquatch."

"I did what I had to do," I choked out.

"And?"

"No going back now," I finished, the words settling upon me like a physical, crushing weight. Like something red-hot had been driven inside me, twisting and burning from the inside out.

"Do you want me to bring the Skull clan in?" Em said, still holding me in place. "Or do you want to take control first? Might be less bloodshed that way. We need to move fast either way."

"What?" My brain felt too full, unable to process what she was saying. "We came for the card and the book—"

"Take them," she said, carelessly. "But we may as well take the clan too. You said we might need a few days to work out the final details. Why not do it here?" She released me and turned back to look over the ledge. I hung back from her, not wanting to see the grisly sight below, but she wasn't looking down. She was looking out over the clan. "If you don't, someone else will."

"I can't just—"

Her eyes flashed with impatience, and she stepped so close for a moment I tensed—as if worried she was going to push me too. Her voice dripped with scorn. "If you want to turn the new tech on, if you want to change the world, then *stop asking permission*. If you want something, *take it*."

Was it really so simple?

Below us, I heard raised voices, men gathering. Em was right: whatever I was going to do, I needed to do it now. The first of the men had found Gabriel's body.

The question was: Was I done hiding? We still had time. We could take the book and the card and leave . . . figure this all out somewhere far away from here . . .

Or, I could find out if the boy Kaden and Issac had left behind was more than just a follower. If I really meant it when I said I wanted to change the world for the better.

I forced myself to walk to the edge of the wall, to look down and see what I'd done. Men gathered below, standing around Gabriel's prone body. But then I raised my eyes so that I was looking beyond the clan, beyond these walls, to the city waiting for someone to save it.

If you want something, take it.

"Men of the clan," I said, my voice growing with each word. "I came here with a secret—one Gabriel didn't want known. He was afraid and wanted to keep all of you in this prison forever with him as your jailor. But that's not what I want for you."

The men below looked up at me, more and more gathering below. Yet all were as silent as the body that lay in the center of them.

"Gabriel tried to kill me, and I defended myself. He wanted to stay in the past because he was afraid of change and afraid of me." My voice grew in strength with each word. "But I'm tired of living inside a jail. Gabriel was a coward who wanted to keep you all under his thumb forever. He didn't believe the world could be better. But I don't see cowards below. I see men who have survived everything—and who no longer want to live in a prison. I ask you to join me in building a new, better world—where no man is a prisoner. Who's with me?"

There was silence, and then, Liam's voice sounded. "I'm with you."

"I'm with you," said another, and another. More and more voices sounded, until it seemed like a mob below—a mob I controlled.

Someone brought a tarp forward, laying it over Gabriel's body, so that he became nothing more than a lump below.

Em took my hand and thrust it into the air, and there were roars of approval below. An icy cold settled over me as I found myself asking a new question: What happens when you become the bastard you were trying to bring down?

~

Three hours later, the Skull clan marched through the gates, and Gabriel was buried. It didn't feel real that he was gone, and I was clan leader now.

The day passed in a blur—there was so much to do and figure out. Some of the things I couldn't wait to do—give men back their guns, tear down the whipping post—but others I dreaded. At dusk I made my way to Addison's door and knocked. I could hear her moving within, but she didn't open the door.

When it became obvious she wasn't going to let me in, I said, "Addison . . . please, can I talk to you?"

Again, nothing. I leaned against the door, and spoke through the crack, hoping she could hear me. "I'm sorry. This . . . this wasn't what I wanted, Addison. You have to know that."

Still, she didn't answer, and I stared at the door, wondering if I should force myself inside. Then I considered how I'd felt the moment I accepted that Kaden was never coming back. How I would feel if I'd met the man who killed him. I closed my eyes and said, "You're free to come and go now, Addison. No one will stop you. But I need to know everything I can about the new tech engineer. I'll send Liam tomorrow to talk to you. You don't have to talk with me if you don't want to."

Again, no answer. I left feeling unhappy, but unsure what else to do. She'd just buried her brother. And I was the one who'd killed him. As much as I wanted the information on how to find the engineer, I wouldn't force my company on her. She deserved that much at least.

That night, I had the men build a giant bonfire from the remains of the whipping post. Someone had shot a deer, and I allowed for double rations to be served. There was an air of celebration, the fire painting faces in flickering flames, and I felt both a sense of victory and uneasiness. Gabriel's body was barely cold, and we were celebrating.

I forced myself to smile and laugh with the others, to talk about how things would be better, how we would turn on the new tech, and all the things we would have again, before I bowed out and made my way to Gabriel's rooms. They were the biggest, and included the warden's office and a back bedroom. Liam had given me the key, but I'd passed it off to Em earlier. She hadn't wanted to come to the celebration, and when I walked into the room, I saw why.

She had an electric lantern set on the table. Spread out all around it where the papers and books I'd last seen with Addison.

"What are these?" I said in surprise as I came to her side. I didn't want to admit it, but I was glad she was here. This room—full of a dead man's possessions—would have been eerie without someone else.

She turned over a paper, and without glancing up said, "You tell me. I got them from Addison's room."

"She gave them to you?" I said in shock. After she wouldn't even open the door for me?

"I took them."

It took me a moment to process that she'd stolen them. *Great, one more thing for me to apologize to Addison about.* "You couldn't have tried bonding with her? You two are the only women here—and she also knew Ara."

Em stopped what she was doing, fixing me with an incredulous look. "Remind me again how bonding with her brother went?" She shook her head without waiting for an answer. "Trust gets you nothing in this world."

"It's how I won over the men of the clan."

She laughed. "No, it wasn't. Trust almost got you killed. What got you the clan was killing Gabriel and then taking it by force. You can't trust anyone, Sasquatch, not in this world. Haven't you been listening?"

The old Sam might have withdrawn, or argued with her, trying to prove himself. But I wasn't that Sam anymore. I stepped closer till I was standing beside her. I closed the book she was looking at, and then took her hand, pulling her away from the table and into me.

"Oh, I've been listening," I said, watching as the ice in her eyes turned to fire. "You told me if I want something, I should take it."

She grinned, lacing her arms around my neck. "And what do you want, Sam?"

"You."

I kissed her—but not the way I had before, when I was a boy afraid of everything. I kissed her like a man who'd lost everyone, who'd killed to survive, who was finally ready to fight for what he wanted.

CHAPTER SIXTEEN—SEVYN

I sat on the cold ground, watching the world awaken around me. Green leaves burst from the trees, the nearby river roared, and soon the sun would stain the horizon red. I hadn't missed a single sunrise or sunset since I'd come to the surface.

I should have been happy today.

My only other clone, the one they called Septimus, was dead. Now that he was gone, I'd been able to focus on finding the original Creation, the last traitor. My link to her had shown me the final piece of the puzzle.

There was a way to destroy the humans forever. In a single strike. The path was hazy still, the details murky, but I knew it was there now. If she had found it, then I could too.

I would wipe the Earth clean—like in the story with God and his flood. Surely following in the footsteps of a god couldn't be a wicked thing? The Creation could begin anew. Talia couldn't claim I was cruel, or unjust—not if I used the weapon the humans themselves had created.

It was an ironic sort of justice. The humans had created me in their image, just as their God had with them, to bring their destruction.

And yet, despite all the steps being laid out before me, I felt that strange sense of emptiness. When the sun rose in all her glory, did she miss the stars she'd burned away?

Around me the Creation slept, as I lay there and watched as the sky lightened bit by bit.

One form slipped away from the others.

I knew at once who it was—no Creation needed to slink away from us. One of the Creation rose to stop her, but I lifted a hand, silently ordering them to stop. I waited a few moments, allowing Talia to draw ahead before I followed her into the growing dawn.

Talia headed for the river, which surprised me. Did she know we feared the water? I had been careful to avoid showing her this weakness, sure the humans would find some way to use it against us. And it wasn't as if the river was safe for humans now: it was cold and far too fast in the early spring—she couldn't possibly cross it. Maybe she thought she could disguise her tracks there? As I followed her, I wondered if I should simply let her go.

The thought was abhorrent.

But why should it be? There was no real purpose in my new plan for her. I needed only to find the original Creation Emma and resurrect this new weapon. I didn't need Talia.

Yet my feet kept me moving forward. I couldn't let her go. It was as if my mind and body were separate—a strange sensation I had yet to experience. In my distraction, I didn't realize her tracks had stopped until she'd stepped out of the brush ahead of me.

She held a gun aimed straight at my heart.

It wasn't the first time a human had tried to kill me. It was, however, the first time I forced myself not to step forward and end her before she could pull the trigger.

Some strange chemical rushed through my blood, making my fingers tingle, my breath come deeper and faster. The wind caught her hair, trailing it across her cheek, her eyes blazing into my own, the dawn behind her.

Beautiful, I thought, but I wasn't thinking of the sunrise.

Was this what the moment before death felt like? It didn't matter of course—if I fell some other Creation would become leader and continue my quest. But I realized I didn't want to die.

We stood there, the sound of the river roaring, impervious to my peril. Maybe even welcoming it.

"Why did you let those people in the mall go?" she finally said, the gun trembling in her hands.

"Why should I tell you?" The wind pushed behind me, as if wanting me to step forward—to death or to her?

"Because if you don't, I'll kill you."

The scents of wet earth, the pounding of the river, the fire in her eyes—this world, it was all so beautiful and painful. So fleeting. I wasn't ready to lose it yet. "I bargained with them. The traitor's life to allow them safe passage out of the mall."

"You spared them?"

"Hardly. I let them flee so my scouts could follow. They'll go to the strongest clan." I smiled. "And to the last traitor."

The hope in her gaze died. She squared her shoulders and swallowed hard, preparing herself to do what she thought was right. "I should kill you."

"You should." I wondered, if she fired, what would happen. When my heart stopped beating, when my blood flowed into the ground, would my soul escape to the same place the humans went?

"Is that all you have to say?" Her hands trembled as she pointed the gun at me, but I said no more. There was no defense I could offer her. No bridge I could build between us.

I took a step forward, then another, and another. One slip of the finger—that's all it would take. So little between life and death. For the first time, I understood what it felt to be human.

"Stop . . ." she demanded. "I'll do it . . ."

"Then do it. You know what I was created to do. There is no bridge between us. I am death, and no one escapes me forever."

My blood rushed and roared inside me, wild as the river as I stepped closer to death, to her, to madness. I didn't stop until I felt the cold barrel pressed against my chest. Until I could have run my fingers across her cheek. Until I could have leaned forward, brought our lips together, and made our breath one.

Her eyes were wide as they stared into mine. I wondered how I'd once thought her unremarkable, disposable. Now the thought of losing her was more terrible than the thought of her pulling the trigger.

She lowered the gun. I watched as she turned to face the river, pulled her arm back, and threw the weapon. It disappeared into the current with a splash.

"You're wrong about humans, Sevyn," she said. "And about the Creation. You don't have to do this."

"Look around you, Talia. I've sent humans ahead to warn them, to tell them to band together to fight me, and all they've done is kill each other."

"They're frightened. There must be a way to bring peace to the city that doesn't involve death."

"There isn't."

"You won't even try to see if there is another way?"

"Why should I? I have never known peace at a human's hands. All I've known is death and violence. All I've felt is hatred and malice."

She stepped forward, and instead of pushing me as I expected, she placed her hands on my chest. My entire body froze beneath her touch.

"And now, Sevyn? What do you feel now?"

The sun lit her from behind. I could feel my heart beating too fast, her hands pressed against my chest. Farther down the river a broken bridge stood, the two ends reaching out to each other, yet never able to meet.

"Nothing." I stepped away from her. "I feel nothing."

I spent the rest of the day watching the river's swift current, refusing to see or talk to Talia. I thought maybe the river would bring some measure of peace. Instead, I remembered all the Creation who had died by human hands beneath the water, choking, screaming, unable to breathe. I saw only the darkness the river hid beneath its current, and a path that was unyielding.

There was only one way forward. The path I'd been made to walk all along.

I made my way back to camp, a plan already forming in my mind. The Creation watched as I walked to the center of them, the darkness inside growing and clawing its way free.

"The humans have a weapon that will destroy the city, and then the world," I announced to them. "And we're going to get to it first."

CHAPTER SEVENTEEN—SAM

Em's hair splayed across the pillow, her face smooth and unworried. Maybe it was wrong to be happy in the room of a dead man, but I'd learned to enjoy moments like these—especially with Em.

I leaned forward and pressed a kiss to her lips. She opened sleepy eyes, then turned over and pulled the sheets over her head.

"It's not even dawn," she mumbled. "Go back to sleep."

She'd woken several times in the night—not screaming as she used to, but shaking and sweat-soaked, moaning about dark water pulling her under. I held her in those moments, whispering comforting words into her ear, till she settled again.

"I want to get an early start." I tugged playfully at the sheet she'd pulled over her head. "Don't you want to join me?"

"No." She burrowed deeper into the blankets. I laughed and decided to leave her be—I liked the idea of her in my bed. Plus, I couldn't lie still another moment. I had so many plans and dreams, not just for the clan, but for the whole city. I dressed quickly and then ducked outside.

While most of the clan still slept, a few men were already up and moving, and they nodded respectfully as I passed. I'd worried about the older men accepting me—but there were no longer the same distinctions there had once been. Young or old, rich or poor, whoever we were before the plague didn't matter. We were all survivors now.

I made my way down to Gabriel's office. I needed to look through the notes and documents, to search for any mention of the new tech engineer. The papers Em had taken from Addison had no mention of him—yet he had to be here somewhere, right?

The room was untouched from the last time I'd seen it. It felt disrespectful, almost tauntingly so, to sit where he had—like making a snow angel on a freshly turned grave. But I had already taken his room; taking his office was hardly any worse. I forced myself to sit. The chair creaked, but when nothing else happened, I began to search through the papers left on the desk.

As the sun rose, I moved from the papers on the desk to the filing cabinets, to journals filled with meticulous notes and schedules. It was soon clear that Gabriel tracked everything, which was both frustrating and impressive. How was I ever going to find mention of a single man?

I'd asked Liam to go talk with Addison yesterday, but maybe it was time I went to talk to her myself. Except every time I thought of seeing her a wave of nausea ran down my throat. How could I face her when I'd killed her brother? What would she say? It was easier to sit at the desk, to keep searching, than to face her. A few hours passed in silence before a knock came on the door.

"Come in," I called out, grateful for a break. Liam stepped inside, his face tense and troubled. "What is it?" I said at once.

"One of the scouts just returned. He needs to talk to you directly. You and you alone."

"Let him in."

Liam opened the door, and a man I knew—one of the few I remembered from the original clan—stumbled inside. I grabbed him before he could fall, helping him into one of the chairs. Liam caught my eye and I gave him a reassuring nod before he closed the door behind him.

"It's Jack, isn't it? I remember you. You were friends with my brother and Issac."

There was a gauntness to his face, an emptiness to his eyes I was beginning to recognize. He nodded, and when he still didn't speak, I reached in the cabinet where Gabriel had stored several bottles of whiskey. *Because, of course, Gabriel would save the best for himself.* I poured two glasses and handed him one.

His hands trembled as he raised the glass to drink. The amber liquid seemed to calm him. "The Shadow Valley clan is gone," Jack said.

"What do you mean?"

"I mean the buildings were burned, the animals slaughtered, and all the bodies had been dragged out and buried."

My legs felt weak. I tilted the glass back and let the whiskey burn down my throat. "They killed them—and then buried them?" *What kind of monsters kill men and then bury them?*

I tried to see this the way a clan leader would. Cold and detached. The Creation were in the city, and now they were moving against clans. Would they continue one by one, till we all fell? Numb panic began to pulse in my chest. I thought I would have more time. I'd only just taken control of the clan. I still didn't have the full plans yet to turn on the new tech. I didn't know where the last key was, or where the engineer was.

"There's more," he whispered. His hands shivered, shaking as he reached into his jacket and pulled out a scroll. "They left a message—dozens of them. They all said the same thing."

I took the scroll from him and opened the note.

Bring me the weapon or the city burns.

~

Outside the sun was high in the sky, the courtyard buzzing with activity. Men called out to each other, but I couldn't make out any of the individual voices. Cold shock made everything around me feel blurry and distant.

The Creation knew about the new tech. They knew it could be used as a weapon.

My knowledge was supposed to be our singular advantage to beating them—and now they knew. Now, once again, everything had changed. This was no longer a race to save the clans, it was a race to beat the Creation to the weapon. Except they seemed to think the weapon was something small that could be brought to them—maybe they didn't know everything yet. Maybe there was still hope. I was so focused on what all this meant that I didn't notice Liam until he stood directly in front of me and cleared his throat.

"Sorry, Liam, I didn't—" I stopped, reminding myself I was clan leader now. "How can I help you?"

"Some men were caught trying to steal weapons and desert last night," he said.

"Where are they?" I said, my heart sinking.

Liam pointed to the top of the wall, where four men stood, tied to the railing. This was one of Gabriel's punishments. Deserters would stand there for twenty-four hours. No food or water. No rest. And then they would each be given ten lashes.

I stared up at the men on the wall, the weight of the clan seeming to press down on my shoulders. What was the right thing to do here? I had to show the men of the clan that we couldn't just run until we were all picked off, one by one. I also didn't want to be like Gabriel.

But if I didn't punish them, then I knew what would happen. I hadn't forbidden Jack to tell the others what had happened to the Shadow Valley clan . . . All the men would know soon enough. They would know that an army was burning clans and killing everyone inside. If I didn't do something drastic, the clan would be over before I ever had a chance to save it.

I couldn't let that happen.

Liam stood waiting for a decision I wasn't sure I was ready to make.

Across the courtyard I saw a flash of dark hair—Em parted the crowd of busy men as she strode toward us. I wasn't the only one watching her. She was like a flame on a cold night, drawing the gaze of others whether she intended to or not.

"Trouble already?" she said, sounding annoyed.

Liam glanced at me, then, when I didn't stop him, and said, "Some men tried to desert last night. They're waiting for Sam's decision. . ." He lowered his voice and added, "Not that I'd ever tell you what to do Sam, but the men are scared."

As they should be. I nodded, and said, "I'll meet you up there, Liam. I need a moment alone with Em."

He nodded, and then proceeded to climb the ladder to where the men awaited their punishment. *This is what you asked for. This is the price you pay for power.*

But first I had another problem to solve. I turned to Em. I was surprised to find her eyes hard, so different from the way she'd watched me last night.

"The Creation know about the weapon." I handed her the note. She read it wordlessly, and when she'd finished and still didn't speak, I said, praying to God my suspicions were wrong, "Do you have any idea how they could know?"

"No." But her eyes were too hard, her voice too even. I didn't want to believe she would betray us. I couldn't believe it. Except it was becoming blindingly obvious that even after everything, she was still keeping secrets from me.

I'd once had a vision: me, leading the clan, and then the city, beloved by all. Em at my side, supporting me, maybe someday loving me . . . but what if all that was just a fantasy?

Em looked up at the men waiting above and said, "You can't show any weakness. I've heard the men talking."

It felt like she'd punched me in the stomach. The first man I ever killed was to protect Em—I'd put an arrow through his neck without blinking. And now Gabriel's blood was on my hands too. Was that not enough? Would it ever be enough?

"I'm not weak," I said. "I'm a leader."

Before she could speak, I turned and started to climb. With each step I felt older, heavier. *She thinks I'm weak. She thinks I can't do what's needed to protect the clan, to save us all. She doubts I can do this—just like all the others.*

I mounted the final step, glancing down at the clan, the life there, and hardened my heart. There was a price to pay, for power, and for peace, and in this world, it was paid in blood. I'd sworn to make things better.

No matter the price.

Liam leaned against the parapet looking as tired as I felt.

Behind him the four men stood, all of them with their hands bound behind them.

The first man glared at me, while the others stood with their heads bowed, likely hoping for mercy.

"This is Cain," Liam said, as we drew closer. "He works with the weapons and—"

Cain spat, and the glob of spit landed on my shoes. Liam froze. I looked down at the spit, not angry. Cold swept over me, as I heard her words, again and again. *Weak. Weak. Weak.*

"I won't follow this boy just cuz he brought that whore and her ugly clan here," Cain said, glaring at me. "He can go to hell."

"Untie him," I said.

"I don't think that's—" Liam said.

"Untie him." My voice was sharp, commanding. The voice of a *real* clan leader.

Liam stepped forward, giving me a look that said he thought this was a mistake. Maybe it was. Maybe this whole thing was one giant mistake. But it was too late to go back now.

As soon as his ropes fell free Cain stepped forward, shaking his fist at me, his eyes angry. "You listen, prick. You think just because you killed that bastard—"

The gunshot took him right in the chest.

The recoil lanced up my arm—such a small physical impact for ending a man. The recoil inside me . . . well, that spiraled and tightened, never ending, so that I would remember this moment for the rest of my life.

Cain staggered back, staring down at the hole in his chest. For a moment he tottered against the edge of the wall—and then he fell. A sickening thump sounded as his body hit the ground on the other side.

The courtyard went completely silent.

I turned to the other men. They all flinched, even Liam.

"Any other objections?" For the first time, the men of the clan watched me in perfect, terrified silence.

"Cut them free," I said. "These three are our first volunteers for our expedition to turn on the new tech, and they'll be guards till then. Should anyone desert, they will take the same punishment."

Then I turned to the courtyard and raised my voice. I had the full attention of everyone.

"The Creation are coming," I said, my voice ringing out strong. "If you desert, they'll find you, kill you. But the weapon is ready and waiting for us. All we need to do is find the new tech engineer. If any of you remember anything about him, you need to tell Liam or me at once. We can defeat the Creation, but only if we work together."

This time the courtyard was filled with an ugly silence, none of the men cheering.

My panic grew.

~

The rest of the day passed like a song that slowly sped up, growing faster and more manic, as I grew more desperate. None of the men seemed to remember the engineer, and the few who did had no idea when he'd left or why. Addison still refused to see me and I couldn't find it in me to force open the door.

I was a murderer, a killer now. Why should she want to talk to me?

At the very least she let Liam in. I allowed myself the small comfort of knowing she wasn't wholly alone—the way I felt now.

Even though I'd sent out a message for all the expedition

leaders to meet at dusk, in the old museum, to make our final preparations to turn on the new tech, I made my way back to my room two hours before the meeting. I'd told Liam I needed to lie down and that I'd meet him there. The truth was I needed a moment without all their eyes on me. Instead of lying down, I paced the floor back and forth, wanting to punch a hole in the wall.

Em finally made her way in, setting a bowl of soup on the small table in the corner. I ignored it and said, "Please tell me you found out something about the engineer." If we couldn't find out more about him, this entire meeting would be pointless and I would look like a fool.

"No. However, I did meet Addison."

I sighed and then slumped into the chair. "Great."

"She mentioned two people Gabriel thought might know him and where he'd be now."

I froze, staring up at her. "Who?"

"Kaden and Issac."

I stared at her in shock. Kaden and Issac? If they knew the engineer that meant I would have likely known him too . . . I sat back in my seat, thinking hard, trying to sort through memories both painful and fond. Kaden had been the best expedition leader in the old clan, and part of that was because he broke Gabriel's rules and ventured outside clan boundaries. He made friends and connections all over the city.

Was it possible I'd met the man I'd been looking for?

"Well, any ideas?" she said, breaking my concentration.

I stared up at the ceiling, seeing nothing. "Not really." Back then the world had seemed different, a place that didn't need saving. I'd been a follower, not a leader. I'd trusted my older brother completely—there was no need for me to wonder what men had done in their earlier lives. Which meant now I had no way of knowing which of the men I'd met might have been the engineer—not without asking Kaden or Issac. I hated the next words that came from my mouth, but I couldn't help it. "It doesn't help us. Kaden and Issac are both dead."

"You never know. Lost things have a way of coming back to you."

I frowned at her—that didn't sound like something Em would say. But then she reached out and tapped the cover of a book lying on the table. "Or something dumb like that."

"Is that a quote from one of my books?" I said in shock. Em had always made fun of my passion for reading. "Did you actually read something I recommended?"

She rolled her eyes, but I saw she was smiling as I picked up the tattered paperback book she'd tapped. It was *Harry Potter and the Order of the Phoenix.*

"You mentioned those books when we first met," she said with a shrug. "I saw it in Addison's room, and I thought I'd give it a chance. I remember Ara loved the movies, way back when." Her eyes flicked up to meet mine and she grinned. "But as soon as you get TV back, don't expect me to read another page."

"Fair enough." I opened the front cover, tracing the worn page before I said, "You really should start with the first book though, to fully understand the journey—"

Em yanked the book out of my hands, pulling me toward her with a grin. "Shut up, Sasquatch. I can think of a few things more fun than reading to do right now."

I grinned and forgot all about the book, leaning forward to bring her lips to mine. *Maybe it's not too late for us to be something real. Today was just a bad day. It'll get better.* She kissed me and my hands roamed lower, when a sudden knock on the door stopped us dead.

"Go away," I yelled, lifting Em onto the table as I muttered, "Can't a guy catch a break around here?"

But I didn't get to kiss her again, because the voice said, "There's someone at the front gate who says he knows you." Em's gaze locked on mine as a strange premonition churned in my chest. "He's demanding to be let in."

"Knows me how?" I said, prepared to tell whoever it was to wait. Instead, the next words upended my whole world.

"He says he's your brother."

PART **TWO**

CHAPTER EIGHTEEN—KADEN

Ara and I stood at the gate, darkness about to fall.

The others were hidden in a grove of trees a half mile from here with strict instructions that, if we shouldn't return, to make their way south without us.

Only standing here, before the gates, did it truly hit me.

Septimus was dead.

I would never again see the wonder on his face as he discovered something new about the world. I would never again joke with him, or laugh at the innocent way he saw things.

Another friend gone, sacrificing himself so I could live.

Matteo had also left our group, only an hour before we reached the clan. He'd spoken to Ara briefly, and I'd seen her grief in the way she'd embraced him. She hadn't given me an explanation and I didn't ask. Our group grew smaller by the minute.

A cold wind blew as Ara and I stood waiting before the Old Pen. It carried with it the scents of the city: the deep breath of the river; the sweet, earthy scent of the sage; the ominous smell of smoke.

Somewhere in the ruins, something burned. I wondered if the Creation had attacked again, if by sparing us we had doomed another group of innocents. Standing before the stone walls, I felt the pull of the open land, beckoning me to run, urging me to disappear into her safety. I didn't move. The lives of others depended on me now. I had to make peace with Gabriel—even if that meant groveling before a man I hated.

Things had once been so simple. Issac, Sam, and me against the world. I'd found my family after the end of the world and had defended them. But now it felt like no matter how hard I tried, I couldn't protect everyone I loved.

"Do you think he's here?" I said to Ara, trying to break the awful silence. Ten minutes ago I'd yelled up at the guard that Sam Preston was my brother—but the guard hadn't given us any information. He'd simply told us to wait.

Ara had her hood on, her face buried in shadow, so that the guards above didn't know she was female. She'd refused to hang back, to let me go in alone. "We should be ready for any scenario," she said.

Hope and despair churned in my chest. I tried to do as Ara said, and prepare myself. Sam could be gone or dead or he could have come to the clan and then left, driven away by Gabriel. But there was also the chance that he could be here. That we could be a family again.

With no warning, the small gate closest to us rattled and began to lift. The guard gestured us forward and called out, "Hurry! Into the Chute!"

At first, I wasn't sure what he meant, but then I saw that there were two gates we'd need to pass through to enter the clan. The Chute must have referred to the long cage between them. Ara caught my eye, and together we stepped through the first gate. I flinched at the thud it made as it sealed behind us.

Ara and I walked down the narrow Chute, and I thought about the old clan—and how it had all fallen apart. Gabriel had kept Ara as a prisoner, and Issac had given his life for Ara and me to escape. During that escape the decoy fire we'd set had spread. Even if it was an accident, we were still responsible for burning the old clan building to the ground. There was too much history between Gabriel and me to ever expect a friendship, but I hoped I could appeal to his pride as a clan leader. Or at least his need to control everything.

As we made our way closer to the final gate, I looked up to the guard now watching us—he was holding a rifle and had ammo strapped across his chest.

"Looks like Gabriel finally got his fortress," I muttered to Ara. "Wonder if he chose stone so we couldn't burn it down again."

She shot me a look that roughly translated to *behave*.

Too bad that's not really my specialty with Gabriel.

The final gate inched open. Through the rising bars I could see a courtyard of stone buildings lit by the dying sun, a single man standing ready to greet us. I steeled myself, pushing fear aside as I fixed a cold, lazy smile on my face. I'd once played this game with Gabriel well—too well maybe.

But when the gate thudded fully open my smile slipped away. Because the man standing before us was nothing like Gabriel.

For one, he was much younger, with hair shaved close to his head and a serious expression that didn't match his obvious youth. He was tall, but lanky, with the look of someone who'd recently grown but hadn't yet caught up to his height.

Then everything changed.

I was no longer standing in the clan—no longer worried about Gabriel. I was fifteen again, in the woods behind the house, a long summer day coming to an end.

"Sam, look, it's that fox again!" I said from the riverbank.

Sam stopped carving his stick and looked across the stream. After a long summer, freckles dusted his face and arms. Together we watched as the fox slunk across the opposite side of the bank.

"Do you think it's the one that killed Jesse's chickens?" Sam said.

"Probably." I reached back for my .22. "I could make you a Davy Crockett hat."

"No!" At the sudden noise the fox bolted into the undergrowth, the shot gone.

Sam's cheeks flushed red at his outburst. I could see he was worried I'd berate him—the way his father always did. But he surprised me. "I don't really need a hat—but maybe we could trap that opossum we saw and put it in my dad's shed?"

I grinned. "That's the best idea I've heard all summer."

The best moments of my childhood, every moment that counted, were with Sam.

He was the center, the gravity. He was the reason I'd crossed state lines on horseback, braving a fallen world to find him.

And he was standing right in front of me.

Somehow I hadn't really expected to find him. I hadn't believed I would ever truly come to this moment.

"Sam?" My voice was a strangled cry. "Sam . . . it's me."

The boy of all my childhood memories wasn't the one who stood before me. Instead, a young man with deep, serious eyes watched me. I could barely reconcile the laughing boy who loved to read with the unsmiling man before me, armed to the teeth and looking fully capable of using the guns and knives strapped to his person.

He was a man of the clan now. He'd grown up without me.

"Sam?" I said again, because he still hadn't spoken.

"Kaden?" he said in disbelief, rocking back a step, as if he'd been hit. Then he rushed forward, and I met him, crushing him to me. There was a strength to him that hadn't been there before. He was taller than me now! I pulled him back, held him at an arm's distance, wanting to see my little brother—only he wasn't so little anymore. My throat thickened as I looked at him. "Look at you! You've gotten so tall!"

"Or you got shorter," he grinned.

I punched him on the shoulder and then hugged him again. There was a hint of stubble on his cheeks that definitely hadn't been there before. Only now did I realize I had expected to find him just as I'd left him—but isn't this what Issac and I had prepared him for? To survive. And it looked like he'd done far more than survive. He'd done what I had never managed to do and found a way to work with Gabriel.

I shouldn't have been surprised: Sam was always the best of us. He had Issac's compassion and ability to dream and forgive, combined with my recklessness and charm. It shouldn't have been a surprise that he was the one who'd finally built a bridge between Gabriel and the men of the clan.

As soon as I released him Ara stepped in to take my place. "It's so good to see you, Sam." She pressed a kiss to his cheek, and he blushed so red I would have teased him if we hadn't literally just gotten here. Then Ara peered deeper into the clan. "Is Emma here? We saw her in the background of the video you broadcast— that's how we found you."

"Ummm . . ." Sam glanced over his shoulder for a long moment, and when he turned back there was some new emotion hidden in his eyes. An evasiveness. *Or a lie?* But Sam didn't lie. "Em's out right now. We're gearing up for an expedition. She should be back soon."

Ara grinned, and I could see the joy and delight on her face, even as I couldn't help the strange feeling that there was more that Sam wasn't saying.

"I just can't believe you're both here!" Ara said, and she stepped forward and gave him another hug. Again, Sam's smile seemed a little wooden, but I guessed it was shock. After all, I'd known for months that Sam was alive, but he'd had no reason to think we were anything but dead.

A few men on the wall were watching our reunion, but no one had approached. Now that I'd gotten past the shock of seeing Sam, I wondered where Gabriel and all his lackeys were hiding. Shouldn't they be gathering, preparing to threaten and imprison us? The sheer looming walls were even more oppressive from the inside: smooth stone with few handholds, a walkway around the top, and a guard tower in each corner. Still, Sam's presence had to mean it couldn't be all bad. He'd chosen to be here.

"So, you're going on an expedition?" I said, trying to decipher the evasiveness of his gaze.

"Yes," Sam said, but again, I felt something missing.

"Who's leading it?" I asked, wondering if there were still men here I knew.

Sam was quiet for a long moment before he said, "I am."

"Sam, that's amazing!" Ara said. "Good for you."

"Gabriel's letting you lead?" *That doesn't sound like him.*

There was a challenge in Sam's gaze when he looked at me, but even so, nothing would have prepared me for the words he said next. "Gabriel is dead. I killed him when he tried to kill me. I've been the clan leader here ever since."

The silence unspooled, growing thicker and colder as Sam and I stared at each other.

It felt like I was trying to swallow something sharp and painful. How could the boy who'd cried the first time he killed a deer have killed Gabriel? How could Gabriel, the man I'd despised and fought with for years, be dead? Yet even as I thought it, I saw the way Sam's eyes narrowed, his fists clenched, and his chin tilted up, as if he were waiting for me to berate him.

Suddenly I didn't care why Gabriel was dead, or why Sam had done it. I'd lost so many people I loved—and like I'd told Septimus, no one survived the apocalypse innocent. Whatever he'd done, I would help him bear it.

"I should have been here, Sam," I said softly. "I'm sorry. Forgive me." I'd always thought that a new clan leader was what I wanted. But I hadn't wanted Sam to pay the price.

He shrugged—a look that reminded me so much of young Sam it almost brought tears to my eyes. "You're here now. That's what matters." He glanced back at the clan, and again that serious look settled back into his face. "We've got a lot to catch up on. But first things first. Ara Edana and Kaden Marshall, welcome to the newly rechristened Mencata clan."

I smiled. Mencata was Issac's last name. We'd once teased him that if we ever led a clan, we would name it after him. I'd never thought that day would come. But Sam had.

We stepped forward, and just like that, I was a man of the clan again.

~

Watching Sam lead the clan was one of the more bizarre experiences of my life. The boy I'd known was gone, replaced by someone so capable I barely knew what to say. Even stranger, some of the men looked at him with something like fear.

We'd told Sam about the others who'd come with us from the mall, and he'd dispatched a welcoming party with impressive efficiency. It felt wrong, not to have time to mourn Septimus, to pause, but all around us the clan was a river of activity, and we were swept along in its current.

Sam wasted no time, pointing out features of the clan as he led us to a back corner where he said an important meeting was to take place soon. "I've ordered all the expedition leaders together—you may as well join us. I'll wait to explain more." There was a grimness to his eyes I'd never seen before. *Of course there is. He's leading the clan. The lives of all these men are in his hands now.* With a jolt I realized I was one of those men now.

My brother led us into a building that looked like it had once been some sort of war museum, with old guns behind glass and other props that had been pushed into the corner. There was a group of maybe twenty men all gathered around a table near the door. They fell into a respectful silence as Sam approached. Ara lagged behind, dipping her head so her face was concealed by her hood. She had wanted to leave, to look for Em, but Sam insisted he would let us know as soon as she returned.

Ara's attempt to hide was almost immediately uncovered.

"Ara? Kaden? What the hell?" A man with blue eyes and curly hair stepped out from the group of men.

"Liam?" Ara and I said in unison.

"I thought you were both dead!" Liam lifted Ara clean off her feet and spun her in a circle before he set her down and embraced me. Other men I remembered stepped forward, shaking my hand, all of them wanting to know where we'd been. To my surprise it was Sam who brought the room to order.

"All right, all right," Sam called out. "We'll throw a party for Kaden and Ara as soon as we can. But for now, we have actual work to do." The noise in the room died at once, and the men all joined Sam around the table.

"Kaden, Ara," Sam said, addressing us, "the Shadow Valley clan fell yesterday and we have reason to believe more of us will fall soon. I've assembled all the expedition leaders today for one clear purpose." Sam's voice was clear and commanding—no precursors as he jumped straight in. "To finalize our mission to turn the new tech back on."

"I thought we weren't going till next week?" Liam cut in.

"Change of plans," Sam said curtly. "We're moving the timeline up."

"Why the rush?" Liam said. "If we do this wrong, we blow the whole city to kingdom come."

"Because someone else is after the weapon now," Sam said, "and if they get there first, they *will* blow the city to kingdom come." The mood in the room suddenly shifted, and there were tense mutterings at this.

"Who?" Someone in the crowd asked.

"The Creation," Sam said, and I met Ara's eyes, the shock there reflected in my own. *He knows.* "They took out the Shadow Valley clan yesterday, maybe others."

"They were at the mall," I said, and stepped up to join Sam at the edge of the table. "They killed one of our group, but the rest of us managed to get away."

There was an iciness to Sam's gaze as he looked at me—a coldness that reminded me eerily of Gabriel. "Is there any chance they could have followed you here?" he asked.

Oh shit, I never thought of that. Our group was full of old, weak men who were still recovering. It wouldn't have been hard for the Creation to follow us.

"I don't think so," Ara said. "We were careful . . . and they had the chance to kill us all and didn't."

Sam seemed to think about this, then slowly nodded. He leaned over the table, pointing at the Shadow Valley clan, and then drawing a finger along the distance between us and them. "Regardless of where they are now, we have to assume they're either looking for the bunker where the new tech weapon is stored, or looking to find someone who knows where it is. The weapon was meant to serve as a backup to turn the new tech on. If the bunker is closed and the weapon goes off, the explosion funnels into the existing system and provides a large enough surge of energy to turn the new tech system back on. But if the bunker is open when the weapon goes off—"

"—then it destroys the entire city," Liam finished.

Sam nodded. "Exactly." He pulled a chain necklace out from beneath his shirt, a card and key hanging there. "I have the access card to open the bunker, and the first of two keys that primes the weapon. Our mission is to find the last key, and the new tech engineer with the launch codes. One team comes to the bunker with me—I need to search all the bodies left there. And another team will go to find the engineer with the launch codes. Which is where you come in, Kaden."

My stomach jolted, as the eyes of the other men turned to me. "I'll do anything I can to help, Sam . . . but I'm not sure what I can do here. I don't know anything about new tech." And I'd certainly never stumbled across a bunker like this.

But Sam didn't pause. "Before he died Gabriel said that the only two men who knew who the engineer was and where he might be were you . . . and Issac."

"I do remember him," I said after a moment. "Though it's been a while, and he didn't technically belong to the clan. He was more of a drifter who liked the clan's safety, and would sometimes stay in the mall, but didn't want to join us. His name was Rahul." I wracked my brain, trying to remember any other details that might help. "I don't think he liked others to know about him working in new tech. He was paranoid someone might think he could get it back on." *Which I guess was exactly right.* "He had a few different hideouts—safe houses, he called them. Places he would disappear to if anything looked like it might go south. He was friends with another new tech engineer, but I never met that man."

"Where is he now?" Sam demanded.

Déjà vu rose in me, of standing before a different clan leader, who always demanded an answer. "I don't know, Sam." *I wish I did.*

"I do," Ara said. "He's at the mall."

"You're sure?" Sam said.

"I am," Ara said. "He was there a few days back. Kaden and I can find him."

"Then we have a plan." Cheers went up around the group, men clapping me on the back as I tried to smile. This was good, right? The tension winding tighter inside me was only from the knowledge that the Creation were out there, and how many things could go wrong with this plan.

Sam lifted a hand, and silence fell as he addressed the group a final time. "At sunrise, I lead a group to the bunker. Kaden and Ara lead a group to the mall to find the engineer. Liam, you'll stay and hold the clan."

"For how long?" Liam said.

Sam's voice was grim but determined. "As long as you can."

CHAPTER NINETEEN—ARA

The trees rippled in the moonlight. We weren't supposed to be out, but rules never mattered to Emma. I followed behind her, watching her black hair flow in the wind.

"Emma!" I called out. "Emma, wait for me!" She kept running. A flicker of fear rose in me—the river was just ahead. I ran faster, the tree branches whipping at my hair and face as I followed her. But the pain didn't matter. Only Emma did. I burst out of the trees, terror rising at the rushing black current—

Then I saw her.

She stood at the river's edge, watching the water with wariness and fear that I didn't see often on her face.

"Do you hear the voices?" she whispered. "They're afraid of the water . . . but they're also in the water."

I made my way to her side, positioning myself slightly in front of her, so that I was between her and the river. "No one is in the water," I said, trying to sound sure, because the current was dark and swift. If someone was in there, they weren't alive.

"But I heard them . . ." she whispered, "calling to me . . ."

"Let's go back," I said, uneasy now. Emma was fearless to a fault. Which was why her words frightened me—if she went into the water, I wasn't sure I could pull her out. "It was just the sound of the river. Or maybe some other campers in the woods." When she didn't move I reached out and took her hand in mine. She started and then looked up as if she'd forgotten I was there—or as if she'd been a great distance away and had only just returned.

"You won't tell Father?" she said, sounding worried.

"Of course not," I said with a smile. "Sisters keep each other's secrets. Always."

My favorite memories with Emma were like that—beautiful, soaring, yet secret. I'd protected her—from our father, others, and even from herself. She always lived on a different frequency than the rest of the world, yet it didn't matter, because she always invited me into her song. She would be back soon, Sam assured me, and after all this time of waiting, searching, and praying, I'd finally be reunited with my sister.

Flickering torches lit the corners of the clan. After the meeting finished Sam had ordered them lit so that everyone could prepare for tomorrow's expeditions. There was a buzz of excitement, and Kaden and Sam were at the center of it. The two of them barely seemed to pause for breath. Once you would have been hard-pressed to know they were brothers—now it would have been impossible to miss.

A strange sort of jealousy churned in my chest as I watched them from my perch on the wall. Kaden was in the center of a group of men, gesturing with his hands, and even though I couldn't hear what he was saying, I could see the other men and

Sam all clearly laughing. This was an adventure again, and they were two brothers reunited before the storm.

I wanted that so badly it hurt.

I looked up at the stars shining bright above us. I wanted to believe that Septimus was up there now, along with Issac and my father, all of them watching over us. Yet as much as I missed them all, Emma was the one my heart longed for. What would she look like now? Would she be excited to see me? I stalked the shadows, torn between surveying the deep, velvety darkness of the night beyond the clan walls and watching the front gate for a glimpse of Emma.

And then she walked in.

Emma, my sister, strode into the clan.

It felt like waking from a dream—or falling into one I'd been seeking for years.

She'd cut her hair short—it suited her sharp, feminine features. Her strides were purposeful, and she spoke to several men who nodded and then moved off at once to whatever demands she had made. My heart swelled to see her, not just whole and well, but strong, beautiful, thriving. My last image of her, the one burned into my mind, was of her staring out the window of our childhood home, with white eyes weeping blood. It had eclipsed too many of my fond memories of her. Seeing her now, older and confident, felt like releasing a weight I hadn't realized I'd been holding.

I smiled as she snapped at two men, who instantly stopped lounging and set to work. She was just as commanding and unapologetically herself as always. She skirted the place where Kaden and Sam still stood talking. I wondered if this was on purpose. I knew only that Sam and Emma had traveled together at some point, but it was strange, thinking that Sam and Emma had been here all along, without us. Or that they might have been friends.

An older man with skull paint on his face stood outside the building she approached, and she stopped and spoke to him. Sam had mentioned the Skull clan had joined recently, but so much had happened I hadn't really thought to ask why. I hadn't seen any other men with skull paint, so I assumed most of them had already assimilated. Not this man though. They talked for a few moments, and then she made her way inside and he stood outside, as if to guard the door.

When she'd disappeared, I climbed down the ladder and made my way across the clan. The men she'd snapped at eyed me warily, as if expecting me to do the same. I only smiled at them and then made my way to where the man with skull paint stood. He looked me up and down as I approached. With the smeared paint on his face, and lit only by the torches burning through the night, he was imposing. If it hadn't been for the fact that Emma was on the other side of the door, I would have turned around.

"I need to go in there," I said, gesturing to the door behind him, unsure if he was a guard. "I need to talk to Emma."

He smiled at me—more unsettling than reassuring beneath the skull paint. But then he stepped aside. Nerves made my hands and legs tingly. I couldn't believe this was it. I couldn't believe I was about to be face to face with my sister. I pushed my way inside, my mouth dry as I tried to decide what to say to her after all these years.

A single lantern sat at a wide desk; behind it stood a large, unmade bed. I opened my mouth, but no words came out. She spoke with her back to me. "Wait outside, Jabari, I'll only be a few minutes."

"It's not Jabari," I whispered.

She froze, her hands still inside the backpack she had been unpacking onto the wide desk. Her back was still to me, but it didn't matter.

She knew me and I knew her. We were sisters—if not by blood, by every way that mattered.

My heart pounded, the only hint that time still moved. Then, without turning, she continued unpacking the backpack.

"I wondered if you'd find your way back here," she said quietly. "You are always good at finding trouble."

"Trouble that you started."

She set the final book on the table, then slowly turned. I drank her in like a person starved. The dark hair. The piercing blue eyes. The cutting gaze. The knowing smirk. She was both exactly as I remembered her and changed: like a knife sharpened.

"You're late to the party, as usual." But then her mouth twitched, the tiniest smirk. "Just in time to make things worse."

"That's what sisters do." I couldn't take it anymore—I crossed the room and threw my arms around her. She hesitated, but then her arms wrapped around me too.

"Emma," I whispered, my throat thick with tears, barely able to believe she was here, she was real. I'd dreamed of this moment so many times, of holding her again, seeing her healthy and strong, that I worried at any moment I might wake up. "I missed you. I missed you so much." I was crying for real now, crushing her to me and never wanting to let go.

"I missed you too," she whispered back, something grudging in her words.

Finally I pulled back and wiped my tears free, wanting nothing to hinder my view of her. I reached out and ran a hand down her shortened hair, smiling as I took her in. "Your hair looks nice short. Really grown up. Remember when Mom cut my hair really short?"

Her nose wrinkled in delight. "You looked like a little boy." Then she looked me up and down and gave me a devious smile. "You still look like a boy. What are you wearing?"

I laughed—of all the things she could have noticed, of course it was this. She wore a tightly fitted black leather jacket with jeans and an olive-green shirt—it looked like what you might expect someone in an apocalypse movie to wear. In contrast, I wore baggy men's clothes that hid my form.

"Kaden and I crossed the city to get here. I didn't want to draw attention." I paused, wondering how much to tell her, how much she knew. Did she know about the cure? Did she know about Father? But I didn't want to delve into all that, not yet. This was a happy moment. A moment I'd dreamed about for years. "You must break a lot of hearts around here."

She smiled, a sly, devastating look. "Just the one. He talks about you all the time."

This comment stopped me dead. Was she joking? Em had never shown an interest in boys. "Who?"

She laughed now, high and clear as a bell. Then she cocked her head sideways, clearly enjoying this. "I didn't think he had it in him to take over the clan. But he surprised me. Maybe you and I are more alike than I thought, going after brothers. Well, half brothers."

Half brothers. It took me too long to understand. And then, when it hit me, I almost couldn't believe it. Kaden had only one living half brother. Sam. I thought back to Sam's video, with Emma in the background. Of course I'd spent many nights wondering how they'd connected, where they'd found each other, but I'd always assumed it had been because they were both looking for me. I'd never considered . . . I'd never thought . . .

"You and Sam?" I tried not to sound shocked and failed miserably.

"Try not to look so surprised."

"No, really I—I'm happy for you both."

She rolled her eyes. "Please, it's not like *that*. He's just . . . We're just . . ." She trailed off, and her smile disappeared. She suddenly turned back to the desk.

"You're just what?" I said, trying to drag her away from whatever was bothering her and back to me.

But when she turned to face me, her eyes were no longer full of laughter. They were cold. "We helped each other," she said. "That's all."

I didn't understand the sudden change in her demeanor. "Okay," I said, not wanting to push her further away. "Are you coming with us—on the mission?"

It was the wrong thing to say. Her eyes flashed. "You want me to come with you to destroy the Creation?"

"No—Emma, that isn't what I meant—"

"What did you mean?"

I stared at her, afraid, because I knew this Emma. She was shutting a door on this conversation, and on me. But I couldn't lose her. Not again. So I said nothing, letting the ugly silence stretch out between us.

She shook her head, looking both disgusted and disappointed. "You're just like Sam. Like all of them."

"What do you expect us to do, Emma? Not fight them?"

A long, ugly moment stretched out, and Emma finally said, "I *am* them."

"You're not. You're my sister." I reached out and took her hand in mine. "You belong to me, and I belong to you. Father and I made a horrible mistake. We never should have left you."

She didn't pull her hand away, but her eyes were still cold. "How is dear old Dad?"

I whispered, softer, "He's dead."

"Then he got what was coming to him."

I flinched as if she'd hit me. Emma said things sometimes like that—to protect herself. "You don't mean that."

"And if I did?"

I swallowed. "It wouldn't matter. You're still my sister. Please, Em, tell me what I can do to make this right. I'll do anything. Say it and it's yours."

She stared at me. But it wasn't the look I'd ached for: one filled with memories of long, summer nights, of laughter weaving through the pines, of bare feet running through grass. It was a bitter look. "Watch over Sam. He'll need you and Kaden, even if he pretends he doesn't."

"Em—"

"No, Ara," she pulled her hand from mine. "I can't stay here."

Panic flooded through me. I'd just gotten her back; she couldn't leave now. "Please, Emma. Please, I'll do anything—"

She gave me a sad smile. "Remember us, the way we were. Two girls who believed they were sisters."

"You *are* my sister, Em. You always will be."

She froze, and for a brief moment I saw another story unfolding: one where we stood together, where we reconciled the past, where we overcame what we'd been created to be and chose a new path together.

Instead, she said in a cold voice, "We stopped being sisters the moment you left me to die. Make sure Sam gets my letter."

~

Kaden was outside the brick building the men used as a sort of cafeteria. He was talking with a group of men there, but as soon as he saw me, he cut off his conversation, hurrying over to me at once.

"What happened?" he said. "What's wrong?"

It was all I could do to not break down and cry. "Can we go to bed?" I whispered.

"Of course."

He took my hand, leading me through the darkness to our room. It had once been a cell, and now held a cot on one side and a toilet on the other, with a sheet hung up where the bars were. I'd slept on the ground in the mountains so often that I didn't care where we were, only that we were alone. I sat down on the cot, burying my head in my hands as Kaden crouched before me.

"Ara? What happened? Talk to me?" He sounded terrified, but I couldn't speak, replaying Em's words over and over again. Why hadn't I made her stay? Why hadn't I told her none of it mattered—not the city or the Creation or any of it? She was more important than it all. I would have crossed hell to find her, to save her . . . Only Em didn't need saving. She never had.

"I talked with Emma," I finally managed.

"Ahh," he said. He sat down on the cot beside me, wrapping an arm around me.

I leaned into his warmth. "She pretty much said she never wanted to see me again. What if she never forgives me?"

"She will. We came back to make things right here, and that's what we're going to do. No matter what it takes." There was a fierceness in his voice, a passion that I desperately wanted to believe in. But I wasn't sure I could.

"She said she couldn't fight with us. Not when she's . . ." I trailed off, unable to say it.

Kaden sighed, but his next words surprised me. "Maybe that's a good thing. She proves that the Creation aren't all bad. Maybe there's still hope. Maybe this can all end in peace."

I wanted to believe him. But when had anything in this world ever ended in peace? It felt like the peace Issac once spoke of only grew more distant. "She's leaving. I tried to stop her. But she wouldn't listen to me."

He was quiet for a long moment before he said, "Sam and Emma are both grown up now. We both remember them as kids, but they aren't anymore. We have to let them make their own decisions—and mistakes. All we can do is try to support them through it."

I snuck a sideways glance at him, measuring his look when I said, "It sort of makes me wonder what it will be like to be a parent? Do you think we'll be terrible at it?"

This time his smile was real. "We'll be great."

"What kind of world would we be bringing children into?"

"A messed-up one. But I think it's always been that way." He squeezed my shoulder now, trying to tug a smile free. "Come on. Imagine a little Kaden, running around the clan butt-naked, trapping raccoons and setting them free inside the walls. Or a little Ara, setting fire to everything she sees. It might be better to be in the apocalypse—we'd never have been able to afford insurance before."

I laughed at this—because only Kaden could make it sound

like an adventure and not a disaster. He was so good at believing the future could be brighter than the present. "You really think we could do it?"

"Sure. We'd figure it out. Like anything else." He pressed a kiss to my shoulder, then the hollow of my throat, then up my neck, leaving a trail of warmth behind. "Isn't this how it usually goes? Survive the apocalypse, discover the cure to a plague, get married, defeat a force of superhuman clones, and then raise a family. Right?"

I laughed as his kisses continued. "Are you trying to distract me?"

"Is it working?"

"No. Try harder." He brought his lips up to mine, and for a moment I let all the worries of the past fall away. Maybe the family I'd been searching for, the past I'd admired and sought, was only that: a memory.

Kaden was my family, and my future, now.

Together we would build something bright enough to burn away the dark.

CHAPTER TWENTY—SAM

It felt like being a kid again, having Kaden back in the clan.

So much so that I decided, just for tonight, I would set aside the burden of leadership, the threat of the Creation, and everything else that kept trying to tear us apart. Till the sun rose, I would let it be just me and Kaden against the world. The way it had once been.

"She okay?" I said, when Kaden emerged from the building. He'd left our group too fast for me to see anything other than Ara looking upset.

"She will be. She talked with Emma. It didn't go well."

I was surprised at this—Em was back? As soon as she'd heard that Kaden was at the gates, she'd slipped away, telling me she needed some time alone. Usually, when she came back to the clan she came to find me first. But I'd long ago given up trying to control, or even understand, Em.

"Em's a free spirit," I said with a shrug. "Give her some time."

Kaden gave me a searching look, and a blush worked over

my cheeks. He grinned. "And how exactly do you know about *Em*?"

I ignored his question. "Come on, I want to show you something. Before someone else needs us."

I led my brother toward a rope ladder that led up the wall, both hoping he would let it go and conversely that he would ask again. I had no idea how to characterize what Em and I were—or if we even were anything. Even though Kaden had once been the person I looked to for advice on women, this was complicated, because he and Ara were a permanent type thing. Emma and I were a whenever-she-decided-she-didn't-hate-me type thing.

We sat on the top of the wall, looking over the dark foothills beyond, the progressively emptier bottle of whiskey perched beside me.

"Remember when we told Issac we were gonna figure out how to get movies back on?" I said. "And that we were going to force him to watch every new Star Wars movie and show?"

Kaden grinned. "And you always asked him to recite the originals, but he couldn't remember in enough detail, so we tried to get the clansmen to do a shot-by-shot live-action remake with Liam as Luke Skywalker and it was terrible?"

"Only because you were an awful Princess Leia."

Kaden tilted his head back and laughed so hard the noise boomed out over the dark hills. "Yeah, I won't argue with you on that." Then he smiled. "It's weird. . . sometimes I miss those days."

"Me too." Kaden had filled me in on some of what had happened while he was away. On how Issac had died and what really happened that night. But knowing didn't make it better. If anything, I missed him more now. "I miss him."

"He's still watching over us."

My smile slipped away. "Not sure he'd be proud of what he's seen me do lately." Only now, without the men of the clan watching me, could I finally say the truth. "I didn't want to kill Gabriel. I keep thinking about it. Replaying it—wishing it could have gone differently somehow. I keep wondering what Issac would say if he were here."

His hand landed on my shoulder. "He would have understood. Issac was for peace—but he understood sometimes you must fight for what you believe in."

I shook my head. "It's just all so different than I thought. It feels like, ever since he died, everything has gone wrong. None of this is how I thought it would be . . ."

"Yeah, I get what you mean. Issac's last words to me were, 'There is only the peace we find.' I thought that meant we'd create some perfect world someday. But I don't think that's what he meant. I think he meant this"—he gestured between us, then to the sprawling night beyond—"these small moments are all we have."

"You know," I said, "I'm pretty sure it'd be a great moral boost if you reprised your role as Princess Leia tomorrow."

Kaden laughed, then reached out and snagged the bottle from me. "Only if you get Em to play Darth Vader. From what I've heard that one is a little too familiar with the dark side."

"You have no idea." I swiped the bottle back, and we sat there, talking and laughing, wasting the night, two brothers once again.

~

I woke alone, wondering why Em hadn't come back to the room.

I hadn't seen her last night—but Em often did her own thing, and Kaden and I had stayed up talking late into the night. The fear of ruling the clan, the crushing responsibility, had begun to abate. I didn't have to rule alone, not if Kaden was here. For the first time I actually believed I could do it: *we* could do it. Save the city. Turn on the new tech. Build a new, better life than the one before. It didn't matter that the old clan had burned. We would rise from the ashes.

All that anger and rage, I could move past it now . . . and while Kaden had shown me I didn't have to do this alone, it wasn't just him I dreamed of building a new world with.

I wanted to build a new world with her. I wanted to find Issac's peace with her.

I sat up, and only now that I looked around the room did I see what I hadn't when I'd stumbled back into the room last night. Her jacket, her gun, her pack, and all the small things she'd left in my room had been neatly removed.

No.

No, she wouldn't. Not again. She couldn't leave me, right when Ara got here. Right when we were about to start our mission to restart the new tech. Right when I needed her most.

Not when I'd been ready to tell her that she was the reason I was doing this. That she was the one I wanted to stand beside at the end of this.

You're overreacting. Maybe it's not what you think. I threw off the covers and stalked to the table in the corner. There were several new books there now, including the few Harry Potter books I'd been missing. Once I would have smiled to see them, thinking they were a gesture that showed I meant to her what she meant to me. Now it just felt like I'd been sucker punched in the chest. Because there was a note folded on top of them, and somehow, I knew what it would say before I even opened it. I stood over the note, breathing hard, fingers trembling, before I finally forced myself to read it.

Sam,

I can't be here for this next step.

Trust yourself, Sam. You are the leader the people need. You are the reason I decided to help save humanity and not end it.

—Em

My chest rose and fell, my hands trembling as I tensed to rip the page, and then couldn't. That was it? I stood there like a fool, rereading it again and again. No sweet goodbyes. No mournful pleas.

She'd cut my heart out and stomped on it a second time, and just like before, I'd let her. Just like before, I was the fool.

All I could think about was our last few days together. It wasn't just the feel of my arms around her, or her lips against mine. It was what she made me believe I could be. What she made me believe I could accomplish.

Now, I felt like I'd plunged back to Earth. Dark rage churned in my chest as I stared down at the letter. Outside I could hear the birds calling—so happy and bright that I wanted to pick up my gun and waste every precious piece of ammo just to watch them fall from the sky.

We're all alone in the end. That's what she'd told me, time and time again.

I hadn't really believed it till now.

Why did it matter if Kaden or Ara were here when the one person I relied on—the one person I loved—could leave me like I meant nothing?

Love. It was the first time I'd used that word to describe how I felt about her. I loved Em.

But in the end it didn't matter. Love was useless.

I lifted my shirt from the place I'd thrown it last night. As I dressed I felt a soul-deep loneliness: one I hadn't felt since my mother died, in those few weeks when Kaden hadn't found me yet, when I was utterly alone in a fallen world. Only back then the loneliness had been a cold thing—now it was hot, burning, explosive.

I wanted to break something.

Kill something.

What was the good of leading the clan, of saving humanity, if there was no one to share it with? Kaden had Ara, and sure, he would help me. For now. Until something came up. Until Ara needed him, and then he would choose her over me all over again.

I picked up my gun, checked it was loaded, and stalked out into the dawn. There was only one person I wanted to see now, and it wasn't Kaden or Ara.

There was only one person who'd never abandoned me. Who had stood by me through all of it.

Or at least she had, until I'd killed her brother.

Only now, with the sun rising like a reckoning, and the full weight of the clan pressing down on me, did I finally understand Gabriel. Leading was a sacrifice. Day by day, minute by minute, it demanded your soul. Until you had nothing left to give.

There was still a guard at Addison's door, but he didn't stop me when I knocked. "Addison, it's me. Can I come in? I need to talk to you."

It was still early, but I knew Addison always did her walk around the clan with Gabriel, and sometimes Liam, before the sun rose. Or she had. I wondered now if I should have offered to take Gabriel's place. Or asked Liam how she was doing.

I knocked again. "Addison, please. Can I come in?"

After Gabriel's death I'd told her guards she had permission to go wherever she wanted—that they were to obey her wishes. Mostly because I wanted her to see that I was better than Gabriel, that I wouldn't keep her a prisoner like he had. Only now did I wonder if it was the world who held her prisoner, not Gabriel.

"Addison?" I leaned my head against the door and closed my eyes, trying to shut out the sounds of the clan awakening. "Please, let me come in. I'm so sorry . . . I didn't . . ." *Didn't what? Didn't mean to kill you brother? Didn't know how to talk to you about it after?*

No answer came.

From behind me the guard said, "She hasn't come out all night."

I straightened and tried to fix my face into one more like a clan leader—and less like a desperate boy begging for a girl's forgiveness. "When was the last time you saw her?"

"Haven't. The guard I switched with hadn't seen her either."

The breeze suddenly gusted, sending a chill straight to my bones. "She's still here though, right?"

"Don't know. You said she was free to go wherever she wanted."

I fisted my knuckles, my nails digging painfully into my palms. *Tell her she can go wherever she wants. Tell her she's no longer a prisoner.* I thought I was being fair, just, kind. I didn't think she'd leave. I turned the handle—it was unlocked. My stomach churned, already knowing the truth I desperately wanted to deny as I pushed. The door creaked open, thudding against the wall, the sound echoing in the space.

The room was empty.

She was gone.

A vice-like grip tightened around my chest. The ground

suddenly seemed unsteady. The room before me blurred. My heartbeat pounded louder and louder, yet the insidious voice in my head grew only more deafening.

Everyone leaves you.

Kaden and Ara came back—but how long will they really stay?

We're all alone in the end.

I lifted my hand to the note still folded in my breast pocket— the one from Issac. I'd once found hope in it, those unread words he'd left behind, but now I could barely hold my shaking hand against my chest. The ground swayed, and I stumbled forward, knocking into the table and then clutching at it like it was a lifeline in a stormy sea.

There was so much I'd wanted to say to Addison. She'd been there when no one else had. But I'd been blind: by ambition, by power, by rage. By the affections of a girl who didn't really care for me.

On the table lay a single book: *Romeo and Juliet.* The last book I'd given Addison. I reached out with a shaking hand and opened the cover to find a note tucked inside. Just like the notes I'd once written to her.

Goodbye, Sam. I know you'll worry, but I'm leaving with Liam to make a new start. I won't say where, but we'll be safe, and we aren't coming back. I can't be here anymore, not after everything that's happened.

I hope you know that I forgive you. And I hope you'll forgive me for leaving with Liam. I know he's your second, but you have Kaden now. Be careful, Sam, that you build a clan and not a cage.

Love,
Addison

The book fell from the table, knocked free by my shaking hands, but I didn't stoop to reach it. I was afraid that if I bent over, if I lay down, I might never get back up. Em had left me. And now Liam was gone too. Maybe I could accept Addison's betrayal—but Liam's? He had been there, for me, for the clan, for so long, I'd always assumed he would be here forever.

Had I been blind, or just stupid?

He's a coward, just like all the rest of them.

He left me, just like everyone does.

I placed my hands flat on the table, feeling the grain of the wood there, trying to still the churning betrayal and rising panic. Did no one believe in me? Did no one want to stay? I pushed aside the panic, focusing on pulling in one breath, then another, then another.

When the room finally settled, my gaze cleared enough to make out the many bookshelves that lined the rooms. Books had once been my salvation. Issac had read me his Bible by the firelight. He'd taught me about God and faith and forgiveness. I'd chosen to live in the old Barnes & Noble, to become a keeper of the stories there. I thought I'd found my salvation in the stories of another time.

Now they watched me in judgment. The same bitter way I watched them.

This room was full of lies, of stories that didn't come true. Good didn't win—it was trampled beneath those who took what they wanted. Love didn't triumph—it wilted. It abandoned you when you needed it most. These pages were full of nothing but empty promises. Looking at them, all I saw were reminders of my failure as a man, a friend, and a leader.

I took a deep, shaky breath, pressed all the pain down, and then covered it with the cold mask of a ruler.

They all wanted to leave me?

Fine. Then I would become the bastard the world had made me.

I would do this alone.

It took everything in me to leave the books where they were, and not burn this room to the ground. I made my way back out to the front, where the guard still lounged, as useless as they all were.

"You're relieved from duty." I strode past him without a second glance. He called out to me, but I didn't turn. The joy of Kaden's return, of me becoming clan leader, all shriveled inside me.

The sun lit a bloody horizon as I took in everything I'd gained—and wondered only how much higher the price to restart the new tech and save the city would become.

At the gate I found out from the men that Addison had left a few hours before dawn to lay flowers on her brother's grave. Liam had accompanied her. She'd taken a large bag with her, and Liam had carried only a gun. No one had questioned them, because Liam was my second, and Addison was free to go where she pleased.

Here I'd thought Liam was going to help me save the clan, and the city, but then he had made his own plans. He hadn't even left a note. No one had seen Em leave, but I didn't doubt she was gone. Disappearing was her specialty. I could tell from the worried looks from the men on guard duty that they thought I was going to punish them. But this wasn't their fault.

It was mine.

~

An hour later, the clan was in a state of mayhem. With Liam gone, Kaden and I leaving, it didn't matter that I was nearing a full-on panic attack: I needed to name a new clan leader. The problem was there was no choice that would make everyone happy. This was beginning to feel like a resounding theme in leadership. All around the courtyard men were gearing up to leave, or preparing for the defense of the clan, all awaiting my decision.

Then, a respite. The guards called out from the wall. "There's someone coming down the road!"

I exchanged a look with Kaden. I'd been cold with him this morning. I knew it was unfair, but I also couldn't stop myself. What was the point of letting him in, of spending time with my brother, when we were all about to go our separate ways? *Everyone leaves you.* That, too, felt like a theme, not of leadership, but of my life.

"Who is it?" I called up to the guard.

"I don't know . . . he looks injured."

Another injured man at the gates—it felt like a strange echo to the night I'd been kicked out. But now I was the clan leader. I got to decide what to do.

"You want me to—" Kaden began.

"No. I've got this. You go help with the horses."

Kaden looked like he wanted to say something but then nodded and ducked off to help one of the older men trying to saddle one of the few horses we had left. Kaden had told me last night that he wanted to take over the stables again, to help rebuild the herd, to start breeding cattle and other livestock and trading with other clans. We'd had to release most of the herd, unable to feed them through the winter, but Kaden said he could get them back and more. All morning he'd helped with organizing men, and it irked me watching him now, seeing how effortlessly he had slipped back into clan life. How he'd returned like nothing had happened and stepped back into his old role. It felt like the price he'd paid to be here was simply forgetting me.

I strode to the front gate, and then called out to the guard, "Open the Chute!"

Maybe it was a bit reckless, going out alone, but all the men were gathered. If this was some kind of trick, or attack, we were ready.

Or maybe I just wanted to be reckless.

The gate inched open and as soon as the gap was wide enough, I ducked into the Chute alone.

"Close it up!" I called out. The gate shuddered and reversed directions. There was a sudden pounding of feet heard over the screech of the gate. I turned to watch Kaden slide cleanly beneath the gate, a moment before it slammed closed, like some kind of Indiana Jones.

I stared at him, part of me impressed, the other part annoyed.

He grinned. "You didn't really think I'd let you go alone, did you?"

"You let me do everything else alone."

His smile fell away. The words were so angry, so bitter, and came from such a dark place inside me, that I couldn't face him for another second. I turned and hurried down the Chute.

"Open the second gate!" I yelled, feeling Kaden at my back, knowing he wanted to speak with me. But in that moment, I would have rather faced a Creation horde than talk with him.

The final gate creaked open and Kaden and I both stepped free. Then there was no time for anything but focusing on the man now coming down the road straight for us. He walked like a puppet with half its strings cut, lurching and staggering. Blood stained his clothing. Bruises bloomed over his face and arms.

I didn't have to look to know that Kaden followed close behind me as I approached the man. Before I could reach him, he kneeled over and collapsed on the road, facedown.

Kaden's and my eyes met, argument forgotten. This man was near death. Whatever information he'd brought, we didn't have much time to get it.

I felt like a boy again as I crouched beside the man's body. *What do I do?* "Sir?" I said to the man, kneeling beside him, hesitant to touch him. The stench of fresh blood greeted me, even with a cold wind blowing it away. "What clan are you from?"

Kaden knelt on the man's other side, watching me. After a moment's hesitation, I decided I had to touch the man. Even if there was a risk he was infected, I couldn't let him die with his face in the dirt.

"We should roll him over," I said. Kaden helped me shift the man so that he lay on his back. Already his eyes held a glazed sheen.

"Can you hear me?" I said again. "I'm clan leader here. Did you come with a warning? What clan are you from?"

"Cloverdale," the man finally answered. "Told to bring a warning. Clan . . . Burned . . . Dead . . . Came to warn . . . You're next . . ."

He took a final breath, and then lay still. I stared down at him, the words repeating in my head.

You're next.

The Creation were coming for my clan—just as I planned to leave it.

We were finally out of time.

But all I could do was stare down at the man and his wide, unseeing eyes. I needed to make a plan. I needed to lead. Yet all I could think was that it didn't seem right for his eyes to be open when there was no soul left inside. Was he with Issac and my parents now? Was he with all those who'd left me behind?

"Sam," Kaden said softly. His words drew me back to the present. I turned away from the dead man on the road to face Kaden reluctantly. Something about his gaze made me feel small—like I was once again a little boy waiting for his older brother to save him.

But I wasn't that boy anymore. The gazes of hundreds of men on the clan wall, watching us, proved I wasn't. They were all waiting for me to make some sort of decision, to lead them.

"Did you hear what he said?" Outwardly my voice was cool, collected, everything a clan leader should be. Inside, I felt the terrifying urge to run down the empty road and never look back.

"Yes," Kaden said, keeping his back to the clan. "We can take smaller teams into the ruins, leave more men to defend the clan—"

"No," I said, shaking my head. "I know the Cloverdale clan. They . . . They didn't have the walls we do, but they had more ammunition and guns." I dropped my voice. "We barely have any bullets left. We can't win in an all-out fight. Not without the new tech weapons."

Is that why Liam left? Because he knew it was hopeless?

"We could send messengers," Kaden said, "to the other clans—"

"The other clans are falling one by one!" My voice was loud and panicky. I forced myself to take a deep breath—these were my people, my responsibility, now.

Kaden didn't let me think long. "I can't think of anywhere safer than behind these walls. They'll just have to hold on till we can get the new tech back on."

But they wouldn't hold on. They would die—just like all the others had.

I needed a place to keep them safe while I turned on the new tech.

Which is when it hit me—an answer that had been right in front of me the whole time.

The answer only someone who'd released the Creation, and who'd spent many nights holding one, would know.

The Creation had a weakness.

It wouldn't help me fight them, but it would help protect my clan.

"No," I said, turning back to the walls of the clan, "We're going to evacuate the clan."

"Evacuate? Where?"

I didn't answer him. Not yet. "Call everyone together in the cafeteria. I have a new plan."

CHAPTER TWENTY-ONE—KADEN

Sam was angry with me.

That wasn't new—we were brothers, after all.

What was new was the warning that we were next. If I didn't make things right with Sam now, I might lose my chance forever.

I followed Sam as he made his way back into the clan, leaving the dead man where he lay. "Sam. We need to talk."

"I'm busy, Kaden."

But I wasn't going to give up so easily. I stepped in front of him. "Sam . . . please. What's wrong? I thought—"

"You thought just because we swapped tales and drank whiskey last night we could just pick up where we left off?"

I stared at him, lost for words, because, yeah, that was pretty much exactly what I'd thought. "I'm here now—"

"You're right. You're here now. You have your mission. I have mine. So why don't we both just get on with it."

He brushed past me, and the Chute swallowed him whole. I

watched him go, trying to figure out what exactly had changed between last night and now. And when my brother had become a man I didn't know.

~

"Where's Liam?" one of the men in the crowded cafeteria hall called out. Everyone had been gathered here and there was a nervousness to the crowd, a shifting energy.

Then Sam paced through the men. He looked older, more serious, and when he climbed onto one of the tables, an expectant silence fell over the crowd.

"Liam is scouting ahead of us," Sam said. There were murmurs, uneasiness in the men. This wasn't what Sam had told me this morning, but I understood the desire not to cause an all-out panic. If it looked like Liam, the second-in-command, had deserted. . .

"Who will lead the clan's defense now?" someone else yelled.

"No one," Sam answered. There were cries of outrage, but Sam stood unmoving. He held up a hand and silence fell at once. "The Creation have taken clan after clan without repercussion. We don't stand a chance without the new tech weapons." Uneasy mutterings rose, and again he raised a hand, like some kind of conductor managing the sway and fall of an orchestra. "But the Creation have a weakness. I've seen it myself. As have Ara and Kaden."

Now the gazes shifted to Ara and me, the other men drawing away from us, as if we were infected. *Weakness? They don't have a weakness!* I'd seen the rows of bodies, the empty towns burned.

But I didn't dare speak, or even move, pinned in place by the stares of the men. Ara caught my eye, and I saw by her look she also had no idea what Sam meant.

But apparently Sam knew exactly what he was doing—and he wasn't afraid to use Ara and me to do it.

He cleared his throat, reclaiming the room. "The Creation fear the water. I've seen it. And so have Ara and Kaden."

The water. Only now, with a pang of heartache, did I remember how much Septimus feared the water. The river that we'd crossed—he'd been willing to take a zip line across it rather than try to ford it. At night sometimes he moaned about green water, then woke screaming, gasping for air like he'd been drowning. Beneath The Last City I'd seen how they'd kept the Creation suspended in glass tanks full of green water—and from what Septimus had told me, many Creation had died in those tanks.

Why had I never put that together before? Was it too painful to think of my friend? To try to use what I remembered of him to defeat the Creation?

I prayed that he would forgive me for what I did next.

"Sam's right," I cut in, the crowd turning to me now. "The Creation fear the water. If you can find a building downtown, across the water, you'll be safe until we can get the new tech back on."

A man from the back spoke. "So, is that it then? Is the clan over?"

"No," Sam said. He pointed to a thin, tall man in the crowd. "Boden knows the downtown section better than any other man. He'll lead all of you there. Cross the water and find a safe place to hole up. Kaden and Ara will find the engineer. I'll go alone and find the key. There isn't time to discuss—this is my decision as clan leader. Now everyone grab whatever you can carry. We leave the Old Pen now."

"When do we know it's safe to come back?" someone in the crowd called.

Sam and I exchanged a look. The last time we'd left, Issac died and the clan burned to the ground.

"When the new tech comes back on," Sam said, but I heard the undercurrent in his voice. There was a good chance many of us would never return.

There was a good chance another clan was finished.

CHAPTER TWENTY-TWO—SEVYN

I stood in the empty courtyard and slowly turned. All the weapons were gone, most of the food too. But what remained—personal items littered in hallways, clothes strewn on lines, a chicken strutting boldly across the grass—told a story I hadn't expected.

They'd left with only what they could carry.

Judging by some of the fires still left burning, we'd missed them by hours.

I'd taken clan after clan, waiting for someone to offer real resistance, to finally make this an interesting fight. I'd expected this clan to put up the greatest fight of all, because this was where Emma, the original Creation, had been hiding.

But she had deserted them too. I couldn't understand where she'd gone or why, only that she'd left. Lucky for them, too, because if she had stayed, I would have known what they were doing and attacked sooner.

I'd been following her movements, tracking her thoughts in my dreams, but it was an imperfect system and it felt as if she'd suddenly cut me off. It made me blind as to her reasoning or new direction. I closed my eyes, trying to reach out to her, but I saw only darkness: black, thick, and suffocating. She was clever, I would give her that. Just when I thought I understood her, understood the humans, they surprised me yet again.

Just like Talia. She never does quite what I think she will.

I opened my eyes, tilting my head back to catch the sun and letting the cool scents of the afternoon wash over me. Across the courtyard two Creation tried to corner the chicken, but it squawked and flew away, escaping them. They let it go. After all, a chicken wasn't the prize they wanted. We'd been cheated of our grand battle. But I knew the biggest battle was yet to come.

They were only humans. They couldn't have gone far.

Making my way to one of the walkways encircling the clan, I stared out at the city beyond, trying to understand the new emotion churning inside me. It irked me that of all the clan leaders, it was the boy leader who had slipped through my fingers. I'd seen his face in flashes, through the eyes of Emma. I thought she had allied herself with the humans. But she'd chosen to leave them. That was what I couldn't understand.

The walkway ended before me and I was forced to turn and stalk back. The hills beyond had grown verdant with spring, filled with scents of wet earth and blooming plants I had no name for. Yet I could enjoy none of the beauty here. I wanted to pretend it was because of the humans and their cowardice, but up here, the hills stretching out before me, I couldn't lie to myself.

"Bring Talia to me," I called down to one of the Creation. "I want to talk with her."

I waited there for some time. When the Creation returned, I could tell there was something wrong.

"Where is she?" I said at once.

The Creation responded in a flat, unemotional voice. "No one has seen her since dawn. We did not realize she was meant to still be a prisoner."

No one has seen her since dawn. The words sliced through me, straight to my core. The last conversation we'd had, the accusations she'd made, roared forefront in my head.

I hadn't expected her to leave.

I hadn't expected the Creation to let her.

But why should they care about her? The Creation viewed Talia as a passing fancy. Why should they notice or admire what they were meant to destroy?

None of them really saw her, none of them cared about her.

Except for me.

"Would you like me to send out scouts looking for her?" the Creation said.

"No. Leave her. She is only human," I said, and smiled at him. I wondered if he saw the falseness in my look. If he saw the way I was becoming like them.

But of course not. He only nodded, turned, and left.

I was alone once again.

She was gone, and everything was as it should be.

She was gone, and everything felt empty and hollow.

I forced myself to turn away from the ruins, to look down to where the Creation gathered below.

"Creation!" I called out. At once, silence fell below, as they all looked up at me.

Looking down at them, at the perfect way they spaced themselves, at the way they were copies instead of unique and different like humans, I felt a sour hatred rising in my chest.

Was that why I'd been drawn to Talia? Because she was something I could never be?

"Rest, Creation," I called out. "Take whatever you wish. The humans have fled rather than face us—cowards that they are. They are planning something new—and as soon as I discover what, we will destroy them."

There were no cheers of support, no mutters of dissent. The Creation followed me absolutely. They were weapons I could sharpen, wield . . . or discard.

But as I looked down at them, I decided that before I found the escaped humans, or the weapon, I would find her. I would make her see that I was right—the humans were the villains, not me. I would make her watch my destruction.

No one questioned me when I left.

CHAPTER TWENTY-THREE—SAM

The wind was my only company as I crossed the ruins alone. It was easier than I'd thought it'd be—handing the clan over to Boden and then walking away. Some of the other men had wanted to come with me, to go as a team. I told them it was better this way—I would move faster alone.

The truth was I didn't want them with me.

It was a relief to not have the burden of leadership or company.

I didn't care that Kaden had caught me just before I left and begged me not to go alone—rich because he and Ara were no longer taking a team on their expedition. I wasn't a boy anymore. Kaden didn't get to tell me what to do. He didn't just get to show up out of nowhere and start bossing me around.

As I walked, I could taste the scents of the coming summer blooming across the land. I had so many plans, so many dreams once: not just to get the new tech on, but to plant crops. To rebuild the dam above the city. To watch the world come back. Once those dreams had felt bright and warm, like standing before a furnace, the heat so powerful it hurt to draw near. Now they felt dim and distant.

Last time I'd journeyed to the bunker, it had been to bring Gabriel there, like some little boy eager to show his elder what he'd discovered.

Now Gabriel was dead. I was alone.

There was no one to help me. No one to care if I lay down and died.

I tried to push away the dark thoughts—it was only the creeping silence of the city, the way things seemed more sinister when you were alone. My path took me through what was once a well-loved park. I remembered it from the before days—my mother had taken me there once, when it was full of families and laughter. Now the playground was rusted and half buried beneath the weeds, the once-open field taken over by waist-high grass and weeds.

I jumped at a sudden movement—but it was only a scrap of fabric fluttering in the breeze. For a moment I had thought it was Gabriel, or the nameless man I'd killed to save Emma . . . it made it worse to run, but I couldn't help it.

My breath came faster, burning up my throat, but even when I felt light-headed, I forced myself to keep moving over weed-filled lawns, through ruined neighborhoods, over streets choked with rusted cars and fallen trees and corpses.

I didn't let myself stop or rest. Closing my eyes for even a moment was unbearable. I found myself checking over my shoulder often, paranoid that I was being followed.

Only when I looked over my shoulder for what felt like the hundredth time did I realize how well and truly alone I was. Alone the way I thought I'd wanted.

Alone in a way that poisoned my soul.

For so long, all I wanted was to belong to the clan and to be a part of something bigger. To make a true difference in this world. Now I was clan leader and going to turn on the new tech. I was going to do what Kaden and Gabriel never had. . .

. . . and it still didn't feel like enough.

I touched the unopened letter in my pocket, tempted to read Issac's final words to me. We had been a team, a family back then. Even with the world in ruins, I was *happy*. Was that just because I was a boy?

Was this the cost of growing up—you learned that the whole world was shit, everyone sucked, and no matter what you did, you always ended up alone?

"Sam? You okay?" Issac glanced at me from across the flames. Kaden had just left with Ara, pulling her through the doors and into the vastness of the mall beyond. She'd looked frightened, and I wanted to tell her she didn't need to be. She was with Kaden.

He had asked her if she wanted a bath, which must have meant he'd taken her to the fountain. I found it strange he didn't ask me to come, but I supposed someone needed to stay and watch all our supplies.

"Why did he take her alone?" I said, annoyed. "I wanted to talk to her too." It had been so long since I'd seen a woman. It wasn't fair that Kaden got to monopolize time with her. And she clearly was more afraid of Kaden than she was of me—I saw the way her eyes tracked him every time he moved.

Issac smiled, that look he sometimes gave me that said I was missing something obvious. "They'll be back soon."

I didn't see how he could be sure of it. But I just shrugged, trying to be as nonchalant as Issac. He could be so quiet when he wanted to be—for me words were rising flood waters that grew higher and higher and then spilled out. I lasted about thirty seconds this time.

"Why did you vote against bringing her back to the clan?" I said in a rush. "She'll be safer there than out in the ruins."

Issac took his time answering. He always did. "You would be safer in the clan. Yet you always insist on coming with us. Why is that?"

I puffed my chest out, indignant. "I'm a man of the clan! It's my job to help out. Someday maybe I'll be more than just an expedition leader. I'll be the person who turns the world back on."

I'd never said that to Kaden, but saying it now, I liked the way the words sounded. Like I could do something as powerful and important as what Kaden did.

Issac smiled at me as if I'd given him an answer. I tried to work out what his look meant and then said slowly, "Are you saying maybe she belonged to a clan and was on her own expedition too?"

"Do you think it's ever right to take someone's freedom?" he said.

"Well . . . maybe only if it's the end of the world."

"The word 'apocalypse' comes from the Greek, meaning to reveal, or to uncover. Maybe God's apocalypse wasn't about destroying the world—it was about revealing the truth of who we are."

I thought about that for some time. Had I found the truth of who I was? I was Kaden's brother, Issac's adoptive son, a man of the clan. Wasn't that enough? Or was he saying I needed to be more— do something big like turn the new tech back on and save the world?

I gave up trying to figure out what he meant—I could just ask Kaden later. And if I asked Issac any more now, he'd probably ask me to read some Bible verse. "Tell me more about Star Wars," I said. "I never got to see that last movie that came out."

"I only saw it once."

"Perfect. Can you describe it, in intricate detail, shot by shot?"

Issac's laugh was warm and deep. "How about I tell you what I remember, and you fill in the gaps with your own version?"

"Fine," I said, smiling up at the ceiling, because this was one of my favorite games. I was good at telling stories. In a life before the apocalypse, I would have been a writer, or a comic book artist, and made stories that people around the whole world would love. But before he could start in on the opening scene, I had one last question.

"Hey Issac? What's one thing you would change? About your time since the plague began?"

I expected one of the answers the other men gave: to have electricity again, or hot showers, or bacon, or chocolate. Instead, he surprised me.

"I would have found you and Kaden sooner."

I smiled into the dark. After we'd finished talking, and Kaden and Ara had returned, I fell asleep dreaming of how I'd one day get the new tech back on, and how Issac would see that I was just as strong and smart as Kaden.

When Issac had gone, he'd taken so much more than his guidance and wisdom.

He'd taken a part of me.

I wished I had asked him more about his life before the end. I know he'd been a father, but I never knew what happened to his wife or daughter, or why he'd adopted Kaden and me? And maybe most importantly, why did he still believe in God, even when it looked like He had abandoned us?

I still remembered that night with Ara: because it felt like one of the last moments when we were all still a team, when everything seemed possible. Kaden was still the center of my world, and I couldn't imagine anything, even a girl, changing that.

Issac had believed the apocalypse was God's test, our chance to see who we truly were. But I wasn't sure I liked who I'd turned out to be: A murderer. A clan leader. A brother forgotten. A scorned lover.

Maybe the only hope I had left, the only way this would all be worth it, was to become the man who turned on the new tech.

All I had left of Issac was this letter. I touched my hand to my breast pocket, feeling the now familiar shape and weight of it. It called to me in a way it never had before, but I only let my hand rest on it.

I couldn't open it. Not yet. Kaden liked to say it was over when the fat lady sang. Well, she wasn't singing yet. I would read it either when I got the new tech on, when I saw the pulsing brightness of lights banish the threat of the Creation, or when all hope was lost.

I would read it when I could answer Issac's question, his God's question, about who I was, who the apocalypse had revealed me to be, in a way that made me proud.

CHAPTER TWENTY-FOUR—KADEN

Ara and I walked alone through the ruins. Matteo had told her of a secret house where he would be bunkering down for a few days, and Ara thought it likely that Rahul had run there. We were quiet in a way we weren't normally as we walked.

I know maybe I should have been worried about the clan; Sam had assigned a new leader, a quiet man named Boden who knew the downtown area well. He would lead them across the water, but all I could think of was Sam. The betrayal and anger in his eyes. He'd gone off alone, and even though he claimed he'd spent the whole winter leading expeditions alone, there was something about his rage that scared me . . . Gone were the days that Sam looked at me like I was some kind of hero. Back when Issac, Sam, and I were all a team, the end of the world was an adventure. I'd thought I would be able to reclaim that here, that one night of bonding would be enough for Sam to forgive me. Only now did I realize how naïve I'd been.

It was my greatest fear that something would happen to him before I could make things right between us.

About an hour in, we passed an old Victorian-style house with a red X across the front, when Ara suddenly spoke. "Care to share what's on your mind?"

I hadn't realized how quiet I'd been, lost in my thoughts of how to fix the mess I'd made. "Sam's angry with me. And honestly, I understand why."

"Do you want to go to the bunker? I could find Matteo and Rahul alone. You could still catch up with Sam."

"Every time I leave you alone, Princess, calamity happens. I'm not letting you out of my sight." I reached out, took her hand, and then pulled her to me and kissed her. For a moment I let myself live here, in just the touch of our lips and hands, before she danced away from me, laughing.

"Excuse me, expedition leader," she teased. "I thought you were supposed to keep a clear head?"

She pulled us forward, continuing down the long stretch of empty road surrounded by abandoned houses. Even if my heart still hurt for Sam, I tried to believe that I still had time. I could still fix this—and finding the engineer was the first step. Together Ara and I crossed over a bridge that spanned a highway, dozens of rusted cars littering the path and blocking the way.

"Kinda brings back old times, doesn't it?" I said as I helped her climb across the top of the massive car jam. I tried not to wonder about all the people who'd been in these cars, just trying to escape the city.

"Evading death in our city? Yeah, it does."

The sun continued its slow march across the sky and toward the horizon as we continued through the ruins. Matteo hadn't given Ara an exact address, only a general idea with land markers, which meant as we drew closer, we had to move slower, working in circles. There wasn't an official clan in this area, but that only set me more on edge. Anyone could be here. And we were drawing closer to the waters of downtown. Where there was a water source, there were people, and where there were people, there was trouble.

We soon left the highway behind and crossed back into neighborhoods. Even though the houses were ruined, with spring in full bloom, the greenery hid most of the decay and devastation.

"You know what I've been thinking," I said as we walked. "Maybe it's time to get rid of all these clan boundaries and territory wars. Maybe with the new tech on we won't need clans anymore."

"You don't think the people need the clans?"

"I think they did—but maybe with the new tech on, they won't anymore. Maybe it'll be a better world and city than the one before."

Ara gave me a sad smile. "You sound like Septimus."

I nodded, my heart suddenly heavy again. It didn't feel like he was really gone. I kept waiting for him to walk around the corner, with some new question I had no idea how to answer. "I wish he could have seen the lights come back on. I wish he could have seen all this." It hurt to talk about him, but I wanted to keep saying his name, to not forget his sacrifice.

Ara reached out to squeeze my hand. "Maybe he does see it all. Maybe he's up there with Issac, watching us now."

I tilted my head back, and then, speaking to the sky said, "Hey, if you guys are up there, can you give us a hint to where Rahul is? We're kinda burning daylight down."

Ara laughed at this. "Come on, it's got to be somewhere—"

Ara stopped speaking, and moving, abruptly. Instantly my gun came up, surveying the ruined houses, the trees, every window pointed at us—but when my gaze stopped on her, I saw she was staring at the ground.

"Ara?" I whispered.

"There's blood on the ground."

I took one last look at the surrounding houses, my heart still racing with adrenaline, before I came to stand beside her. She knelt beside the smear of blood while I kept my eyes up, watching for any threat.

Then she stood and made her way to a nearby tree. There, on the smooth bark, lay the bloody outline of a hand. *Shit.*

Ara and I exchanged a glance, having a conversation without words. We could leave, right now, and avoid a potentially dangerous encounter with either an injured person, or whoever had done this to them.

But we nearly were where Matteo said he would be. There wasn't a clan in this area, which could mean it was Rahul or Matteo who'd left behind the bloody handprint.

We had to finish our mission, or all this would be for nothing.

I nodded once at Ara, and she immediately started forward, tracking the blood trail. I kept my eyes up, ready for anything. I heard every creak, every whisper of wind, every creak of trees.

Suddenly she held up a hand and we both froze.

"There is someone behind those trees," she whispered, pointing to a thicket of trees just off the road.

Neither of us moved, and before I could decide what to do, a figure staggered out of the trees. I trained my gun on their chest, but it was quickly obvious they weren't armed, and further, looked badly injured.

Even stranger, it was a woman I recognized.

"Talia?" Ara said in a shocked voice.

"Ara," Talia whispered, her voice hoarse and breathless. "You made it back."

Then she collapsed.

CHAPTER TWENTY-FIVE—ARA

I ran forward, too late to catch Talia before she hit the ground. "Talia!" I said, alarmed. "What happened?"

It felt kinder to say that than what I was truly thinking: *What the hell happened to you?* She looked nothing like the Talia I remembered, who was cocky, self-assured, with midnight-colored hair and bright eyes. This Talia looked half-dead, and only the fact that her eyes were clear—and not white and weeping blood—convinced me she wasn't infected.

She tried to speak, but all that came out was a croak. I pulled out my water container and held it to her lips. Her hands trembled as she drank, but most of the water escaped, running down her dirty cheeks and onto her filthy T-shirt. She coughed, a wet, retching sound, and then shivered.

The day wasn't cold, but I looked up at Kaden, who seemed to read my mind. He immediately pulled off the small pack he carried, pulling out the tightly rolled sleeping bag. As he did I unzipped my jacket, draping it around her. Now that I was close to her, I saw that despite her shivering, there was a sheen of sweat on her forehead.

There were a thousand questions I wanted to ask her—but suddenly we didn't need to find Matteo just for the engineer. We needed him for Talia. He was our best chance at getting her medicine.

"What happened?" I said to her, worried she would pass out again before I could figure out what was wrong with her. "Where are you hurt?"

"Ran into . . . group of men," she whispered, her voice hoarse. Kaden and I exchanged alarmed glances at this but said nothing. "One shot me—managed to get away. . . but not feeling so good now." Her eyes closed, and I wondered if she had passed out.

I looked up at Kaden. His eyes were tight, his lips pressed together.

"We have to find Matteo."

Talia could barely speak, let alone walk. The bullet looked as if it had gone through her middle and even though she'd wrapped the wound well enough that it didn't seem to be actively bleeding, something was clearly not right. In the end, Kaden carried her in his arms while I scouted just ahead of them, looking for the easiest path and any sign of Matteo. It was dangerous, stupid even, to travel this way. But we couldn't leave her to die, and I didn't know what else to do. We needed help.

She didn't seem fully conscious of what she was saying, whispering, "Don't tell him. Don't tell him."

"Don't tell him what?" I finally said, when Kaden was forced to set her down.

She looked at me, her eyes clear for a moment. "Don't tell Sevyn the humans did this to me." There was something tortured in her voice, and Kaden and I exchanged an alarmed look. She couldn't mean Sevyn—the Creation leader? Worse was when her whispers changed to, "I need to find him again."

Given her present state, I wasn't entirely sure we could trust anything she said, so I simply squeezed her arm and then said, "Save your strength. It's going to be all right. We're going somewhere safe."

"I need to find him."

"Let's get you well first."

She nodded, her eyes closing and her face going slack again. I didn't like the sheen of sweat on her face, or how weak she looked.

"How much farther do you think you can carry her?" I said to Kaden.

"As far as I need to," he said. But I could hear the exhaustion in his voice, see the way his arms shook. "Help me lift her again."

I helped him lift her, and this time she didn't stir at all, which felt like a bad sign. He didn't suggest splitting up, but the threat of it hung over us as we struggled onward.

It happened so fast I didn't have time to warn him. I was walking forward, watching the buildings over us, when my feet caught on a line of wire that ran through the grass.

Cans shook in the trees next to us, giving away our position.

"Put your guns down or—" The deep voice trailed off. But instead of freezing in terror, my heart soared. Because I knew that voice.

"Matteo?" I called out, close to crying. "We need you."

CHAPTER TWENTY-SIX—KADEN

Talia rested in a cot pushed into the corner of the small attic room Matteo had brought us to. We'd managed to get some broth in her, and now, as Ara crouched beside her, I took the chance to examine Matteo's hideout. The building lay on the edge of the flooded downtown, with large windows that gave a bird's-eye view of the surrounding area. From outside it looked like a run-down rental complex—the kind of place I would have bypassed as an expedition leader. The first two floors were empty, but the attic in which we now stood was stocked with supplies and could only be accessed by a trapdoor ladder.

It had been a nightmare to get Talia up here, but it was a great hideout. Which was sort of the problem. We didn't need a hide-out. We needed to find Rahul and get him to the bunker before the Creation did.

"Thanks for taking us in," I said to Matteo. He grunted, and even if I knew that I should try to butter him up and ease into it, we didn't have the time. "We're looking for Rahul. It's important we find him as quickly as possible—lives depend on it. Do you know where he is?"

Up to this point, Matteo had barely looked at me. Now he turned to me, his eyes narrowing. "What do you want with Rahul?"

"We need him to help turn the new tech back on. Have you seen him?"

Matteo went back to watching Ara, his gaze inscrutable. "No."

Before I could question him further, Ara stood up from Talia's side and made her way over.

"She's sleeping," she said. "I'm not really sure how much of what she was saying was true. She said she'd traveled with Sevyn and the Creation from The Last City to here. She wants to see him again."

"She wants to see Sevyn? Did you ask her why?" Matteo said, stealing the question before I could ask it.

Ara sighed. "Yeah . . . she said she needs to stop him." She shook her head. "It doesn't really matter what she means unless we can get some medicine for her. Any ideas?"

Matteo glanced out the window at the rapidly darkening ruins. "I don't have anything here—but I've never crossed the water to the hospital."

"I have," I said, slowly, hating the look of hope Ara gave me. *No matter how hard you try, you can't save them all.* "But we need to be heading downtown—to help Sam." I gave a pointed look at Matteo, trying to clue Ara in. Sure, he *said* he didn't know where Rahul was. But if Ara asked . . . well, we stood a much better chance of success.

Except Ara didn't ask—I don't even think she saw me. All Ara could do was stare over at Talia, who looked even worse than when we'd found her. We'd cleaned out the bullet wound, but as we couldn't find an exit wound, it looked like the bullet might be inside her. Her body radiated heat, and there was a grayish pallor to her that I didn't need a doctor to tell us wasn't good.

I hated this part of being a leader: of choosing who lived and who died. Sam was priority number one . . . but Talia was Ara's friend from The Last City. I couldn't just let her die.

Not when I'd already failed Septimus.

"How about this," I said. "I'll go search for medicine. Maybe some sort of general antibiotic could help? And you two can talk while I'm gone. But we need to leave at dawn to meet Sam at the bunker. He's counting on us."

I gave Ara another look, and this time she glanced at Matteo and nodded, clearly understanding the deal here. She needed to find out where Rahul was while I was gone. Matteo's eyes narrowed further at our interaction. I didn't like being quite so obvious, but time was of the essence.

"All right. I'm going to head out," I said. "I'll be back at dawn."

I opened the trapdoor, packing only my knife and a headlamp Matteo had lent me, wanting to move fast. But before I could climb down Ara caught my hand.

"Be careful."

"Careful? That doesn't sound like me." I winked at her, but her smile didn't quite reach her eyes. Matteo had moved to the far corner of the room, so I dropped my voice and said, "There's one more thing. Whatever happens, if I'm not here by dawn, take Matteo to find Rahul and then head for the bunker. Even if I'm not back in time, you need to promise you'll go. I'll meet you there."

"What about Talia?"

The next words were harder to say. "If the Creation beat us to the bunker, and set off the weapon before us, everyone in the city will die. We can't sacrifice everyone for her." It was harsh, cruel even, but it was true. "Promise me you'll leave by dawn."

There was a heaviness to her gaze now, but she nodded slowly. "I will. So long as you promise you'll meet me at the bunker."

"I promise I'll always love you." I pressed a kiss to her lips and then started down the ladder. "And I promise I'll see you at the bunker."

Outside, the last of the daylight was fading. My back and arms ached from carrying Talia, but even though I longed to lie down, I knew I wouldn't sleep tonight. I couldn't. Not when Talia lay there dying. Not when the Creation were out there, working to find the weapon before us.

I could feel time growing short, like a noose tightening around my neck.

~

Even though I was a strong swimmer, I wasn't crazy enough to try to ford the flooded waters of downtown at night. The currents were swift, cold, and unpredictable—even in the daylight it would be dangerous to try to swim it. Plus, I was exhausted from carrying Talia. I needed a boat.

So, I began my search, following a path Issac and I had taken once. I knew a few men who'd lived in this area, who had boats for fishing. The trick was finding where they'd hidden them. Ideally, I'd have another person to help me handle it, and wait till sunrise—but I wasn't sure Talia had that long, and Sam definitely didn't. We had to get to that bunker.

Matteo had given me a headlamp, and when dusk faded, I flicked it on. It burned through the dark, lighting crumbling buildings to my right, and the black surface of the water to my left. It was a risk, but everything was a risk now.

An hour in, near an old apartment building where I knew some men lived, my flashlight lit on some brush haphazardly thrown over something clearly meant to be hidden. I smiled, and then made my way forward, bit by bit uncovering a canoe. *Thank you, God.* It looked like it hadn't been used for some time, but there were two paddles tucked within, and it was far enough from the water it hadn't taken any damage. I stared at it, wondering how hard it would be to handle alone, in the dark, when the voice broke through the night.

"We meet again, human."

I spun as a tall form stepped out of the darkness. Then the surge of hope in me died, and I felt like I'd been punched in the stomach. Because for one brief moment I thought it was Septimus standing before me. I thought he was alive, and what we'd seen by the mall was a mistake.

But there was none of the kindness or curiosity of Septimus in this man—only cruelty.

"Sevyn," I said, my hand going for the knife at my hip. "Won't pretend I'm happy to see you."

He strode closer, something almost predatory in his move-ments. "I thought you would be the boy leader." He sighed, and then pulled out a gun from beneath his jacket, holding it in that same way Septimus had, like he was touching something rotten. "How disappointing. Would you rather I killed you with a gun or my bare hands—it makes no difference to me."

"Well, if you're asking, I'd rather you not kill me."

He smiled like this was funny. "And why should I not kill you?"

"Well for one, I've got some unfinished business to attend to." I wasn't sure why I said what I did next. Maybe it was the final bid of a desperate man. Or maybe it was the way Talia seemed so desperate to talk to him—as if it was the only reason she clung to life. "And I'm looking for medicine to save Talia. She's hurt."

His eyes darkened, and for the first time, fear ran up my neck. Because, unlike most men who'd threatened to kill me, there was something about Sevyn that made me think he could. Easily. Without remorse.

I would die here, and I would never see Ara again or keep my promise to her. I would never start a family or—

He lowered the gun.

CHAPTER TWENTY-SEVEN—SEVYN

I'm looking for medicine to save Talia.

He was lying of course—humans were known for it. All he was trying to do was save his own neck. He and the others were on some idiotic quest to get to the weapon before I could. . .

Yet there was something honest in the eyes of this human. They were a shade of green that didn't seem natural. The same color as the green water that had imprisoned me. It made me dislike him more than I already did. I wanted to see him the way I did all the other humans, with the same crude, unremarkable features.

Now I realized those green eyes and golden hair would be forever burned into my memory. I would always be able to pick him out from a crowd. He didn't realize how lucky he was to be wholly unique, to not have copies of himself. That was part of why I'd killed Septimus—I wanted no other versions of me.

I was singular. I was unique. Even if I had to kill to be so.

It would be so easy to lift the gun and squeeze the trigger.

Too easy. If he died, I'd never know if he really was trying to save Talia.

"Where is she?" I said, not yet decided whether to kill him. "Tell me and I may spare you."

"If I tell you, then you'll have no reason to spare me."

"True. What do you propose?"

"A temporary truce. You help me find the medicine to save her."

I ground my teeth together. It would be easier to kill him. But he had known Talia's name. And there was something about him, some expression of honesty I hadn't seen in other humans, that made me think he was telling the truth.

Or he was especially adept at deception. "All right, human," I said, because it would be easy enough to kill him later. "How do we reach the medicine?"

He glanced behind me, at the buildings rising beyond the water. "Are the rest of the Creation here?"

I smiled. *As if I would ever tell you.* "They are exactly where I've told them to be."

Even though my gun was lowered, his hands were still on the knife at his waist. He finally seemed to realize this, and lowered them slowly, his gaze not shifting from me as he said, "Before we start, I need your promise. A temporary truce till dawn. You keep your Creation from attacking my people, and I'll help you find the medicine that will heal Talia."

A truce with a human. It was such a strange, new curiosity—like a mortal suggesting a truce with God—that I couldn't help but indulge him. I could kill him at dawn just as easily as now. What were a few more moves in the chess game when the end was already decided?

"Fine," I said. "No Creation will attack a human tonight. But at dawn, I make no such promises."

"Great." He reached down into the long wooden boat he'd been pulling brush off, then tossed me a paddle. I caught it, then eyed it skeptically. It looked like some kind of child's toy—not something you would trust with your life.

"We need to get moving," he said, pulling the rest of the brush off the wooden boat. "I have an idea for somewhere to look—but it'll be dangerous."

"I fear nothing a human can do."

He laughed. "We'll see."

~

Humans were foolish, violent, unforgiving creatures in general.

But this human, with the poison-green eyes and maggot-colored hair, also seemed to have a death wish. We had dragged the wooden boat, which he called a canoe, to the edge of the water, and now he insisted we could use it to cross the dark water to the hospital beyond.

"It will sink," I said as I glanced out at the treacherous currents. The rippling surface hid unknown depths, and it seemed like a monster waiting to swallow me whole. *Green water. Hands pounding against glass.* I had felt hundreds of Creation die this way, unable to help them.

"It won't," said the human. "It's our only chance to find the medicine. It's our only chance to save Talia."

Talia. Was she really in danger? Only at the mention of her name did I step forward.

"You take the front," he said. "Jump in when we get a few feet offshore and I'll push us off." The water swirled, making strange sucking noises as we waded in. I felt a sudden sharpness in my lungs. It felt like I was already drowning as the water lapped at my legs, reaching higher with each step. I froze, unable to go farther.

"She's running out of time, Sevyn," the human said.

Anger flared in me—strong enough to bury the fear. "Do not use my name, human." I stepped into the boat, a flash of terror nearly blinding me. The entire thing wobbled, unstable as we drifted away from shore and out onto the water. Instant regret filled me, but then the current swept us away and it was too late to change my mind.

"My name is Kaden," he said.

"I don't want to know your name," I spat. "I will kill you as soon as dawn comes and this damned truce is over." Unless this entire thing was a ploy to kill me. Why hadn't I thought of that before?

But even if it had been, so what? He couldn't overpower me. If I drowned, I would pull him down with me. The canoe teetered treacherously as the current pulled us deeper into the flow, buildings rising like black looming giants all around us.

"The current is high with the spring," he said.

He seemed to muse on this for a while before I snapped, "What does that have to do with us and the medicine? If you don't have a plan, human—"

"I have a plan," he said. "There's an old hospital that the current is pulling us toward. Since the plague it's been surrounded by water and hard to get to. There's a chance there might be something left to help Talia there." His flashlight moved over the water, casting strange, horrible shadows on the buildings and the current below. I tried not to look at the choking, swirling water, not imagine it closing in, suffocating—

"You seem to know a lot about this place, human," I said, more to not have to think about the water. It was easier to focus on my hatred rather than my fear.

"I spent time here as a kid," he said, and he dipped his paddle in the water, straightening out the canoe. "My dad lived in Montana, but my mom was here. And after the plague started, I came here. To find my brother, Sam."

Sam. The name rang a bell in my head. The boy leader was his brother. Of course he was. Trouble ran in his blood.

"You seem to really care about Talia," he said.

I froze, and there was only the sound of his paddle, dipping into the water again. "You have no idea what you speak of."

"If you say so."

There was something a little too knowing in his voice. Something that made me want to push him right out of the boat, hold him under the water, and watch him drown.

"So typical of a human," I said, sneering at him while wishing I didn't need him to steer this pathetic excuse for a boat. "Always thinking of themselves—when really the world would be better off without you."

But he only smirked, like I'd walked right into whatever deceptive trap he'd set for me. "So why are you here then?"

I didn't have an answer for that. But I decided that as soon as we had the medicine and found Talia, I would kill this human.

~

The hospital was a red brick monstrosity that loomed out of the darkness. We nearly overturned as we both struggled against the current.

"Paddle! Harder! Come on, Sevyn!"

"I'm trying, you human fool!"

He let loose a string of colorful curse words I'd never heard before—but would use if we did survive this—and then finally he said, "There! That window! We can get inside!"

I turned just in time to see an enormous, shattered window looming out of the darkness, the water high enough that we could coast inside if we were lucky. Together we dug our paddles in, and I bent over as we ducked to make it through.

Except we weren't lucky. The boat hit something, and then tipped over, and I knew only panic.

Swirling darkness.

Blinding water.

Cold like daggers.

I thrashed beneath the surface, drowning, dying—

—and then strong arms seized me, yanking me out of the water and dragging me out of the current and back through the window. As soon as I felt the floor beneath me, I surged up and shoved him off me.

"Release me, human!" I spluttered, spitting out water and struggling to breathe.

But the human didn't notice my wrath. "Help me get the canoe!" he yelled. His headlamp spun wildly as together we both worked to get the canoe inside the building. The current was trying to pull it back out through the window, and it took both our efforts to drag it away from the window and farther inside to safety. Though perhaps safety wasn't the right word: now that we were inside, water lapped at my thighs, the ceiling hung low and oppressive, and the headlamp's light seemed like a tiny match before a gale.

We were both breathing hard, the sound of rushing water all around, when the human started to laugh.

I glared at him. "Stop laughing. This isn't funny."

This only made him laugh harder. He bent over his knees now, laughing so hard it looked like he was crying. "No one survives the apocalypse, Sevyn," he finally managed, still chuckling. "You may as well laugh."

I stared at him frowning, unsure what to do. Should I take one of the paddles and smack him over the head? But no, I needed him to find the medicine and get back across the water. I couldn't just kill him now.

Finally, he managed to get a hold of himself and gestured forward. "Come on. Let's go this way."

He tied the canoe up, and then we waded through the knee-deep water into the hallway. Even with his headlamp, my eyesight was better. "Look!" I said, pointing to the wall. "A map."

He sloshed through the water, making his way to the map. He examined it for a few moments before he said, "I think we should try the top floors."

"So long as you hurry, human."

"So long as you learn my name first."

"It's not 'human'?"

He laughed, and then set off down the corridor. I followed him, wondering why he dared present me his back, why he laughed when faced with death . . .

. . . and why, after I'd threatened to kill him a dozen times, he'd saved me.

CHAPTER TWENTY-EIGHT—SAM

Finally, I reached the outside of the bunker. Dusk was falling but I wasn't tired—I was numb. I made my way through the gaping entrance, past the shriveled corpses, through the cold hallways, then gave a bitter laugh as I stood before the stairwell that led down to the weapon.

It felt like this was all I did now: venture farther into darkness, alone.

I saw it all in flashes.

Everyone who'd left me. What I'd traded, what I'd done to bring the power on.

Standing here, alone, it suddenly all felt so empty. But I'd gone through too much to give up now. I turned on my flashlight, which flickered ominously, and then stepped into the darkness.

Descending into the bunker had once felt like an adventure—now it felt like descending into hell. And like hell, the twisting metal hallways were filled with the dead. Above ground they were shriveled, but down here they were preserved—as if they wanted to cling to their stolen humanity and forever protect their secrets. I'd never noticed before what they looked like, the way their limbs twisted. It felt sacrilegious, not just to be down here, but to search their bodies for the missing key.

"Hello, Phillip," I said dully to the guard at the bunker. He didn't respond.

And then I froze.

Because, farther down the wall, where before there had been nothing, now another guard was leaned against the wall.

A corpse that hadn't been there before.

Either the dead were walking, or someone else had been down here.

I wasn't sure which was more terrifying.

I pulled out my gun, and then stood in perfect, terrified silence. Every scary book I'd ever read, every tale of monsters or the undead all came creeping back to me. The one thing in common those stories had was some stupid side character who ventured into a creepy place alone and then died a horrific death. That was me. I was the dumb character. *Just breathe, Sam. Monsters aren't real. The dead don't reawaken. They're just stories.* Yet the darkness beyond the beam of my light felt like a physical force trying to creep closer, wrap around me, and suffocate me.

My heart went into overdrive, so that I could hear every thump in my ears, even as I became hyperaware of my surroundings. The deep, metallic scents of the underground. The faint odor of bodies slowly rotting. A distant sound of dripping water.

I tried to reason, tried to *think*.

Someone else was either down here in the darkness with me or had been.

If they had moved bodies, did that mean they were searching

for the keys? Could the Creation have figured out the location and beaten me here?

So was the last key gone? Was I too late?

To hell with this. I called out, "*Hello? Is anyone down here?*"

Something moved in the darkness.

I felt the terror like a white-hot blade.

"*Who's there?!*" I shouted. The shadows were monsters of the dead, of every man I'd ever killed, waiting to devour me. "I'll shoot—I swear I'll kill you!"

A form stepped around the corner. I nearly squeezed the trigger—but then the light outlined a shape.

Her shape.

I was frozen there, unmoving, as she slowly walked forward, step by step, the light burning her shape out of the darkness. Still, I didn't move, frozen as she came closer, until the glare of my flashlight blinded her.

"What are you doing here, Em?" My voice was cold, calm—even as the turmoil swirled within. I forced the gun, and light, to lower, to rest on that tension-filled space between us.

You can't trust her. She's just like all the rest. She left you. Everyone always leaves you.

But knowing that didn't stop the fact that I had taken a step closer. I was sucked into her gravity—I always had been.

"I'm sorry I left," she whispered. "I was afraid that Sevyn would come for you because of me. He knows about the weapon. He knows about me. He can see flashes of what I'm doing. I thought it would be safer if I came down here. If I stayed in the darkness where he can't see what I'm doing. I didn't want to leave you . . . I was trying to protect you."

My heart gave a lurch at her admission, but I tried to ignore it.

Because she'd still left me. I was still angry at her... I couldn't keep doing this, forever waiting, and wondering if she really wanted me.

"Do you just expect me to forgive you?" I said coldly.

"No. But maybe this will help." She reached around her neck and pulled out a chain—with a key hanging around it. The last key.

She had found it.

She stepped forward, all the way up to me, and then placed the chain around my neck where it settled with a sort of finality. I touched the key, needing to feel that it was real. I'd been driving toward this goal for so long, I'd almost started to believe it was impossible.

I lifted my eyes from the last key to her. She watched me with something like worry in her eyes—as if she were afraid I would say no to her. As if she didn't know I was completely in love with her.

And then it all clicked.

She didn't want to be alone either. She'd pushed me away because she cared for me the same way I cared for her. Maybe I wasn't the stupid side character who got killed in the creepy basement. Maybe I was the side character who fell in love.

I laid my gun down, then set the flashlight on the ground, pointing up, so that it cast a halo of light around us. I closed the space between us, tilting her chin up so that I caught the full devastating impact of her smile.

"You know," I said, "We really need to go over gun safety again. I could have shot you. I thought there was a monster down here."

She smirked before she kissed me. "Who said there isn't?"

CHAPTER TWENTY-NINE—ARA

I stood before the window, waiting for Matteo to finish making food. As I waited, I watched the stars above. Growing up in the city, I'd been able to see a smattering of stars, but most were drowned out by the city lights. Now it was like an entirely different sky stretched out. The Milky Way wove like a spider's web, the individual stars glittering and sharp. I'd once wanted to study astronomy, but I never had the chance. Now I didn't see them for their beauty but for their help with navigation. They would chart a clear path to the bunker—but what about Kaden's path? Had he found the medicine yet?

I hated that there was nothing I could do to help him.

He had his part to play—and I had mine.

I turned away from the window and made my way back to where Matteo was fixing us a late supper: some dried deer meat with a can of beans. I took a seat on a crate beside him and then picked right back up where we'd left off an hour earlier. "Please, Matteo. We need your help. Imagine how having the new tech back on would change things."

"More power isn't always a good thing." He dumped the beans into a pot. I'd told him I could eat it cold, but he insisted on warming it up.

"But don't you want to help the rest of this city? Please, Matteo, just tell me where to find Rahul."

He was silent for a long time. "You don't need to find Rahul."

"Yes we do—"

He held up a hand. "Rahul was a new tech engineer. But he's not the one with the codes, or the one who knows how to get the new tech back on. I am."

I stared at him for a long time, but he didn't look up from stirring the beans. I tried to process the fact that he'd been the one we needed all along. Then I decided it didn't matter. All that mattered was getting him to help us now.

"Will you help us?" I asked.

He sighed, and then said softly, "Before I say yes, I want to tell you a story. And then it's your decision. If you ask me again, I'll say yes . . . but if you don't, I would understand."

"Then tell me."

He gave me a long look, then began. "I was in the bunker with another man—his name was Phillip Constantino. He was a good man, a real rule follower. We had both been in the military most of our lives, so when we were told that a plague had started in some other cities, and that we were being called in, it was just another order we had to obey. Before I went in I told my wife and girls to stay inside our house, to barricade the door, to not let anyone in but me. We were well prepared—had a backup generator, food and water stores, a garden. Everything you're supposed to have." His eyes had taken on a faraway look. I'd never heard him talk about his family beyond showing me his house—and it scared me what was coming next.

"For three weeks, I stayed in that bunker as things got worse and worse in the city. I kept telling myself they would be fine, we were prepared." He stopped for a moment, and then said, in a voice that seemed to hold years of grief, "And then we were given the order."

"The order?"

"To destroy the city. My city."

The way he said it—so cold, so hopeless—sent a shiver down my back. I burrowed deeper into my jacket. Once I'd thought I'd damned the world, because the cure for the plague had been in my blood all along. But I felt as if I'd found some redemption. I couldn't imagine being asked to destroy everything and anyone you ever knew. There was no redemption in that.

He suddenly stood, making his way to the window. For a minute he stared out at the city beyond—yet I had the feeling he was seeing something different than the starlight above and darkness below. "My orders were to set off the weapon and destroy my home. And my family with it."

"But you didn't?"

"No," he said. "I couldn't. Not when I knew my girls were out there." With shaking hands he reached into his jacket and unzipped an interior pocket. Then he pulled out an envelope. It was veined with creases and faded yellow, as if it had sat inside his jacket for years. "I was supposed to type in the codes and turn the key. But I couldn't do it. Not when I knew my girls were still alive.

"I tried to leave, and Phillip confronted me." He closed his eyes, his voice dropped. "He demanded I return to my post. I gave him my key, told him I couldn't do it, to find someone else. I opened the door of the bunker, only to discover that everyone outside it was dead. He demanded I return, but I refused. We fought and I . . . I shot him."

I stared at him, not knowing what to say, or if I should even say anything.

He continued. "I thought when I got home that it would all be worth it. I thought the order was rushed, or exaggerated—but during those weeks when I was in the bunker the city had changed completely. There were bodies in the street. Cars on fire. Gunfire in the distance. Abandoned tanks everywhere—like a war had been waged. But I didn't doubt that my wife and girls would be there. Then, when I got home, I saw that my house . . . had the red X."

Finally, he turned back to look at me. "I'll help you, Ara. But I want you to know what you're asking. There is always a cost for our actions. Are you ready to pay it?"

"I am," I said, even though I felt a shiver of premonition as I said the words. "We'll leave at dawn."

He nodded, and just like that, I'd done my part.

But I didn't feel triumphant.

I felt terrified.

~

It was a struggle to sleep. Every time I closed my eyes, I was brought back to the day my father had sprayed the red X on our door. Again and again, I saw Emma, with white eyes weeping blood. No matter how I tried, I couldn't picture Boise as it had once been. All I could remember was driving across a city filled with flocks of black birds. And my father telling me not to look at what they were eating.

Issac, Septimus, my mother and father, Gabriel—there were so many dead and gone. Every time I got up to check on Talia, to make sure she was still breathing, I grew more worried, fearing she would end up on my list. But I clung to the hope that Kaden would find something to help her.

I must have slept, because I woke, groggy and not at all rested, to Matteo shaking my shoulder.

"Ara, wake up."

I came instantly awake, fighting my blankets as if they were an enemy and reaching for my gun before he said, "Take a breath—no one is attacking."

"Kaden?"

He paused, and then said heavily, "He's not back."

My stomach dropped, a hundred different scenarios flashing through my mind: Kaden, wounded in the ruins. Kaden, overturned in the water. Kaden, taken captive and needing me. Then I looked over to where Talia lay, horribly still.

"Talia?" I said.

"She's still alive."

Something about his tone scared me. When I stood over her, my breath caught in my chest, so that it suddenly became hard to breathe. The light breaking in through the window showed the horrible truth that last night's darkness had hidden. Her skin was gray—for a moment I thought she was already dead. Her breath came in slow, uneven gasps. Staring down at her, I felt as hopeless as if she was already gone.

"What do we do?" I whispered. I couldn't just leave her. Not the way I'd left Emma. Not when she was on death's doorstep and Kaden wasn't back yet.

Matteo came to stand by my side. I couldn't help but notice

his jacket was on, his backpack fully packed, his shotgun at his side.

A horrible flash of déjà vu hit me. I'd once left Emma just like this.

But she hadn't died.

She'd survived.

Maybe while Kaden was still out there, there was still hope.

"I opened the windows," Matteo said softly. "She'll have the breeze on her face, the sun coming in . . . there's nothing more we can do for her."

"We can be here with her when she . . ." I couldn't say it. Couldn't form the words.

"Or we could let her sleep peacefully. Trust that Kaden will make it back with the medicine. We could do what we promised, and finish this."

There will be a cost. Make sure you're ready to pay it.

I bent over and pressed a kiss to Talia's forehead. She didn't wake, and something told me that this would be the last time I ever saw my friend. This was my final goodbye. I would remember her the way I had in The Last City: fearless, bold, and beautiful.

"Goodbye, Talia. I'll always remember the adventures we had together."

Then I turned and told myself not to cry. Matteo passed me my backpack and I settled it on my shoulders. It felt twice as heavy as it had yesterday.

CHAPTER THIRTY–SEVYN

We spent several hours searching the remains of the hospital, eerie with its white empty hallways, thick coats of dust, and general feeling of abandonment. Even with Kaden, who *claimed* he was excellent at finding things, we had little luck. It was clear someone had cleaned out the place long ago. I'd given up trying to refer to him as *the human*. It was too exhausting, especially when he insisted on talking to fill the silence. I now knew where he'd grown up, what kind of food he liked, the three times he'd gone to the ER as a child, his favorite breeds of horses and dogs, and several other details I highly suspected he gave only so that it would be harder to kill him.

As if that would make a difference.

"Are you sure this is what she requires?" I rolled the small glass bottle between my fingers. It annoyed me that Kaden had found it and not me. Staring down at the tiny bottle was terrifying and humbling. How could something so small be the difference between life and death?

"No," Kaden said bluntly. He stood across from me, opening and shutting cabinets. His flashlight's beam was beginning to grow dim, and I was trying not to think about crossing the water with only its weak light.

"You said medicine would save her."

"I said it *might* save her. I'm not a doctor."

I resisted the urge to throw him out the hospital window. Knowing humans, or at least knowing this particular human, he would survive the dark waters and emerge twice as strong and ten times as annoying.

Plus, we had made a truce. Unlike humans I honored my word.

I tucked the bottle safely inside my jacket and checked the last set of cabinets. Nothing. Outside I could glimpse the faintest light on the horizon. Dawn was nearing. I should have been cheered that we wouldn't cross the water in darkness, but the light felt like a cruel warning.

Kaden pushed aside a hospital bed, then swept his light over the room. The beige colors were muted by dust, but even trying to imagine everything here as new and clean, I still couldn't see how this place had ever been comforting.

"Did people really come here when they were sick?" I touched the bed, and it crinkled. "I think I'd rather die beneath the sky."

"Me too," Kaden said, and I immediately regretted saying anything. I didn't want to have anything in common with him. "We should head out," he said, his flashlight moving over the room a final time. "I don't think we're going to find anything else and Talia needs that medicine as soon as possible. Make sure you don't drop it."

"Do not tell me what to do. When the truce breaks—"

"Yeah, yeah, we kill each other."

Apparently, I'd made too many threats without following through—a lapse I would rectify as soon as the sun breached the horizon. Or, at the very latest, the moment I got Talia the medicine that would save her.

~

The journey back was even more terrifying. Kaden clearly chose the most dangerous, difficult path—I was sure of it. Even with the light of dawn breaking between the buildings, every jostle of the boat, every splash of water felt like the hand of death reaching out to me, reminding me how many of the Creation it had already claimed. How happy it would be to claim yet another.

"Do you know where we're going?" I snapped as water surged over the front of the canoe.

"Kind of."

"Kind of? What the hell kind of answer is that? I thought you were a leader among your people?"

"It's been a while," he said. "Issac was better with the water navigation and boats. I was always better with horses."

Of course he was better with horses—they were as temperamental and short-sighted as he was. But I was stopped from saying so when icy water splashed over the side and nearly upended us. Kaden barely managed to keep us from pitching into the dark waters. I felt doubly angry—because of his obvious ineptitude and because it was growing more difficult to refer to him as *human* instead of *Kaden*.

I cast him an angry look when the canoe steadied. "Why did you not bring this Issac now?"

"He's dead."

I nearly mocked him—human death was my purpose, after all. Instead I felt curious—this could very well be my last chance to learn about humans before I destroyed them.

"This Issac—what was he to you?"

Kaden smiled—a strange thing that was somehow both sad and happy at once. "He sort of adopted my brother and me after the plague. He became a father figure to both of us. Helped us find our way, survive, and grow up, I guess." He chuckled. "Not that I ever really grew up." He paused, and then added. "And he taught me about God. About mercy and faith. I owe him a lot."

Creation did not have fathers. We had a single creator, and I'd killed him. Maybe that was why I asked the next question. "How did he die?"

"I was being chased by hounds. They had me cornered. And then someone started firing from the darkness—Issac. He saved me. But one of the bullets hit him during the fight. He died, but he wasn't afraid to go, to meet his God."

Of course he had died in a violent way. There was no other way with these humans. Couldn't they see the world would be better off without them? I wanted to make him see this.

"And you think your God will forgive you for all you've done?"

"I guess I won't know till I get there."

In true human form, his answer wasn't what I wanted. Or expected.

Before I could question him further, the current dragged us between two tall buildings, into a narrow channel, then shot us out the other side and into a vast swirling pool. I was growing more confident with the paddle, but even so, I flinched when water splashed over me. Cold drops ran down my face like some chilling mockery of a lover's hand. The current spun us in several slow circles, as if it wanted to show us the beauty of the dawn, the last vestiges of the human world before it sucked us into her dark depths.

"You really hate the water, don't you?" Kaden said. And then, so softly a human would have missed it. "You must really love her."

I stiffened at his words—so casual, so careless—and so close to the truth. I forced myself to unlock, to dip the paddle into the black water as if I didn't fear it.

"Do not speak of things you know nothing of," I said quietly. *Maybe I should kill him now. He knows too much, sees too much.* But I needed him to bring me to Talia. Something told me time grew short.

"I know something of love," he said, clearly as stupid as he was loud. "I just got married."

"If you're expecting a congratulations, don't hold your breath. Or do. Just point me in the right direction first."

He chuckled at this. "I'm only saying, maybe we aren't as different as you think."

"We are nothing alike. When the truce breaks, I will prove it."

He sighed but fell blessedly silent, only speaking when telling me to paddle.

"There," he said at last, pointing to a place where the current cut into a rise of land. "We can get to shore there. Paddle hard."

"What do you think I'm doing?"

We were not a good team. I would have happily thrown him overboard and waved as the current carried him away, but I needed him still. The canoe crashed into the bank. I immediately leapt free and left him to struggle alone to pull the boat to shore.

"Sevyn! Help me!" he yelled. He had made it onto the ledge, but the current was pulling the canoe back out.

"No. Let it sink for all I care."

He gave up and let go, letting the water pull it away. *Good riddance.*

"You could have helped me drag it ashore," he said, annoyed for maybe the first time I'd seen.

"For what purpose?"

"To use later! That was a good canoe."

"It was a death trap, and it is of no use to me."

"Come on." He shook his head, wiping off a band of sweat. "We're burning daylight."

Burning daylight.

It was a strange saying, so deliciously human that I was tempted to ask him what it meant. And then I realized I recognized it because I'd heard it in a memory. Septimus's memory.

That was why I had the strange impulse to like this human.

Because Septimus had once liked him.

So, I stayed quiet. I didn't ask him about what he'd shared with Septimus about his life, his God, his faith—and why he'd also told me. I didn't ask why a human would befriend one of the Creation, or why he would help one now.

Because the more you knew about someone, the harder it was to kill them.

~

Kaden led us along the outer reach of the water's limits. The brighter it grew, the more I could see beneath the depths of the water. There were cars, streets—a whole world down there. A world the humans had lost.

As I walked, I wondered why I was here, with a human who

had saved me, when I should have been with the Creation. Was I indebted to him now? I rejected the thought immediately. We'd agreed on a truce—I would uphold our agreement and not kill him. That would be his repayment.

All that mattered was Talia. I would find her, heal her, and then take her to the other Creation. I could destroy the city—and take Talia in the bunker with us. This city would be finished—and I would never think of these people again. If Talia was my one weakness, then so be it. The humans had thousands. Why shouldn't I have one?

Finally, Kaden stopped. "It's just ahead," he said, slowing. He turned to me, glancing at the gun at my hip. "You promised—"

"I won't kill you." *Yet.* "Now lead on."

He didn't look happy, but he did as I said. For the first time it was me smiling—not him. I was in control now.

He led me to an old building. It looked abandoned, but I supposed that might have been the idea. As we climbed to the top, I caught the scent of something like smoke and meat. Humans had definitely been here. A ladder led to the top floor. Kaden pulled back, gesturing to let me go first. I eyed him suspiciously—was this some sort of trap?

But he just shook his head, and then climbed ahead of me, and I followed him up.

"She's over there," he said.

But I heard him only distantly because a low buzzing had begun in my ears. It felt like I was suffocating, breathing in only water. Like I was slowly drowning and there was no one to save me.

Step by step my feet drew me forward. I stared down at her, unable to match this person on the bed with the Talia I knew. She had been healthy when I'd last seen her. It was as if an entirely different person lay there. For a wild moment, that's what I believed had happened. That the humans, like the Creation, had other clones of themselves. And this was simply another clone of Talia. The real one was still out there in the ruins. The real one was still shining brightly, somewhere safe from the reach of this world and myself.

"Talia?" I said, praying that I was wrong, that it wasn't her.

But her eyes opened. I saw her, and the truth. There was only one of her. The human's God was cruel and wonderful in that way. It took her a moment for her eyes to focus on mine.

"Sevyn," her voice was a hoarse whisper, and she smiled. Something dark churned in my chest, like a storm was building there, about to break free.

"Why is she alone?" I demanded, turning to Kaden, hating that he was here, hating the look of grief on his face.

Kaden shook his head. "I had to leave her to find the medicine."

"What happened to her?"

"She was shot." Attacked. By humans. Of course. They were the villains, the monsters I sought to end. I reached inside my jacket, bringing out the medicine, and thrust it at him. "Give this to her. Now. If she dies, you do too."

He did as I said, not even protesting or begging for his life. "I'll leave you alone," he said after, turning to go.

But before he could, Talia spoke. "Wait," she whispered. "Help me go outside. I want to feel the sun on my skin. One last time."

My heart lurched, and I didn't allow myself to look at Kaden. How many years had I dreamed of simply feeling the sun on my skin, the wind through my hair?

Together Kaden and I managed to get Talia down the ladder.

As soon as we were past the ladder, I lifted her into my arms, refusing to meet Kaden's eyes again. I didn't want to see the pity, or the truth there. The next time I looked him in the eyes, it would be just before he died.

Finally, I knelt in the grass outside the building, Talia cradled in my arms as I held her tightly against me. I didn't care if Kaden saw, because this was what I had wanted all along. To hold her against my body, not in secret, but in the light of day, with everyone watching.

I watched her chest rise and fall, the way she struggled for breath. Why wasn't the medicine working?

"The medicine will work," I said. "We crossed the water to find it. You would have liked to see it—I had to work with a human. You'll feel better soon." Even as I said it, I heard the lie. When had I started lying? When had I taken up a habit so horribly human? I ran a hand across her brow—feeling the heat, the sickness. But then, because I didn't see the point in pretending anymore, I let my hand drop, and I traced her lips, her cheeks, her jaw. Touching her like this was forbidden, against the laws of the universe—but what did they matter anymore? When had they ever served me? Her eyes opened and met mine, and I saw the truth there.

I was too late.

Dawn was breaking all across the sky—and I was too late.

Too late, because no god would ever let someone like me be with someone like her.

"You found me," she whispered.

"I told you that you would never escape me."

"Sevyn," she said, her voice slow, less labored now. "Can I ask one thing from you?"

I traced her hair, the line of her jaw and wondered what

impossible thing she would ask: To spare the humans, or the city? To deny who and what I was? To protect the very souls who had done this to her?

"Anything," I said.

"Kiss me."

It should have been a war, a division of what I was or what I wanted to be. But it wasn't. I leaned forward and brought my lips to hers.

I kissed her, and felt what I'd known from the beginning—that the only path for us ended in death.

I held her in my arms as the day awakened around us, and she slipped away from me.

Her chest rose and fell a final time, and just like that, she was gone.

The darkness inside began to swirl and multiply. I leaned forward and pressed a final kiss to her lips—wondering if her fate had been sealed from the moment she'd first met me.

I didn't know how much time had passed. Only that the sun was as traitorous as the humans, marching across the sky when it should have fallen.

"Sevyn," I heard his voice from a great distance, and when I opened my eyes, it all came crashing back. The human I hated— who talked so much, and yet for all his words of God and love, was only full of empty promises.

"I'm sorry," he said. "We can bury her—"

"No. Leave her here. Beneath the sky." I didn't want her buried beneath the ground, a prisoner forever. Not like I had been. Now she was free. Free in a way I longed to be.

Kaden moved, and I had the gun up and trained on his chest before he could take another step. He froze, those awful green eyes meeting mine. Behind him, the sun rose. The truce was broken. It was time to finish this—forever.

But I didn't want to kill him, not this way, not over her body.

I lowered the gun and turned back to her still form.

"Go then," I said softly. "Run and know I will follow."

He took a step back, then another and another. I could feel his fear, finally. He was nearly gone, about to disappear around the building, when I called out.

"Know this: My mercy died with her. Next time we meet, it will be as enemies. You saved my life, but I hold you responsible for hers. Say your goodbyes, Kaden. I will finish this, one way or another."

CHAPTER THIRTY-ONE—KADEN

Kaden.

He'd finally used my name. As I ran it reverberated inside me. It wasn't an olive branch or a gesture of friendship. It was a promise.

He was letting me know that he knew my name—and that he was coming to kill me.

There would be no peace between us now. That hope had died with Talia. When I'd looked into Sevyn's eyes, I'd seen the truth.

It was us or them.

The Creation or the humans.

I forced myself to run faster, fighting the fatigue as the sun crept higher over the ruins. I'd had sleepless nights before, but never after carrying a woman through the ruins, exploring a hospital all night, then paddling across treacherous currents. But I didn't dare stop to rest. I needed to beat Sevyn and the Creation to the bunker.

I prayed that Matteo, Rahul, Ara, and Sam were all already there with some kind of brilliant plan that would save us all.

The sun rose and beat down on me, promising a hot day. The greenery had taken over since I'd been here, covering entire buildings and cars and lampposts, but even so, I couldn't help but try to imagine what it would look like when we got the new tech back on. Would I miss it—this world where it was kill or be killed? Maybe in some strange way I had found a belonging here. I was good at surviving.

Would I be good at surviving in whatever world Sam would turn on? Because I didn't believe it would bring back the old world. That world was dead and gone now. Whatever we resurrected, this new world would be built on the skeletons of everyone and everything we'd lost.

I turned the corner of a massive building and froze.

Standing not twenty feet in front of me, its coat lit a golden red from the dawn, stood a beautiful horse. He looked like Red, my old horse, but then he moved, and I saw it was a mare. She was a bit smaller, shaggier than Red, and there was a white patch in the center of her forehead. But like Red she looked at me with deep, black eyes, taking me in with a mixture of caution and curiosity.

I blinked hard, several times, to make sure this wasn't a hallucination brought on by lack of sleep.

Instead of running, she looked at me for another long moment, then went back to grazing the fresh shoots of grass pushing up through the concrete.

Suddenly it felt like Issac, or his God, really was watching over me.

Because I'd just found my ticket across the city. Even Sevyn couldn't move his Creation faster than a horse.

"Hey, girl . . . hey, there," I said gently. I thought she would bolt but when I came closer, her soft muzzle butted against my jacket pockets, like she was expecting some kind of treat. When I didn't produce any, she went back to grazing, but allowed me to stroke her long neck and back. She didn't have a bit in her mouth, but there was a handmade bridle around her neck. I waited a few minutes, testing the weight of my arms on her back, and then climbed on. At once her head came up, and when I took hold of the bridle she turned as I pressed it against her neck. A path opened up in my mind, the route Sam had shown me to reach the bunker. I knew exactly where to go.

But I didn't push her forward.

Instead, I waited, glancing at the ruins all around me.

It took me a moment to realize what I was waiting for. It wasn't the horse's owner—I guessed they were dead if the horse had been left here alone.

No, I was waiting for Sam to come bursting out of the under-growth, laughing and yelling that he wanted to come along. I was waiting for Issac, his ax strapped to his side, to come ask me what my plan was, where I was going, and if I'd thought this through. I was waiting for Septimus to tell me how horses were *magnificent but ultimately unreasonable beasts.*

I was waiting for a life that was gone now.

I hoped they would forgive me for moving on, for turning on the new tech without them and beginning a new story.

"Guess it's just us two today, girl," I said, and pointed her in the direction of the bunker. Then I urged her forward, and she took off, running at breakneck speed, as if Death himself were chasing us.

Maybe he was.

CHAPTER THIRTY-TWO—SAM

Em lay in my arms, the two of us wrapped in the blankets we'd found in one of the other rooms. There was nowhere to sleep but on the floor of the bunker, and even pressed against her warmth, the cold of the ground seeped through. The walls of the bunker rose sheer and unrelenting all around us, but even in the dark the strange silver metal of the weapon shone softly. Down here, there was no way to tell day from night—but somehow that felt right.

Down here we could escape judgment.

We could forget what came next.

I smiled sleepily, wondering what Ara would say if she caught me and Em like this. Maybe after the new tech started, we could wipe the slate, clear away all the ugly history, and start fresh. It wouldn't matter what we'd done to get here. Only that we'd done it.

Em and I could build a new life together, with Kaden and Ara beside us.

Suddenly Em muttered, her head thrashing back and forth in

her sleep. I was used to this—her nightmares that ended in her screaming, and me comforting her—but before I could do or say anything, she surged upright, gasping for breath. Her chest rose and fell, her eyes wild. I froze, knowing she was likely to attack me if I moved too suddenly. The soft glow of the weapon behind us was the only thing that gave the cavernous space light.

"Is something wrong?" I said, careful to make no sudden movements. I wanted to reassure her, to pull her back into my warmth, and tell her everything would be all right. We were together, we had the two keys, and soon, Ara and Kaden would be here with the engineer. Everything was falling into place.

But I'd learned with Em to wait for her to come to me. She didn't answer or even look at me. After a few moments I reached out and touched her shoulder. She flinched at the contact and I pulled my hand back regretfully.

"Something's changed," she whispered. "He's changed his mind. I . . . I can't see him anymore."

"Can't see who?" I said.

"Sevyn."

The cold and darkness suddenly seemed deeper, sharper.

"He can't get to us here," I said.

She turned away from me and wrapped her arms around her knees. She stared at the darkness with an intensity that told me she was far, far away from here.

I sighed and then sat up, pulling on clothes before I made my way back to the computers. I'd spent the last few hours tinkering with the system, and I'd been able to get two of the aboveground surveillance cameras working again. They showed me blurry pictures of the streets above. The computer came to life, and when my eyes adjusted I could see from the two working cameras that the sun was high in the sky—we'd slept late. *Imagine that. Can't remember the last time I slept in.* In the clan I never slept in. But now that I didn't have the burden of responsibility, to feed them, or to lead them, I felt lighter. I hoped they'd made it downtown and were safe across the water now. Boden was a good man; quiet, but well liked. He would lead them well.

Maybe even better than I would.

As I worked at the computer, trying to bring more of the cameras back online, Em paced back and forth. It took everything in me not to ask her what was wrong. I knew if I tried, she would only snap at me. Still, my eyes were on her more often than on the computer.

Then she stopped and whispered, "Something's changed with Sevyn. He's coming . . . I made a mistake."

My stomach dropped. "About what?" *Please don't say me.*

She stared at the vault-like door to the bunker when she said, "I need to tell Ara I'm sorry. I was so mad at her. I'm *still* mad at her. But if we die here, I don't want that to be the last thing I ever say to her. It can't be." Then her eyes lifted, and I saw they were filled with steely determination. "It won't be. I'm going to go find them."

She turned and strode over to the door of the bunker. I barely had time to grab the access card before rushing after her. "Em, wait!"

The lever that sealed the door was massive and ungainly, and had taken all my strength to open. Yet she had nearly opened the door when I caught the other side of it and stopped it.

Her eyes flashed dangerously. "Let go, Sasquatch."

"No," I said coldly. "You have to make a choice. You can't keep doing this."

"Doing what?"

"Leaving me."

The words hung between us, and finally she stopped trying to throw open the door, crossing her hands over her chest as she glared at me. I crossed my hands over my chest and glared back, mimicking her, and this pulled a smile from her.

"That wasn't what I was doing," she insisted. "I'm just used to doing things alone. I don't want to be held back or contained by anyone." She gave a deep sigh. "So many people have let me down. Either by trying to put me in a cage or by leaving me."

"Have I ever done either of those things?"

"No. You haven't."

"You said before that you wanted to be with me. That you wanted to do this together. Do you still mean that?"

She rolled he eyes. "Yes."

I reached out, hesitant at first, but then with confidence when she didn't pull away. "Then stop trying to run away from me, Em. Give me a chance. Give us a chance. That's the only way this works."

She looked me up and down, arching an eyebrow when she said, "When did you grow up, Sasquatch?"

I grinned. "I wouldn't go *that* far."

~

We spent the next few hours in the bunker. There wasn't all that much to be done other than wait, though Emma insisted she should go out into the city and search for Ara and Kaden to see what was taking them so long. I made the same argument but in reverse: she should stay here, and I should go out. Mostly we just argued.

Then, just when I was about to give up and let her do what she wanted, something moved on the camera screen.

"Quiet!" I yelled.

"Don't tell me to—"

"Someone's outside," I said, and she instantly fell silent and came to stand beside me. The two of us stared at the camera image.

"I don't see anything," she snapped.

"I did, just a second ago."

"Can you rewind it or something—"

Em reached forward for the keyboard, and I caught her hands. "Don't touch that!"

She grinned. "I like it when you get all mad and demanding."

"Can we not right now?" I said, exasperated but also trying not to smile. Em seemed to like kissing just as much as she liked arguing. Neither of us moved, staring at the camera screen. It wasn't connected to audio, but even so, I held my breath. The oppressive silence of the underground pressed in on us.

"All right, new plan," Em said. She pulled away from me, lifted her gun, and cocked it. "We go upstairs, and if they aren't friends, we kill them. Cool?" But then she paused, looking at me with raised eyebrows, and I realized what she was doing—or at least trying to do. She was including me. *Holy crap, are we finally working together?*

Suddenly I didn't care if it was a shit plan. I lifted my gun, and grinned. "Let's do it."

She laughed at this, and then took off, me following close behind.

When we made it to the ground level, she stepped out first, gun held aloft. I would have preferred to go first, but I figured I'd better take this whole working together thing in baby steps. At least I was *here*.

After being in the bunker, even the musty hallways smelled fresh. I breathed deeply, aware of every scent, noise, and movement as we paced forward. Em opened the door that led directly to the front of the building, blinding us both momentarily with the sudden influx of sunlight.

I was about to speak when Em held up a hand, and then pointed to the opening at the far end, where the building had been blown apart. Nothing but the wind reached out to me.

Then, a steady clomping sound.

Is that a horse?

We both lifted our weapons, waiting, as a group of three people stepped into view, leading a red horse behind them.

"It's them," Em said in disbelief, lowering her gun.

It took me a little longer, because for a moment I thought I was looking at Red, Kaden's old horse. For a moment I felt like I'd gone back in time.

They approached, none of us speaking.

It was Kaden who broke the silence, wearing his trademark grin. "Fancy meeting you two here."

CHAPTER THIRTY-THREE—ARA

I didn't wait for Emma to speak. Life in the apocalypse had taught me how fleeting life could be. I just crossed the space between us and pulled her into a hug. She stiffened, but after a moment she wrapped her arms around me, crushing me so hard it hurt. I held her with the same fierceness.

"I didn't mean what I said," she whispered.

I didn't want to let her go—I just wanted to hold her here against me. "I know. I love you."

"I love you too," she mumbled, like a teenager responding to an overbearing parent. It made me smile because it reminded me so much of old times.

Finally, she pulled back and I released her. She turned to stare at Kaden and Matteo with a grimace. "Who are the strays?"

Matteo's eyes narrowed, but Kaden grinned.

"Emma, this is Matteo, he was the clan leader in the mall," I said, and then paused. For so long I had wondered how this moment would go. How the two most important people in my life would meet. I hadn't envisioned it like this. "And this is Kaden, my, ah, husband, I guess."

"You guess?" Kaden staggered back dramatically, his hand over his chest like he'd been wounded. "*You guess?* Wow, I clearly should have got a bigger rock." But he was smiling when he said it.

"You two got married?" Matteo frowned. "Aren't you both a bit young for that?"

Kaden and I both laughed at this, even though I was pretty sure he wasn't kidding. Emma shook Kaden's hand like she was trying to break it. "Ara always had a weakness for blonds," she said, sounding suspicious.

Kaden winked at her. "My brother always had a weakness for brunettes."

I stepped in between them. "Okay, now that everyone knows each other, can we move this into the bunker?"

"That's probably a good idea," Sam said, his gaze going to the far end of the wide room, where it opened to the outside. A cool breeze swirled in behind us, mixing the stench of rot with scents of new growth. I took in the building: the greenery contrasted with the scorch marks on the walls and floors. The front entrance had been blown off, like some kind of battle had been waged here. There were a few dried corpse-like shapes covered in leaves and debris I didn't want to examine too closely.

"Are you going to bring the horse?" I said to Kaden.

He sighed. "No. I guess not." Then he patted her on the back and removed the rope from around her neck. Her ears swiveled to the opening, but she didn't move, clearly not realizing she was free. Matteo and I had found Kaden riding the red horse across the ruins and flagged him down. I almost hadn't believed it when

I'd seen him. There had been moments since my father died when I thought I saw my loved ones in the ruins. I would see Emma's dark hair or my father's tall form in the shadows, but when I looked closer, it was never really them. So when I saw Kaden, riding a red horse through the ruins, I thought maybe I was seeing things.

But he was real then. And he was real now.

"This way," Sam said, and our group left the red horse standing there. When the horse saw we didn't pull her after us, she turned, walking back for the entryway, and I saw the sadness on Kaden's face. *There'll be time for other horses soon.*

Even though normally I hated the idea of hiding deep beneath the ground, right now a very solid door between us and everything out there sounded like a good idea. Emma led the group of us to a dark stairwell. The others stepped through the door, but before Kaden could follow them, I caught his hand, pulling him back.

"Hold up a sec," I said to him. "You know I love you, husband?" I said, putting my hands on his chest, wanting to feel that he was alive and well.

"Oh, *now* I'm husband?"

I stepped forward and kissed him the way I'd wanted to before but couldn't with Matteo watching. His hands came against me, rough and gentle at the same time, one lacing fingers through my hair and the other against my waist.

Matteo poked his head back out from the stairwell, frowning at us, and we broke apart.

"Come on," he said, sounding annoyed. "There'll be time for that *after* we save the world."

Kaden sighed, and then opened the door for me, gesturing me to follow Matteo into the dark stairwell.

"We're coming, Dad," I muttered.

"I heard that!" Matteo called back, and Kaden and my laughter echoed as the door sealed us into the dark.

~

"The two keys have to be turned at the same time," Matteo said when we'd all gathered in the bunker. It was far bigger than I'd imagined. The top level we stood on was like the tip of an iceberg, the lower levels spiraling down so far I couldn't make out the bottom. In the center of it all was the weapon, giving off a faint, sinister glow. "And it's essential the hatch stays closed. If it's opened when the weapon goes off, because the weapon was trained on the city last, it will destroy the city. If the hatch is closed, it starts a sixty-second countdown, and when the weapon goes off, the surge of energy will restart the new tech system."

"And there's no way to turn the keys and get out?" I asked.

Matteo shook his head. "No. Once either key is turned, the door locks. Whoever is in here . . ."

He trailed off, but I finished for him, "Whoever is in here either dies in here or destroys everyone outside."

Matteo nodded, the entire group of us somber at this news.

"I'll do it," Kaden said first. "I'll find a way to turn both at the same time—"

"No," Matteo jumped in. "I'm older than all of you. It was my job, I should have done it—"

"What if *none* of us does it?" Emma's cold voice cut through the men's loud one. All of us turned to her. She was lounging against the wall, out of the reach of the bright lantern Sam had set on the table. Even as we all looked at her, she stared at the weapon, as if she'd forgotten she'd spoken.

"Em?" I said gently.

Her eyes rose to mine alone. "What if we tricked the Creation? Got them all in here? Got *them* to turn the key?"

The silence stretched out.

Matteo said, "That's a very dangerous gamble. . ."

"A gamble that saves the lives of everyone in this room," I said, wanting to stick up for Emma.

"Or ends the lives of everyone on this planet," Matteo said.

Then Kaden, the last person I expected to support Emma, spoke. "I like it. Go big or go home." Matteo glared at Kaden, as if his worst suspicions had been confirmed, but Kaden only turned to Emma. "Do you think you can sell it to Sevyn? From what I've seen, he isn't easily tricked."

I saw the weight of her answer as she pushed off the wall and came to stand in our circle. "Yes . . . I can sell it to him." Then she added softly, "I am one of them, after all."

Matteo stiffened at her words, and the rest of us exchanged glances. I hadn't expected her to reveal this, and clearly Sam and Kaden hadn't either. I wasn't sure what to say. But I definitely didn't expect Sam to reach out and take her hand in his.

"No, you're not. You're one of us."

She smiled at him gratefully—and my heart lurched.

Because I saw it, just then. I knew Sam loved her, but I thought that was it. Now I saw the truth, and it hit me with the same force it had when I'd first seen her, all grown up.

She loved him too.

She'd told me that there was something between them, but I thought it was fleeting. I hadn't expected the warmth in her eyes when she looked at him, or the way her lips crooked up on one side when he smiled at her.

"I'm in too," I said, and everyone turned to me now. "Either all of us die or none of us. We're a team."

Matteo ran a hand over his face, looking like he had no idea how he'd come to be here, in a bunker, surrounded by people all half his age suggesting this crazy plan.

"Come on, Matty, roll the dice with us," Emma said, something teasing in her voice now. "We all gotta die someday."

I shot her a look, trying for the classic older sister's glare, before I remembered that had barely worked before the plague.

Matteo looked between Emma and me, and then shook his head. "You know, I didn't see the family similarities at first, but now I do. Ara's got a thing for fire, and you for exploding things. How on Earth did your parents keep a roof over your heads?"

"They didn't," I said. "I burned it down. But to be fair, it was an accident."

The group laughed, but then to my surprise, it was Sam who called us back to order.

"All right, we don't have much time, and we're only gonna get one chance. Here's how I'm thinking we play this."

CHAPTER THIRTY-FOUR—SEVYN

She was gone.

How could the sun still shine on this wretched Earth without her? How could plants grow? How could the wind move and whisper, when she never would again?

I knelt by her body the entire day. It felt like I had become a captive again, but instead of the green water holding me prisoner, it was her body. I couldn't move, because how could I move or laugh or smile again when she didn't?

The sun was a traitor, walking across the sky and then sinking into the horizon, painting the whole world red. Just the way I would soon.

I stood, and then forced myself to remember her, remember this. Then I turned and left her there.

I wanted it to be finished.

Forever.

~

I reached the stone building where I'd left the Creation at dawn. I could travel faster than humans, sleep less, but instead I'd planted one foot in front of the other, moving as slowly as the humans did. I wanted to soak in the feel of the wind on my skin, the light of the moon shifting through the clouds. I wanted to smell the scents of the grass and the trees and the small flowers I had no names for, that pushed their way up from the wet earth.

They were all ready, waiting for me.

I hated that they knew.

I hated that they could feel what I did.

"Follow," I said, turning and walking into the ruins. They followed—the slow and steady march of the dead.

CHAPTER THIRTY-FIVE—ARA

We'd spent several hours planning, hammering out every tiny detail. While I didn't feel confident, I was at least hopeful that our plan would work. The trickiest part was that Emma mostly had to be excluded. She wasn't sure how much Sevyn would be able to hear, so she didn't want to risk it. She stayed in another room, and when night fell, she told us, "They'll be here tomorrow at noon."

"We'll be ready," Sam said, and I hoped that was true. Sam and Emma decided to stay in the bunker for the night, but he told us there was an old apartment complex just across from the street. Kaden and I made our way there with Matteo.

Matteo had taken a room down the hall from me and Kaden. It made me smile that Sam and Emma had chosen to stay together in the bunker. I hadn't commented on it—I'd just gotten Emma back after all—but I would definitely have some questions after this.

When we'd found a room to sleep in, Kaden and I spent several hours talking. He'd told me what happened with Talia. My heart hurt for the loss of another friend, but it was the way he spoke about Sevyn that unsettled me. He made it sound like Sevyn cared deeply, or maybe even loved Talia, which made no sense. How could someone so committed to destroying humanity care for a human? At the very least, I took comfort in Kaden's description of Sevyn's fear of the water. The clan would be safe—as long as our plan worked.

I'd woken early, the lightening on the horizon indicating that dawn would be here soon. My heart thudded faster. After waiting so long, it would end today.

"Are you ready?" I said, tracing my fingers over Kaden's back.

Kaden rolled over on the bed, his eyes sleepy as he mumbled, "I was born ready."

A sudden pounding came on the door. "Rise and shine, love-birds," Matteo said in a grumpy voice. "You've got five minutes to get outside."

"He really doesn't like me, does he?" Kaden said, as if he thought Matteo's dislike was hilarious.

"He takes a little while to warm up. Give him a chance."

"Don't worry. I can be very charming when I want to be."

"Why do you think I married you? Now come on, we said we'd be there early."

Kaden groaned from his spot on the bed. "I'm all for saving the world—but can we do it at a more reasonable hour? I thought they weren't gonna be here till noon?"

I laughed at this, and then lowered my voice. "Actually, there is one more thing I want to talk with you about before we meet up with the others."

~

An hour after dawn, we'd all gathered in our places. Emma had been told what she needed to do, and I didn't like not being able to see her now. Her role was easily the most dangerous part of the plan.

Kaden and I stood on the road, waiting. He was quiet this morning, lost in his thoughts. His left hand didn't release mine, though I noticed that his right constantly went to his hip, checking for the gun that wasn't there. Emma had insisted we would be safer without weapons, but it still felt wrong.

"So I was wondering," I said, "after we get the new tech back on, what's the first thing you want to do?"

"Kiss you."

I laughed and shook my head. "No, it has to be something you couldn't do before!" Then I added. "Sam said the clan horses are gone, maybe we could rebuild the herd? Do you want to be an expedition leader again?"

He thought about this for a moment and then said, "At first, I did. I thought that would make Sam forgive me . . . but now I wonder if the time for clans is over."

"Really?" This surprised me.

"If this works, and the new tech comes back on, then maybe we can help rebuild the city. We can get our own house somewhere. That's what I want. A place of our own. Maybe a big farmhouse. Or a ranch. There's some not far from the Old Pen—we could still help out Sam and Emma. I feel like they'll have their hands full."

"It sounds perfect," I said. I could see it already: the house, the land, the horses. Us, a family.

"It will be. I promise."

We stood there, the two of us grinning stupidly at each other, imagining a future that felt even more precious for the danger approaching.

Then the radio crackled at my side.

Matteo had found the radios, but it was Sam who had been able to get three of them working again. My mouth went dry, my heart pounding, knowing what this meant. I lifted the radio with a shaking hand. "Hello?"

"They're coming," Matteo said simply.

Kaden's eyes met mine and I could see the fear there even as he smiled to hide it. *If our plan didn't work . . . if we'd made a mistake . . .* but it was too late to change our path now. Kaden held my hand in his, the two of us standing there alone, waiting for the Creation.

The wind blew through the ruins, but when they came around the corner, it was with no sound at all, like they were ghosts, and I was once again seeing the dead.

Ice ran down my back.

An entire army marched toward us, so quiet I could hear the wind whispering through the windows, hear my heart beating in my chest.

Leading them was Emma and a man who looked exactly like Septimus.

A man who had to be Sevyn.

CHAPTER THIRTY-SIX—SEVYN

I stared at the two humans waiting for us.

Emma had told me they wanted to meet, to discuss some sort of truce. I felt empty inside. I knew this only ended one way.

Hadn't I specifically warned Kaden to leave? I'd threatened him, *promised* him that if I saw him again, I would kill him.

Now he would finally see that I kept my promises.

"Good to see you again, Sevyn," Kaden called out to me.

"I made you a promise last time I saw you, human," I said coldly. "Have you already forgotten?"

"Are we back to the 'human' thing?"

He clearly had a death wish. For the first time I took in the young woman standing beside him. I had seen almost no human females in the cities we'd destroyed, so it was odd to see her here. She had red hair, auburn eyes, and stared at me in defiance. Memories stirred in me—of the two sisters, one dark haired, one red haired, who'd haunted my dreams. The woman was Ara, the last she. The sister who had betrayed and abandoned Emma.

It all made sense—why Emma had come to me. She wanted revenge.

"We want to discuss peace," Ara said, and without meaning to I flinched—because her voice had been plucked straight from my memories.

"It's too late for peace." I turned to Emma now. "You said they have the key—retrieve it."

"We're here to make a compromise with you," Kaden said before Emma could move. "I helped you before, Sevyn. Let me do it again."

It was the wrong thing to say. Because he hadn't helped me.

He'd taken the only person I'd ever loved away from me.

I motioned the Creation forward—I didn't even watch the brief scuffle that broke out. Instead, I stared up at the blue sky high above. Never once, in all my years locked beneath the earth, had I dreamed that the sky would be such a color. Or that the scents on the wind could remind you of a person, of a time that was gone.

Was Talia up there, watching me? Was the God Kaden spoke of kind enough to give her a place there? Or was he as cruel as the humans he'd created?

When the scuffle was over, I turned back to face Kaden. His eye was blackening—he'd clearly put up some kind of fight, but even though he'd been defeated, he still watched me with something like pity in his eyes.

I hated that look—as if he were somehow better than me. I strode forward, and then ripped the metal chain from around his neck, on which dangled a key.

"Where is the other key?" I said to him.

He glared at me, his jaw set hard. "We came to meet you here in good faith, Sevyn. It doesn't have to be like this. We can find a way to coexist. We can find a way to peace."

"That possibility died when she did."

Kaden exchanged a look with the woman beside him, and it irked me that I knew him well enough to recognize the sadness in his gaze.

I turned to Emma. "You said there were two keys? Where is the other?"

Her ice-blue eyes were as cold and sharp as ever. "The boy leader has it. He's in the bunker. If we bring Kaden down there, we can use him as leverage to get the door open."

"Fine," I said, and then gestured forward. "Lead the way."

Let it be finished.

~

"How do we get him to open the door?" one of the Creation asked. I stood before the massive, metal bunker door. There would be no breaking in, not even with the full strength of the Creation behind me.

But I didn't need the might of the Creation.

All I needed was the weakness of humanity.

"Bring me Kaden," I said.

They dragged him forward, and I wished yet again I hadn't learned his name.

"Tell your brother to open the door," I demanded.

"Sevyn, we can still work this out. Please, listen—"

His words cut off with a strangled scream. I'd only broken his pinkie finger, but he clearly hadn't expected it, hadn't seen how fast I could move. His mocking smile was gone now.

"Please, Sevyn—"

"I will not ask you again, Kaden."

His eyes flicked to the door, and then back to me, before he lifted the radio. "Sam"—he paused, looking at me, and then said, all in a rush—"don't open the door no matter what—"

Again, his words ended in a strangled scream, another finger broken. This time he fell to his knees, his face pale and pinched.

"I grow tired of this, Kaden."

But I didn't need to say more. With a sudden hiss and grinding noise the bunker door opened, and there, at last, stood the boy leader. He was taller than I thought he'd be. Taller, but also younger. He didn't have the strange green eyes of his brother, and his hair was shorn close to his head, but there was still something about him that reminded me of Kaden. Maybe the cut of his jaw, or the set of his eyes.

He held something in his hands, but it wasn't a gun.

It was a lighter, held beneath a slip of paper.

"Hurt Kaden, or Ara, or any other human, and I'll burn the launch codes and you'll never turn the weapon on."

I wanted to roll my eyes. This was their incredible plan? I didn't have time for this.

"Take him," I said.

The Creation moved forward without hesitation. To his credit, he tried to light the paper, but it was all too little, too late. I felt that same surge of emptiness, of disappointment, the hole in my chest I had never been able to fill . . . except with her.

"Should we kill him?" the Creation asked.

I stared down at the boy leader, now on his knees before me, and examined him. He did look a bit like Kaden, but the biggest difference was that Kaden always seemed on the verge of a smile. This boy stared at me with hatred in his eyes, like if he had the chance he would kill me. He was closer to what I expected from humans—he wanted death, not peace. Had it been him, not Kaden, who had helped me, I doubted both of us would have survived till dawn.

"Search him," I said coldly.

He fought, but it was hardly a struggle. Soon they produced not just the final key, but also an unopened envelope with what looked like a letter inside. Even though I already had the keys and launch codes, I examined the envelope with curiosity.

"No, please," the boy leader said from his knees, his face bloodied. "That's personal. It doesn't have anything to do with turning on the new tech."

"And I'm supposed to believe that?" I was about to open the sealed envelope when his desperate voice stopped me.

"*Please*, it's a letter from a man named Issac," he said, and now my fingers paused, because I knew that name. It was the man Kaden had said taught him about God. The man who'd died to save him. The man who'd acted like an adoptive father to them both.

"You haven't read it?" I said derisively. Why wouldn't he have opened this letter, all this time after his death?

The boy leader, Sam—I supposed I couldn't deny I knew his name now too—looked up at me with haunted eyes. "I wanted to wait," he said, and for the first time I saw the boy in him. "Till things were so dark I needed his words."

Had these humans learned nothing? I wanted to laugh, but couldn't, because I knew the answer. No, they hadn't learned, and they never would. Something about his voice, so like Kaden's, made me step forward and put the letter back into his pocket.

Then I smiled down at him, a look with all the venom and hatred I had left. "Then, go, boy. Read your letter. It's time."

I nodded to the Creation, and they released him. He scrambled to his feet and ran for the door without looking back.

When his footsteps had faded to nothing, I stared down at the two keys and the slip of paper. The power to destroy a city held in my palms. Was it really so easy? Had the humans really been so foolish?

I already knew the answer.

Of course they had.

"Get all the Creation inside the bunker," I said, staring through the open door to where the weapon gleamed faintly, as if lit by moonlight. But there was no moon, no sun, no stars down here. It was as if we'd returned to the underground lab where we'd been created. As if it would end where it began. Beside the door, propped against the wall, lay a single human corpse, with a name tag that read, PHILLIP CONSTANTINO.

You will soon have much more company, Phillip. The thought was as heavy and suffocating as this underground place.

"What of the humans?" a Creation said. "We found an older man with a radio—and we're holding the green-eyed one and the woman in separate rooms down here."

I waved a hand. "Let them all go." Then I paused and turned back. "Strike that. Bring me the green-eyed human. Alone."

~

It didn't take long to gather all the Creation inside the bunker. Not when they followed me completely. There were multiple levels, spiraling down into darkness, and the Creation filled all of them.

Yet they stood in that strange, perfectly spaced way they always did when gathered. It was the exact distance they had kept us in those tubes, all those long years. Just able to see each other, but never to embrace or comfort the other. I wanted to shout at them now, to tell them they could gather closer, to feel the warmth of another's skin . . . but what was the point? It was too late.

It had always been too late.

Kaden was brought in last. He looked more haggard than I'd ever seen him, one eye swollen, clutching his arm with the broken fingers to his chest. Despite all this, when the Creation thrust him forward, he still managed to stand and look me in the eyes.

"Don't do this, Sevyn. It's not too late."

It was too late the first moment I breathed. Or maybe it was too late the last moment she did.

The computer was already on—I'd put the codes in. It was so easy.

Too easy.

How could this be where it ended?

Was I strong enough to do it?

That's why I'd brought Kaden here—I had to hear the story one more time. The story of Issac was so different from everything I'd witnessed from these humans so far. Kaden had made it sound like he wasn't afraid. Like he'd given his life as a sacrifice to let others live.

But why? Why would he do this, knowing the people he saved would continue to do wrong?

There was a radio connected to Kaden's side, and it crackled now, a female voice sounding. "Kaden? Kaden, where are you?"

Even though endless turmoil churned inside me, my heartbeats numbered, I couldn't help but give him a cold, mocking smile. "Aren't you going to answer that?"

There was something tormented in his eyes. The voice came again. "Kaden? Where are you? We're heading free of the tunnels."

"I can't answer when I'm being held like this," Kaden said, managing a weak smile.

I nodded to the Creation, and they released him and then left us. Once again, it was just me and this perplexing human. Still, he didn't answer the radio. Instead, he reached down with his uninjured arm and turned it off. Then he said, in a soft, almost pleading voice. "Don't do this, Sevyn. Don't set off the weapon and kill everyone in the city."

"Let us be honest with each other, Kaden, for once." I saw the flicker of fear in his eyes before he hid it. I was beginning to know this human well.

"I don't know what you mean," he said carefully.

But you do. You know exactly what I mean. "Your plan was so pathetically thought through—even if I hadn't seen the truth from Emma, I would have guessed it at once."

He stared at me, and I saw the realization, followed by despair. He glanced over his shoulder at the sealed bunker door, likely thinking of all those on the other side. "You know," he whispered.

"That you schemed with your human friends for the Creation to come in here, turn on the weapon, and all die? Of course I did."

He paused a long moment, and then those green eyes met mine. "So what are you going to do?"

The dark hole in my chest swirled with pain, fear, turmoil, regret. "I want you to tell me the truth—about Issac. What really happened that night?"

He looked confused. "I told you. I was being hunted. The men had caught up with me—I couldn't go any farther. Issac defended me, and he was shot. He died beneath the stars."

"And he could have left? Saved himself?"

"Yes."

"But instead, he chose to give his life for yours?"

"Yes."

"I don't believe you. I have seen nothing in humans to show this could be true."

Kaden stared at me, something shifting in his eyes, and I had to look away, because again, I felt like he saw too much. It was as if his green eyes gave him some ability to see beneath the surface, and I hated it. Hated that a human could *know* me. I wouldn't be known by them. I wouldn't be understood by them.

But even though I'd broken his fingers, even though I'd murdered hundreds of his people, he stepped closer. "What are you really asking me, Sevyn? What do you really want from me?"

There was no hiding from it anymore. "There will be no peace. I said from the beginning that this ends only one of two ways: with your death or ours. Which is why I brought you here to make a choice. You said your friend died to save you. That he loved you. So prove it. Prove that humans are worth saving."

His gaze was heavy, his eyes sad, and I saw he understood the gravity of the question even when he said, "How do I do that?"

"Simple." I held out the key. "You turn this."

He stared at the key held in my hand. Such a small thing with so much power—like the vial of medicine I'd held for Talia.

Kaden reached out and took the key from my hands. Then he said, heavily, "Can I have a moment to say my goodbyes first?"

I nodded and he turned the radio on, fumbling to lift it while only using one hand. Before he could speak, the female voice came again, clearly agitated, "Kaden? Are you there?"

Watching him prepare to say goodbye made me feel tired.

Tired as if I'd drowned in blood and pain and emerged from the other side, not reborn, but ancient and bitter and used.

Kiss me. That's what she had asked of me. Her final request wasn't to save the humans. Her final request was for me. I wonder if she knew that she had changed me regardless. I wonder if she knew it wasn't blood or violence or words that made me decide to give humanity another chance.

It was her.

Kaden held the radio in his hand, but he hadn't spoken yet. He swallowed and I saw it in his eyes now. The understanding. The pain. The acceptance. So, he was really going to do it. He had really passed my test.

He lifted the radio to his lips. "Ara? Are you there? It's Kaden."

I closed my eyes and prayed. I prayed that God would be lenient. That He would accept someone who was created and not born.

But mostly I prayed that wherever I went, she would be there.

CHAPTER THIRTY-SEVEN—KADEN

"Ara? Are you there? It's Kaden." I lowered the radio, my hands shaking, as I waited for her response.

It didn't take long, and I could tell from the other end she was breathing hard. Good. I hope that meant she'd been running as far away from this place as she could. "Kaden? Where are you? What's happening? Why aren't you at the checkpoint?"

We'd already agreed on a place to meet that was far enough away from the bunker to avoid danger. Matteo wasn't sure what would happen to the surrounding tunnels when the explosion went off—likely some of them would collapse. But if Ara was at the checkpoint, then she would be safe.

Relief, followed by a strange sort of numbness, engulfed my body. I didn't even feel the pain from my broken fingers, so consumed by what I'd learned, so at a loss with what or how to tell her. *He knows. Sevyn knows what we planned. But he's offered us another way out. A way that ends with my death as well as theirs.* How could I tell her that? How could I tell her that the true cost of defeating the Creation and turning the new tech back on was my life?

"It worked." I heard my voice as if from a great distance. "The Creation are in the bunker. They have the keys and the codes."

"Thank God," her voice came back. "Where are you? Are you clear?"

I closed my eyes, soaking in her voice, and suddenly I wasn't in the bunker. I was back in the bed, lying next to Ara, listening to the news she wanted to tell me before we met the others.

Her cheeks were rosy from sleep, and I pulled her closer to me, wanting to kiss her again. She laughed, pressing a finger to my lips.

"I really do have something to tell you," she said, mock sternly.

I kissed her finger and winked. "I can multitask."

But she suddenly fell quiet and swallowed, a serious, almost somber look in her eyes. I sat up on the bed, concerned.

"Are you okay? Is something wrong?"

"No . . . Nothing's wrong. It's just . . . Well, I'm not sure how to say it, or if I even should." She couldn't meet my eyes, and now I really was worried.

"Is it the plan, because we can change it—"

"No, Kaden . . . I'm late. And I threw up a few mornings ago."

I didn't understand, staring at her in confusion. Late to what? Had she eaten bad food?

Then she smiled, tears in her eyes when she said, "I think I might be pregnant."

The words took my breath away. I couldn't speak. Could barely even think.

She looked worried when she whispered. "Are you happy?"

"Am I happy?" I leaned forward, kissing her fiercely before pulling back and kissing her stomach. Then I let out a whoop.

"Am I happy? No man has ever been happier than I am in this moment."

Her words had changed everything. Everything I'd once thought was important didn't matter.

All that mattered was keeping Ara, and my future family, safe.

Even if that meant I followed Issac's path, I would do it. I wasn't afraid of death, not if it brought them life.

"Ara," I said into the radio, a feeling of calmness settling over me now. "I need you to tell me. Are you all clear?"

"Sam and Matteo and I are at the checkpoint," her voice came back. "We're waiting for you and Emma. Kaden, what's happening?"

"Ara, listen to me," I said, my voice deceptively calm. "Sevyn has offered me a choice. To prove that humanity is worth saving. To prove that love is worth dying for. And I'm going to take it. I'm going to show him we are worth saving . . ."

Sevyn watched me as I took the key in trembling fingers. Two of my fingers were broken, but I still had enough control for this final act. I made my way over to where Matteo had shown us where the two keys would be inserted. My feet felt heavy, my hands numb, but my heart was sure.

My hands trembled as I placed the key inside. Once I turned it, there was no going back.

Once I turned it and Sevyn did the same, I would stand before God. I would see Issac again.

Time was warping and bending. Ara's voice crackled over the radio, panicked now. "Kaden, no, whatever he says, whatever the choice is, say no! Please come back to me. I can't do this alone."

"You won't be alone. I'll always be there with you. Ara, listen, we don't have much time. I need you to do something for me." My fingers shook as I turned the key. Lights came on in the bunker, a low alarm sounding. "Tell Sam I love him. Find a house by the river. Teach our little one to ride. Tell them about Issac and me."

I think I was crying. Moisture ran down my cheeks. My hands were shaking. But the fear was gone now. I'd once thought that I couldn't save everyone. That I'd watch everyone I loved die, one by one, and there would be no way to save them. No way to protect them all.

Now I finally had my chance.

Sevyn made his way forward now.

"I love you, Ara," I said. "Everything I did—it was for you and Sam. I'll miss you so much. I choose you. I'll always choose you."

I finally lifted the button on the radio so that Ara could respond, and I could hear her voice one last time.

"Kaden, please don't leave me! Kaden!"

Then the whole room began to shake.

I closed my eyes. I wasn't scared—not when I knew when I opened my eyes again, I would see Issac, Septimus, and everyone I'd loved and lost.

I said my final words on this Earth.

"I love you, Ara."

CHAPTER THIRTY-EIGHT—ARA

The whole room shook—like a distant earthquake.

The weapon just went off.

It felt like the very Earth I stood on, the axis the Earth rotated upon, had suddenly tilted, even as I shook my head and refused to believe it. It couldn't be . . . he couldn't be . . .

Matteo stood beside me, staring out the window, frozen.

I couldn't accept it. I had to know what had happened to Kaden. I had to know he was safe. I picked up the radio, my voice shaking as much as my hands. "Kaden? Kaden, are you there?"

No voice came back.

I kept calling, again and again on the radio, till my voice was hoarse, till the radio was dead.

Till Sam pulled it gently from my hands, and then held me as I wept in his arms.

Kaden was gone.

Everything inside me went black.

PART **THREE**

ONE WEEK LATER

CHAPTER THIRTY-NINE—SAM

The new tech system was back on, and soon the lights, the city power, it would all be back. But it didn't matter.

Because Kaden was gone.

I stared out at the horizon where the sun was just breaking free. A beautiful dawn that Kaden would never see.

I'd always known there would be a cost.

But if I'd known the cost was Kaden's life, I would have never begun this. I would have left the new tech buried beneath the ground forever. It wasn't fair that I'd gotten Kaden back so briefly only to lose him all over again.

After the weapon had gone off, we'd spent several days searching the rubble around the bunker for Emma and Kaden. The surrounding tunnels off the bunker had collapsed in places, and we all hoped that maybe Kaden and Emma had gotten free in time. But the more we searched, the more hopeless it became.

Four days after the weapon went off, when we'd still found

nothing, Ara, Matteo, and I had made our way back to the Old Pen. Only it didn't feel like a clan anymore. I'd told the clansmen to return when the lights came back on, and even though the new tech system was technically working, there was one last mission needed to release all the power to the city. Matteo said he knew how to do it, that it was as simple as finding and turning a single switch, and he and Ara were going out tomorrow to finish it. Then lights would blaze through the darkness, then the men would return, then the city would come back to life, and we could bury the violence and horror . . .

But I didn't care.

If the men came back here, looking for a leader, I wouldn't be here for them. I couldn't lead them anymore. I couldn't be *here* anymore. Not with Kaden gone. Not with Emma gone. I knew Matteo believed that Kaden and Emma were both dead, but I didn't believe that of Emma. I'd seen her break away from the Creation just moments before they'd let me go. She'd gone down a different tunnel. Unlike Kaden, I believed she'd made it free.

She'd chosen not to come to our checkpoint, because that was just who she was.

She was the girl who disappeared.

The girl who always left me broken and bleeding.

This time, if she did come back to the clan, ready to apologize, I wouldn't be waiting for her.

Now, exactly a week after the weapon had gone off, I sat on the wall of the Old Pen, letting my feet dangle over the side. Once this place had held so much potential, represented so much, but now all it seemed to me was an abandoned prison with memories best left forgotten. Sitting there, looking out over the land, I realized that the time had finally come.

This was rock bottom.

I pulled Issac's letter out of my breast pocket, smoothed out the crinkled envelope that looked as weathered as I felt, then broke the seal. In the light of dawn, I read his last words to me.

Sam,

I'm leaving this letter here for you, because I know how this world works. I found something strange, and, while I trust Kaden with my life, I don't trust him not to go charging into the unknown to investigate. I'll leave the map coordinates below, and while I hope to go with you, I'll warn you now not to go alone. Of course, I imagine you and Kaden may go charging off together, but if you do, be careful. Remember a few things this old man taught you.

Now, because I have the paper, and I've felt lately that the time is coming when I'll see Gracie and my wife again, I want to tell you a few things I've learned in the years I've been lucky enough to live on this Earth.

You are blessed, Sam. I can see you rolling your eyes, but I mean it. The world fell, but that doesn't mean we lost everything. It doesn't mean God abandoned us. He simply gave us a chance to love each other better than we did before. Don't forget that, Sam. Don't lose hope if you lose me, or even your life, because there is a bigger plan for you.

I'm sure you're about to stop reading, but before you do, I have one last request for you. Write down your story—all that's happened to you. Write down and remember the mistakes you made and what they taught you. Write about the people you met, the things you learned, the ones you loved and lost. You always loved stories, Sam—so write yours and remember it's what makes you human.

I'll end with this: there was a time I felt lost, when I thought God had abandoned me. You and Kaden were the hope I found. You were the peace I found.

Issac

I cried as I held the paper to my chest, feeling like I'd released a piece of him forever now. These were his final words to me. There would be no more.

I would never hear from him, or Kaden, ever again.

It was over.

I sat there a long time, holding the letter and looking out over the city. I'd done what I'd set out to do, but now that I had, I didn't want to be here anymore. I couldn't. Not when this place was full of the memories of everyone I'd lost.

I opened the letter and this time I examined the map coordinates written neatly on the bottom of the page. What did he mean he'd found something strange? The coordinates were somewhere to the south—I'd need to find a map to find out where, but I was pretty sure I had one in my old Barnes & Noble hideout.

Suddenly, I knew where I would go next. I would find out what lay at those map coordinates. It didn't matter that Issac had said not to go alone. We were all alone in the end.

I made my way to the stables. There were only three horses left, so I chose the spirited black one. I couldn't bear to take the one with a reddish coat. It reminded me too much of Kaden and his horse, Red. Another lost friend.

I brought only the essentials—well, that and an empty journal I'd found in one of the cells. Something about Issac's request stuck in my head. I'd always found an escape, a release in stories, and even if it was far too painful to imagine taking pen to page now, maybe I would someday. Maybe I would write my story—and Kaden's and Ara's and Issac's. Maybe they could live on in that way.

"Sam? What are you doing?" Ara's voice rang through the barn. Once I would have turned to her immediately, smiled at her, been glad to see her. But too much had happened.

"I'm leaving," I said.

Ara made her way through the barn to my side. Kaden's absence felt like an actual physical force hanging between us. It was as if the tie that had bound us together had been severed forever. I couldn't look at her without seeing him. I didn't want to see the ring I knew she still wore on her finger. I didn't want to see the way her eyes were ringed in red, dull instead of bright.

I thought she would tell me not to go. Insist I stay. But she only helped me check over the saddle and the two bags I'd tied on. I knew it was Kaden who'd taught her how to ride and work with horses like this. The punch of pain hit me all over again.

"Where will you go?" she said simply.

"I'm not sure. Issac left some map coordinates behind. I'll go there first. Then maybe I'll find out how to get the new tech back on in other cities."

Ara nodded. "Promise you'll call when you figure it out? Matteo's got a radio up and running."

I nodded, that lump in my throat impossible to deny now. "Of course, Ara."

"There's one more thing," she said quietly. "But I'm not telling you to make you stay. I'm just telling you because you should know. And because I hope you'll come back someday." She paused a long moment and then said, "I'm pregnant, Sam."

And then I did turn. I saw the devastation, the grief, but also the blazing hope in her eyes. "You . . . you're . . . with Kaden's . . . ?"

Ara laughed at this, and I flushed. "Yes, with Kaden's child. I hope you'll come back someday to meet them. And to see the city again. I know you think it's your fault what happened, but it's not, Sam. Kaden made his choice to save us. There was nothing any of us could have done. And Kaden is with Issac now."

"It was my fault," I said softly. "I was the one who found the new tech. Who wanted to turn it back on." And now, because of me, Kaden would never meet his child.

Ara's hand landed on my shoulder. "He loved you, Sam. You can't carry that burden. He wouldn't want you to."

I'd once remembered her as the girl who'd taken Kaden away from me. But now I saw her differently. I saw her the way I would write her: as a girl with auburn hair and hazel eyes, who'd returned to the city to find her father and had found a man with green eyes instead.

"I still can't stay here, Ara. I'm sorry. Will you forgive me?"

She stepped forward and hugged me. It was strange, being taller than her now. "There's nothing to forgive. Promise me you'll come back some day? Promise me you'll come meet your niece or nephew?"

I nodded, my voice thick. "Yeah, I will. I promise."

"I'll keep looking for Emma," she said, her name like a knife to my heart. Even Ara believed she'd made it free but decided not to come back to us. "If I find her, I'll send out a message on the radio. We're going to start a broadcast from Boise when we get the power up. See if we can get some people to come back. We'll have the city back up before you know it."

Even through the grief, I tried to smile at her. "I believe it."

I wanted to tell her what Emma had said, that lost things had a way of coming back to you, and that maybe I was one of those lost things now, but I wasn't sure I could say the words without crying. I gave her a final nod, and then swung up onto my horse. I paused, looking out the stable door, at the long, terrifyingly empty road before.

But then Ara came to stand beside the horse, giving him a pat before she smiled up at me. "Well, we're burning daylight."

This time both our smiles were real. We both had loved and lost—but a bit of him lived on in each of us. So, I would remember what Kaden had taught me: that each new day was an adventure waiting to be embraced.

"Burning daylight," I said, then kicked the horse forward and left the clan behind.

~

It felt good to be back in the saddle, even if the sun was too bright, the day too beautiful. I rode down the road to the river. At first, I didn't even think about why I was going this way, besides wanting to water the horse. Then I realized I was heading for the spot Em had taken me the day we'd slept on the riverbank, beneath the trees. There she had told me she liked the spot because it was unchanged. There she could imagine the world as it had once been.

When I came closer, I dismounted and then led the horse down to the beach. I bent to the water, cupping it in my hands—and then saw a flicker of movement in the reflection.

I lifted the water to my lips, drinking, and then casually dropped my hand to the pistol at my side. I was about to draw it when her voice cut through the day.

"You weren't actually going to leave without me, were you, Sasquatch?"

I spun, nearly falling into the river as I did.

She stepped free from the trees, limping on one leg, blood streaked across her face. Even so, she grinned as she looked at me.

"Em," I whispered, unable to say more. How could she be here? How could she have found me? She limped the last few feet forward.

"I barely made it out. I was still in the tunnels when the weapon went off," she said. "Half of them collapsed and I had to dig my way out."

"Are you okay?"

"Depends. Were you really going to leave without me?"

I shook my head, almost not able to believe she was here. "I thought you'd left. I thought you didn't want to come back to me." My heart beat faster, both wanting and terrified in the same moment. "You said we're all alone in the end."

She limped the last step forward, her ice-blue eyes shining up into mine. "Maybe we could be alone together?"

I stepped forward and kissed the girl I'd been in love with since the first moment I'd seen her. The girl I'd killed for. The girl I'd risked my heart for, again and again. The girl who I didn't care was human or the last Creation, because she was mine and I was hers.

Finally, she pulled back, grinning up at me. "So, Sasquatch, where were you off to in such a hurry? Found another girl you want to share all your books with?"

"No. I read the note Issac left me. There were map coordinates on it."

She lifted a brow, her voice that sarcastic, cutting drawl I knew too well. "I swear to Creation, if you say there's some kind of safe haven, untouched—"

"No," I cut her off. "He said it was dangerous. Warned me not to go alone. What do you think?"

"You'd really go off on an adventure with a monster?"

The Creation had been many things, but I wondered, if in the end, they weren't monsters. If the reason Sevyn gave Kaden a choice was to give humanity a chance to do better.

"Well, I am a Sasquatch after all," I said with a grin. "Maybe we're perfectly matched." I swung onto the horse's back and then held out a hand to her. "But first we have to go tell Ara you're alive. She's got some news for you."

"I think we can manage a quick pit stop." She took my hand and I pulled her up. The horse pranced beneath us, eager to run, to leave this place behind. But I held him steady, just for a moment, to turn and look at the river, to take in my city.

The sun lit the river in a golden strip, the full green leaves hanging over it, beautiful and heartbreaking all at once.

I decided that Issac was right. I would write my story—Kaden's story. And someday I would come back here to see what had become of my city that we'd sacrificed so much to save. I'd come back and meet Kaden and Ara's child, and I'd teach them to ride horses and be wild the same way Kaden had taught me. But for now, I had to leave. Not because I was running from my past. But because I was seeking a new future with her.

I kicked the horse, and we rode forward, leaving our past behind.

CHAPTER FORTY—ARA

We crawled over the debris, the beams of our flashlights cutting through the dark, eerie underground, only a couple hundred feet from where the bunker had been. Matteo had sworn this was the final step to turning on the new tech across the whole city. The shadows moved oddly, and for a split second I saw him: Kaden, standing behind one of the concrete slabs.

My heart stopped, and then my flashlight moved, revealing only a long pole—nothing close to a man. It wasn't him.

It never was.

This wasn't like the way I'd once seen my father and Emma in the shadows. It was a thousand times worse.

An entire week without him—and the only way I survived, the only way I kept from collapsing, was knowing that a tiny part of him still lived on inside me. I couldn't give up, because this wasn't just about me anymore.

"Let's try over here," Matteo said, and I nodded, numb as I followed him.

This morning, I'd woken before dawn, and reached over to touch Kaden's warmth. For one small moment I'd forgotten what had happened that day in the bunker. Then my hand touched cold blankets.

My flashlight beam hit a massive panel on the wall, and I saw that it matched the picture Matteo had drawn for me. Once I would have been ecstatic. Now I could barely manage the energy to say, "Matteo, over here."

He hurried over to me, his flashlight beam joining mine on the wall. "That's it," he said, and I heard the relief in his voice. "We did it. We found it. This will release the new tech energy to the city."

The new tech system was on—but we'd been searching for this panel to release the energy stores to the entire city. Some of the men of the clan wanted to control access to it—but I didn't care what they said. Kaden had given his life for this power. It belonged to everyone. No more rationing or power plays.

This was the last step in finishing what Sam had started. The final step in releasing what Kaden had given his life for.

"Together?" I said, staring at the massive panel.

"Together," he echoed. We threw our weight against it. It groaned, fighting against us as we slowly forced the metal switch off the wall, and then, when it passed the midpoint, it slammed upward. For a moment nothing happened.

"Did it work?" I whispered.

Matteo didn't have time to answer. A low, buzzing, rumbling noise came from above us, and suddenly, blinking and stretching like they'd almost forgotten what their job was, the fluorescent lights above us struggled to life. It showed the full lights of a tunnel that led all the way one way, then another, rocks and boulders strewn throughout.

"I think we did it," I said.

"Come on," Matteo said. Together we wove through the rubble, all the way to the access hole we'd found that led down into the tunnels. It had taken us most of the day to find an opening that wasn't caved in. Matteo let me climb out first. For so long the city's nighttime dark had been broken only by stars and the moon.

Tonight, lights blazed through the darkness.

It was beautiful, glorious—and heartbreaking. Because for every light that blazed in the darkness, I was reminded of all those who hadn't made it here.

Matteo made his way up the stairwell, breathing hard as he came to stand beside me.

"We did it," I said, feeling empty inside, the joy of our accomplishment poisoned by the cost. "We got the power back on."

"What now?" Matteo said, his eyes serious as he looked out over it all. "Are you going to start a new clan? Or take over the Mencata clan?"

Sam had left—but I couldn't hate him for it. He was off on a new adventure, and now, I supposed, I had to choose mine. "The time for clans is past. This time we start a city. That's what Kaden wanted."

That's what *we* had wanted.

Looking out over the blazing lights of the city, I tried to see the possibility and hope. A new beginning. A new world. *And a chance to do better*.

I wondered if that was why Sevyn had chosen what he did. Had it been to give humans another chance? Or was it because he couldn't live in a world without her? I would never know for sure now, but I hoped that he had been reunited with Talia. I hoped that Issac, Kaden, my father, Septimus, and Sevyn were all together now. Even after all of it, I still believed there was a forgiving God watching over us.

"What do you think they'd say if they were here?" Matteo asked.

"I think they'd say, 'there is only the peace we find. And that this is a pretty good start.'"

~

Even though it was well past sunset, I told Matteo I was going to hunt for some fresh meat. The lights coming on after years of darkness would be like stirring still water—all manner of debris and animals would be shaken up. He nodded, understanding my need to be alone.

I held my rifle casually as I walked, not in the mood to kill anything. Whole sections of the street had collapsed around where the bunker lay, revealing a massive network of tunnels underneath. Now that the lights were on, it illuminated even more of the rubble. It had taken Matteo and me a long time to find one of the places where the underground opened just enough to allow someone to slip inside.

I still see him in the ruins. I can't stop seeing him. I'd told Matteo the way he haunted me, the same way my father and Emma, once had. The way I saw him in my dreams. In the shadows dancing away from me. In everything I wanted and couldn't have.

I paused at the edge of a large section of rubble I'd walked past before. Now, the lights showed me something I'd missed: a small opening that looked like it led directly down into the tunnels.

And there, even more impossibly, lay a set of footprints. Rising out of the rubble, leading away from the wreckage.

My heart, my world, everything stopped.

You can't always trust your eyes. They'll deceive you. Matteo's words.

But what, I wondered, about trusting your heart?

The lights of the city seemed to thrum all around me. It was like going back in time. But there was no going back in time to save Kaden. There was no going back to the beginning, not for me. Not this time . . .

Except the question remained: *Who came up from the rubble?*

I spun in a slow circle, searching the buildings around me. I had almost opened my mouth, to call Matteo, when I saw it.

A flash of golden light—or was it curls?—disappeared around the corner in front of me.

Once again, I was a girl running through the ruins, not from him, but toward him.

What did it matter, darkness or light, human or Creation, peace or war? I didn't care if I was the last she, or if I was the world's salvation or doom. I would forever see him wherever I went: in the shadows, in the ruins, in my dreams. He was my beginning and my end. He was the peace I found.

I turned the corner and smiled.

"Kaden?"

ABOUT THE AUTHOR

H.J. Nelson is an Idaho native who graduated from the University of Wisconsin with degrees in creative writing and wildlife biology. She began writing on Wattpad in 2015, where her story *The Last She* garnered over twelve million reads. It became one of the most-read Science Fiction stories on Wattpad in 2016 and 2017 and was acquired by Wattpad Books for publication as a three-book series. Since then, Nelson has had her work optioned for television by Sony and translated for publication into French (Hachette) and Italian (Mondadori).

A winner of the 2023 Early Career Alumni Award from the University of Wisconsin, Hannah has also written for brands like General Electric, National Geographic, and Writers Digest. When not writing, Nelson has lived on a boat in the British Virgin Isles, worked in two zoos, and ridden an elephant through the jungles of Laos—though she considers raising two daughters her most dangerous adventure yet. You can sign up for her newsletter at hjnelsonauthor.com, or find her on Instagram at @h.j.nelson.